COMING TO TERMS

COMING
TO TERMS

Richard Greensted

LONDON NEW YORK SYDNEY TORONTO

Printed and bound in Great Britain by
Mackays of Chatham PLC, Chatham, Kent

COMING TO TERMS

ONE

The police work to their own timetable. Their rules of day and night are not the same as those of the public they protect. When the phone rang on my bedside table, it was four o'clock in the morning. The bell did not wake me; I had been lying sleepless for many hours, as often happened. The officer who spoke was courteous, and professionally uninformative.

'Detective Inspector Barham would like to speak to you, sir. Would it be all right if he came round to see you now?'

I rubbed my face with my free hand. 'That'd be fine,' I replied. I put the phone down and swung my legs out of bed. I walked into the bathroom, which no longer smelt of Anna's perfume, but which still betrayed the physical influence of a woman. Her make-up bag, and other toiletries, were still arranged on the shelf above the wash-basin, just as she had left them. I had even continued to replace the soap with her favourite, gardenia.

After showering I shaved and dressed, ready for

work although I suspected I would not be visiting the office. I was down in the kitchen when the door-bell rang. I walked up the stairs to the hall, and opened the front door. Two men stood at the top of the steps. One smiled at me, the other stood slightly behind him, solemn and short of sleep.

'Good morning, sir. Detective Inspector Barham. Sorry to raise you so early. May we come in?' He showed me his police card, and I turned back into the hall. Both men followed me inside.

'I'm just making tea,' I said. 'Come downstairs.' I walked down the stairs with the men still behind me. Once in the kitchen, I waved them to the chairs at the large pine table. They sat down, and I started preparing tea.

'Have you heard from your wife yet, sir?' Barham asked. It was a question that he put in such a casual way that he might have been asking after a mutual acquaintance we had once discussed. They must practise that at police school, I thought.

'Nothing, officer. If I had, you'd have been the first to know.'

'Yes, well, it's about your wife, sir.' Barham shifted in his chair, and looked at his unnamed colleague. I filled the teapot, and turned round to face them.

'Have you found her? Do you have some news?' I gripped the work surface with both hands, feeling a sudden rush of adrenalin.

Barham and the other man looked at me for a long moment. The house was entirely silent. No cars drove past in the street.

2

'Why don't you sit down, sir? Challis can make the tea, can't you, son?' The enforced informality of the remark did little to change the feeling of deadness. I sat as suggested, facing Barham, while Challis rose as instructed. Barham took a breath that seemed to steady him.

'We've found the body of a woman who matches your wife's description. We can't say definitely yet. We need to ask you some questions.' Challis, who was behind me now, dropped a teaspoon.

A thousand questions seemed appropriate, but I could only think of one. 'Why can't you say definitely? You've got photos of her.'

Barham took another steadying breath before answering. 'I'd rather not discuss that just yet, sir. As I say, we need to ask you some questions first.'

The most innocent of men will behave differently in front of authority. The presence of the police in any situation, however innocuous, has a strange effect on us all, similar to the presence of death. I laid my hands flat on the table in front of Barham and said nothing, looking into his face for any sign of unspoken information. Challis placed two cups of tea in front of us. Barham reached into his pocket, and produced a packet of small cigars and a lighter.

'Would you mind if I had one of these?' he asked me. I shrugged and shook my head. Barham took out a cigar, and offered the packet to me. I put my hand up to decline.

'Do you own or rent any other property in London?' he asked, after lighting the cigar and inhaling

3

deeply. Barham was in his mid-forties, slightly over-weight and with a grey skin brought on by too many years of working on cases like this. He was trying to be friendly – not, it appeared, from training, but out of some sense of social etiquette.

'No,' I replied. 'We have a house in the States, on Cape Cod, but nothing else here. Why do you ask?'

'Does your wife have anything? Or any other members of your family?' Challis was now sitting with us again, stirring his tea and studying a black notebook.

I thought of my brother, who lived in Hampstead. I told Barham this. He raised his eyebrows, but said nothing. He puffed again on his cigar, then sipped his tea noiselessly. At last, he spoke.

'The body was found in a flat near Baker Street. If, and I stress the if, it is the body of your wife, we need to know what she was doing there. We thought you might be able to help us on that.' Barham looked at me, then at his cigar. He was not planning to volunteer any further information. He waited for a reply.

'I'm afraid I have no idea,' I said, shaking my head slowly. 'What do you have to do to identify the body?'

'That's the other point, sir. We'd like to have your wife's dental records, to see if they match. Could you arrange that?' I agreed that I could, hoping that this small gesture might help me to get more details. Challis wrote something in his notebook. Barham reached into his jacket pocket, and produced a card. 'My number's on here. Give me a call when you've

4

spoken to your wife's dentist. And if you think of anything else, please let us know.' The interview was clearly over. The two men rose from the table, with Barham still holding the stub of his cigar. They walked to the stairs, and I followed them up to the hall. As Challis opened the front door, Barham turned to me.

'While I remember, there was one other thing. When you reported your wife's disappearance, you said you thought that she had taken no clothes and no jewellery. Have you had a chance to check that?'

'As far as I can see, nothing has gone,' I replied, trying to find some significance in the question.

Barham barely nodded. 'Well, as I say, do call if you remember anything. Thanks for the tea.' The men walked into the emerging dawn, and down the steps. I closed the door behind them, and stood still in the hall, hardly breathing, hardly alive.

Once in the kitchen, I rinsed out the teapot and boiled fresh water. I turned on the television, hoping for some news on the event that Barham had just mentioned. He had disclosed little to me, so I doubted that he would have said more to journalists, but I was still hungry for news.

One phrase, which Barham had not used, floated to the front of my mind: 'Missing, presumed dead'. I wondered if that was now the accepted description of Anna. The room smelt of Barham's cigar, and his visit had left little more than the trace of smoke. Barham's words meant less than the things he didn't say, perhaps intentionally. I stood looking at the silent screen of the television. The kettle boiled, and I filled the teapot. Whilst the tea stood, I looked up the phone number of our dentist, written in the address book in Anna's neat hand. I left the book open, and took two mugs out of the cupboard in front of me. I poured the tea, and milk, and took the two mugs up to my bedroom on the second floor. I set one mug down on a bedside table, and carried the other into the bathroom.

In the mirror, there was no trace of anguish or pain in my face. I looked the same. Anna's things remained untouched, inert reminders of her presence: missing, but still with me. In the two weeks since she had disappeared it was only her physical absence that had altered the aura of the house; nothing else had changed.

I turned away from the mirror and walked back into the bedroom. Mechanically, I walked to the window and pulled back the side of the curtain. I looked down at the empty street. The whole world seemed lifeless, and my weariness perfectly matched it. I let the curtain fall, and sat down on the edge of my bed.

The figure in bed moved, and turned towards me, eyes still closed. 'What time is it?'

I looked at my watch. 'Five-thirty. I've made you some tea.'

The face smiled, then returned to stillness. I stroked the crown of black hair above it, then stood up. Here was my point of comfort, a passionate, unquestioning body in which I would envelop myself when the horror of it all became too much and I needed a refuge from relentless reality. Recognised by both of us as such, the relationship filled the lowering void created by Anna's departure.

I wanted to call my son, Nick, but couldn't decide what to tell him. Barham's words could not easily be translated; the message behind them remained unclear. Nick would ask me questions that I wanted to ask; I had to be in control of our conversation, our relationship, and I needed the power of information to achieve that control. I stared at the body beneath the bed covers, jealous of its untroubled calm. My eyes felt swollen. I returned to the bathroom, picked up the mug of tea, and went back down to the kitchen. I heard a pair of feet walking along the pavement, a woman's step, and thoughts of Anna returned.

Missing, presumed dead, described a physical condition – but the accoutrements of life, severally and jointly, served to hold the suggestion of Anna's spiritual presence in this house, our home. Numbers in a phone book, gloves wrapped in scented paper and stored for next autumn, tins of special tea – all testified to her existence, whether missing, alive, or dead. I studied a photo carelessly attached to the fridge: Anna and I sitting together at a beach bar on the Cape, both pinkened from the day's sun and smiling at the camera. Nick had taken the photo; Anna had laughed and worried about her hair being blown by the sea breeze, but the shot captured her well, happy and beautiful, and mine.

I heard noises upstairs, the shower pump working and water running through the system. The world had started again; I turned up the sound on the television for the national headlines, but saw nothing about Anna. Leaving it on, I went upstairs again and saw the empty bed and a crumpled shirt. The curtains were still drawn shut, and no light had been switched on. The bathroom door opened. In the frame of the door Sarah stood naked, her wet hair brushed away from her face. Without speaking, she walked towards me and pressed herself gently against me. My hands ran down her back and we kissed, an early morning kiss, slow but full of intent. As we lay together on the bed, the spectre of Anna's things disappeared, like Anna herself.

TWO

The Indian man who beckoned me up the stairs had thick black hair that was swept back from his face. His skin was the colour of butterscotch, and was shiny. He smiled at me, pulling his hand towards him to suggest that I should follow him. The walls of the stairwell were freshly painted, an odd blend of burgundy beneath the dado rail, and eau de nil above it. When I reached the top of the stairs I turned left and saw a door with a pane of fireglass in it. I looked through the glass and could see Anna, half-turned away from me. The room was obviously an exercise studio, and she knelt on the floor, naked, nodding slowly and repeatedly, as if in some form of meditation or worship. She raised her arms above her head, and I could see the glistening smooth skin that ran from her elbow down to her breast. Then my focus changed and I could see two men over the other side of the room. They were watching me watching Anna. I recognised them as Barham and Challis.

I didn't awake with a start, but drifted out of

the dream back to reality. I was lying under my bedclothes, alone. I looked at the clock. It was eight-thirty. There was no sign of Sarah. The panic that I should have felt about work would not surface. I would ring them and tell them the truth: the police had visited in the middle of the night, and I needed to do some things. The disruption to my working schedule, which spilled over into my whole life, was becoming a routine in itself. Since Anna's disappearance, I had missed half and whole days of work, talking to police and reporters, friends and relatives, trying to explain to myself, through my conversations with them, the new realities of my life.

I showered, soaping away the remaining traces of Sarah and her scent. I changed into more casual clothes, a yellow cotton shirt and dark blue corduroys, and went downstairs to begin the round of phone calls I needed to make. The kitchen still smelt of Barham's cigar, and the smell reminded me how much Anna disapproved of my smoking in the kitchen. I picked up a box of Cuban cigars that lay on the work surface, and pulled out a panatella. An unsmoked cigar is one of life's most sensuous gifts: harmless, but promising great pleasure with its shape, its velvety skin, and its gentle aroma. I cut the end and lit it, converting the promise of sensual pleasure to a harsher reality, still pleasurable but very different.

The phone was mounted on the wall next to the fridge, and I called work first. They were suitably concerned, assuring me that I should take all the time I needed. This was the agony and ecstasy of my job; as a foreign exchange dealer, the markets would still be there when I got back, ready to swallow me up and spit me out if I called them wrong, and always willing to take my bets.

The call was brief; I did not want to mix my office and home lives, and I gave them the barest of details about the reason for my absence. Soon enough they would know what Barham had told me. If Anna had been found in mysterious circumstances . . . The thought arrested me, and I called Nick. I had to leave a message; he would still be in bed, but would ring back and reverse the charges.

The dentist's assistant took my request silently, as if any question, or my answer to it, might have disturbed the manufactured calm of the surgery. Then I called the number Barham had left me; he was not there, but I left details of the dentist so that he could pick the records up. The cigar had gone out, and I relit it and sat down at the table. Outside, the street was full of noise. I sat quietly, occasionally pulling on the cigar, and thought again about Barham's visit. I needed to know what he knew. I briefly considered driving to Baker Street, then dismissed the idea. I turned over the events of the last month in my mind, but the journey was broken by the sound of the letter box flipping shut. I went upstairs to the front door, and picked up the letters and the papers that lay on the door mat.

Anna still received mail, as if the world had refused to accept that she was gone. Occasionally she would receive personal letters from people I barely knew, and I would write or phone to explain the position. I carried the bundle of paper downstairs, dropped it on the table, and made coffee. Reading the papers might reveal more information, and I sat and scanned the three – two broadsheets and a tabloid – with a confused mix of dread and hope. There appeared to be nothing. I leant back in my chair, and turned my mind again to the news Barham had given me. An image of Anna passed across my mind, not dead, but as she was in the photo – smiling, in love with me, careless. I wondered if Barham or Challis could understand the relationship Anna and I had enjoyed.

I picked up the pile of letters, and opened each one. Most were bills, or requests for money from charities, our names faithfully reproduced, like a thousand others, by a word processor. There was one letter for Anna, in a plain white envelope with the address written neatly. I opened it, guessing that it was from another distant relative or friend. Inside was a notelet, a coloured card with a painting of freesias on the front. Inside, a few words were written in the same neat hand.

A—

I've tried to call, but you're never there!

I have some very bad feelings about you – I think you may be in trouble, even danger. I am very worried about you, and want to see you soon. Please get in touch!!

G

For a moment I closed my eyes tightly and breathed in very deeply. The words seemed like any other words. I re-read the note. The two words, 'even danger', caught my eye persistently. It was as if they were written in larger letters, or even a different colour, to the rest of the script.

The handwriting seemed feminine, and the card wouldn't normally have been chosen by a man. I looked at the postmark on the envelope: London, SW3. I reached back behind me to pick up the address book, and looked under 'G'. Some mutual friends were listed, but no one with a first name that began with G. The notelet lay open in front of me, the message clear but its meaning to me distorted by the two words. I flicked back the pages of the address book to the beginning, and started to read all the entries. My coffee sat beside the pile of other letters, untouched. As I ran my finger down the pages of Anna's writing, the two words continued to resound in my brain, like a tune one hates but can't stop singing.

The search proved useless; there was no one in the book who matched the profile I had put together from the letter. I read it once again, trying to see something that would give me a clue about the sender. I stood up, gathering the other envelopes and screwing them up before putting them in the bin. I walked to the window at the front of the kitchen, and looked up at the feet walking past on the pavement. I could hear a brewery dray down the street, the barrels of beer being rolled along the tarmac, with the draymen shouting abuse at each other. The notelet remained on the table, an ugly intruder in my private space.

The phone rang. I let it ring for a long time before answering.

'Dad, it's Nick. What's up?'

When Nick was born, he had been a very sickly baby. He was in intensive care for the first four days, and had to be fed with a tube through his nose. It always seemed to me that his hold on life remained tenuous: sometimes I even pictured him as vaguely translucent, and photos of him seemed to have the same temporary quality. Anna never understood this feeling, looking practically at Nick and seeing only dirty ears and bruised legs. I did not fear Nick's early death, but expected it.

This expectation made my reaction to, and relationship with, Nick very unusual: at times, I could not accept any of his behaviour, believing everything he did to be an imposition on our lives, and looking upon him as malicious and malevolent. These periods of disaffection could last for months, with Anna patiently waiting until he, or I, changed mood. He was a bright, articulate child; he loved his mother passionately, and loved me in a different way.

When we were getting on well, we were inseparable, playing football in the park or reading books together. In Nick I saw the opportunity to create the better man: polite, intelligent, good at sport, and successful. Whenever he deviated from these, our relationship suffered.

Anna and I agonised over boarding school: I had been sent away when I was seven, and had loved it, but Anna knew that my brother had been deeply unhappy and had suffered unnecessarily in pursuit of a better start to life. We compromised; Nick stayed at home until he was thirteen, attending a private school in Chelsea that ensured that Anna was able to fulfil her objective of always being there to meet him in the afternoon. He never seemed stretched by school work, and won a minor award to a public school in Surrey – near enough in the event of a crisis, but a world away from Chelsea and grimy city life. He thrived; he played the piano, got into the sports teams, and did well in exams. If he had adolescent crises, he kept them quiet from us. He was popular with boys and girls, and success came easily to him. But at the start of every holiday, the reports sent the same message: 'Could do better.' Nick never changed gear; he pursued everything at the same speed, with the same determination, but gave up if the first attempt was unsuccessful.

His sister, Emma, could not have been more different. For her, education was an optional extra, a diversion from life which concerned her little. She was bright, pretty, and good fun, but adolescence brought a quiet rebellion, one in which she turned away from work and family and asserted her independence through absence rather than confrontation. Emma and Nick did not like each other, and their rare moments together were charged with mutual disdain.

Nick was calling from a phone box, and I took the number and called him back.

'It's about Mum,' I said. 'The police have been round.'

'What did they say? Have they found her?'

I hesitated, almost immediately regretting that I had started the conversation. 'They've found a body that they say might be her. They won't give me any details. They've taken her dental records.'

Nick didn't need, or want, to ask why. 'Should I come home?' he asked.

'There's nothing you can do. It'll be better if you stay put. I'll call you as soon as I have any news. How's life?'

'Fine. Dad, is everything all right? Are you OK?'

'Yes, no problems. I can deal with this. I'll call you.' I briefly wondered whether to ask Nick about 'G', but decided against it.

'OK. Let me know. Bye.' We hung up at the same moment, ending a conversation that we both knew was starting another phase of our lives without Anna, with new challenges and problems. I wanted Nick insulated from these, but he had to be involved. We had agreed that he should continue his studies at Durham; he was reading History, in his first year, and had been happy and settled there. Bringing him home would have brought the problem nearer to both of us, something we wanted to avoid.

I returned to the kitchen table, clear now of all paper except the notelet. I turned it over, so that the writing was face down. For the first time since Anna's disappearance, the house intimidated me. It was big, and quiet, and very empty. I stood at the table, hands resting on it with my weight on them, and my breathing seemed erratic, caught by small contractions that I couldn't control. My eyes stung, and I forced myself to keep them open, focused on nothing. I knew I must get out of the house. I looked around for my keys and my wallet, and set the answering machine. As I was walking up the stairs to the hall, the phone rang once, before the machine answered the call. I could hear the message that was left very clearly.

'It's DI Barham, sir. We need to speak to you very urgently. Please call me as soon as you can.'

I looked at my watch, without noting the time, and my hand hovered on the latch of the front door. Urgent messages always presaged bad news, and the dread of further revelations drove me to open the door and walk briskly away from the house.

THREE

Anna disappeared two months before our twentieth anniversary. Invitations for a party to mark the event had gone out, and I had never rescinded them. Friends needed to believe that I believed Anna was coming back. It was easier to comply with this than to state the obvious explicitly.

I had never seriously considered any state other than marriage. Anna and I were conventional: we courted, we married, we had children. Her disappearance broke the convention in a way that threatened our circle of friends; even divorce was preferable to the sudden, unexplained, and unexplainable break in our conventional continuum.

Even our first meeting had been conventional: we both went to a party given by a mutual friend, where all the guests were young, most were rich, and some were already married. I was twenty-two, Anna was nineteen. She was beautiful then, in a different way. She was quiet, had a gorgeous smile, drank a little too much, and was interested in me. We always described her as well-covered: she was curvaceous where it mattered, and had wonderful legs and ankles. We did not sit apart from the other guests, but we talked together for a while, and I resolved to take her out. I was not a natural suitor, preferring the company of men, but Anna waited for me to make a move, and we duly began the rituals of mutual attraction.

I knew that I would marry her from quite early on, and pursued her with that end in mind. I met her parents after we had been going out for three months; we visited them in Gloucestershire, staying the weekend. I was serious with them, something they mentioned to her later. Our time alone was different; I had already caught the scent of serious money in the City, and was working for an American bank in their dealing room. Three years at Oxford had served to mature me so that I could already see my life, with Anna, mapped out before me.

I had a flat off the Fulham Road, but Anna refused to move in with me. She preferred to live in a house in Belsize Park with a strange mix of friends who did not like me. Anna worked as a secretary in a publishing house, but her work was unimportant to her. She wanted what I wanted, an end to the misery of singleness. We were together for barely six months before we married, in the town hall at Chelsea. It felt as if life had finally started.

We were passionate lovers, spending long evenings in our first flat together in Oakley Street making love and eating take-away food. I was making a reasonable amount of money, and suggested that she gave up work and we started a family. Anna was delighted. She was pregnant three months after our wedding, and we ached to know what life would be like with a baby. Nothing prepares you for parenthood – books and manuals conspire to hide the facts about families – and our early days with Nick were miserable. Anna suffered bad depressions, Nick was awake and crying most nights, and the flat could not contain the explosion of items that were vital to keep an unhappy baby alive. Work was a soothing panacea of which I took increasing advantage; I could stay out late, I could go in early, ostensibly in pursuit of a great career, but covertly used to avoid the terrors of home life.

Anna's friends evaporated, and new ones appeared, all with children. Talk was always centred round babies. I hated it. On the very few occasions when we made love, there was little passion, all emotion exhausted on keeping Nick docile. We did not discuss our problems, assuming that each other held the promise of better things intact. That promise lay beneath the small shadow of Nick, and the other children we knew we must have. The curious logic of parenthood suggested that we should have another child soon, and get the pain behind us to allow us to enjoy the golden years that we believed lay ahead. Emma followed twenty-two months after Nick, entering the world peacefully and causing anxiety only to Nick, who saw her as a thief of our previously undivided love. Nick cuddled her too harshly, hit her surreptitiously, and experimented with her flexibility and resilience forcefully. Through it all, Emma stayed serene, her sixth sense silently counting and recording the blows and hurts.

The progress of a marriage can be charted as a W curve. Emma's birth found us at the lowest point of the first stroke of the W, not out of love with each other but entirely disaffected with the environment we had built. The death of Anna's father helped us physically; he left her enough money to place a deposit on the house in Redesdale Street, which needed complete renovation. We looked ahead to the golden years, and lived in the house that time and money would convert to a home. Nick's first days at school confirmed that he too, aged three, wanted another life: he would not discuss his time away from us, feigning poor memory and keeping secret his other world. His absence from home gave Emma and Anna time and hope. They were climbing the curve.

At work, I became a master politician, reaching for jobs that gave me power and money, the two axes on the chart of my career. With every bonus cheque and every pay rise, we started another project on the house. We learnt to live with plaster dust, bare floorboards, and the permanent presence of builders and their detritus. Anna was excited by the home we were creating; I was merely frustrated that it couldn't be delivered sooner. The children slept well, while Anna laid swatches of fabric and snippings of wallpaper before me. Anna's taste was immaculate – not culled from magazines and friends, but carefully considered and developed. She began to buy clothes for me, with the same forethought and planning she gave to dressing our home. The early crises of our marriage were behind us.

When the children went to boarding school, the weekends took on a new significance for us. For the first time in our marriage, we were free to act as a childless couple. Anna hated the idea of sending Emma away, and accepted the decision with tears. I was sure that both Emma and Nick would flourish, and was determined to act with even-handedness. If Nick went, so would Emma.

Our childless weekends were the test of our unspoken promise. We rose to the challenge as if our lives depended on it, which they did. Saturdays always started in the same way: I would get up at six-thirty, make Anna a cup of tea and take it to her in bed, then drive down to Wimbledon, ready to tee off at seven-thirty. I had played golf with Douglas for ten years. He was my accountant, and had become a friend, uninterested in what I did at work, someone who asked few difficult questions and whose own life matched mine. We played golf, drank two whiskies, and went home.

I had tried to interest Nick in golf. It didn't work. He resented the early start, and was overly frustrated by every poor shot he played. Golf is not a game for boys: it requires a level of concentration that they cannot reach, and an ability to forget each mistake immediately they have learnt from it. We would return from the course barely speaking to each other, and Anna eventually intervened to stop my efforts. His rare weekends at home became his own, and I struggled to communicate with him.

Anna and I rowed less than we had when the children were at home; we had less to row about. Occasionally we might disagree about something trivial, but we no longer seemed to have the energy for full-blown confrontations. Anna had never really enjoyed arguments, preferring to give in to my demands or use the children as a defensive barrier. Most of my aggression could be released at work; I had little left for home life.

Anna was not a shopper. If we needed something, she bought it. Our definition of needs may have varied, but she was decisive, and never made speculative shopping trips. This suited me. Saturdays were spent in the pursuit of our common interests. We normally lunched in the King's Road, rarely visiting the same restaurant more than a couple of times. We would have an aperitif, share a bottle of wine, and I would smoke a cigar with my coffee and armagnac. We talked about our weeks, trying to bring a detached perspective to events. We discussed the children, and reminisced. After lunch, we would stroll through the Royal Hospital Gardens, often in silence. Once home, we would go to bed, make love, and sleep for an hour, before preparing to go out to the theatre, the cinema, the opera, or whatever Anna had booked for us.

Sundays were quieter. We lay in bed, ate croissants, read the papers, listened to the radio, and occasionally talked. Sunday lunch, so long an icon of family life, was light and brief. We might walk, or visit the children, in the afternoon. The torpor that engulfs the Christian world on Sundays permeated our lives, like smoke filtering through the letter box and windows. By the evening, Anna and I would both be ready for me to go back to work.

We were happy. We were mastering the W curve together. We had a beautiful home, fine children, and each other. We needed nothing else.

When I returned to the house the red light was flashing on the answering machine. It was three o'clock, and the afternoon was warm and hazy. I put the small bag of shopping on the kitchen table, and listened to the messages, starting with Barham's. Anna's mother, Kate, had called, 'just to see how you're getting on'; the last message was for Anna, announcing that her new dress was ready for collection.

I poured a whisky, added a little still mineral water, and sat at the table. Accidentally, I had placed the shopping on top of the notelet. I did not move it. I sipped the whisky, and stood up to make the phone call. On a management course many years ago, I had been taught that standing up when making a call improves one's phone manner, and I wanted to be sharp when speaking to Barham. He was a little intimidating, always giving the impression that he knew much more than he said, and this unnerved me. I wondered if he would be standing when he spoke to me.

Barham was not there, but Challis was. I resented

speaking to him, but he failed to notice.

'Yes, DI Barham is very keen to talk to you. There've been some developments on the case we mentioned to you this morning. We've looked at the dental records, and we'd like to see you. Would it be convenient for you to come to the station?'

The request was phrased with the curious civility that the police believe they have to use, even in the most uncivil circumstances. It was an order with a redundant question mark. I needed to assert my control; if they had the information that I feared so much, I wanted it delivered on my terms and in my time.

'Can't we discuss this now?' I asked, knowing the answer.

'We'd prefer to see you here, if you don't mind, sir,' Challis replied, still playing the game.

'If you insist. I'll be there in half an hour.' I put the phone down before Challis could confirm whether this suited them. I called to order a taxi, as parking would be impossible, and I anticipated a long wait.

I had visited Lucan Place, the local police station, when I first reported Anna's disappearance. There was irony in its location: a street named after a family that had much interested the police for years. No one was standing at the front desk, and I pushed a button to call for attention. A uniformed officer eventually appeared, took my details, and then disappeared after offering me a seat. I stood. Challis opened a door to the left of the reception desk, and nodded.

'Thanks for coming in, sir. Please come this way.' I followed him through the door, past several closed doors, until he turned to his left and opened a door marked INTERVIEW ROOM – 1. He pushed a blank sliding panel on the door so that it covered the word 'Vacant' and revealed the word 'Occupied'. We walked into a freshly painted room, bluish-grey, and he invited me with a hand gesture to sit on a plastic chair at a table. The table had a complicated recording machine on it, with two tape decks.

Challis did not sit down. 'DI Barham will be with you shortly, sir. Can I get you a cup of tea? It's out of the machine, I'm afraid.'

'No thanks,' I replied, and stood still as he closed the door and left me alone. The muscle and skin over my heart trembled, and my hands would not stay still. I put them in my pockets and clenched them.

Barham walked in. He was carrying a large clear plastic bag.

'Good afternoon, sir. Many thanks for coming in. Has Challis offered you tea?' I nodded, and he put the bag down on the floor next to the chair on his side of the table. We sat down together. I waited for him to start.

'I've got some things here that I'd like you to have a look at.' He nodded towards the bag on the floor, then leant to pick it up. He undid an elastic band that was holding the neck together. He reached inside and pulled out a belt, with a cardboard tag tied to it. He laid it on the table in front of me.

I shook my head slowly. 'I've never seen it before,' I said. There was no reaction from Barham. If he had body language, it was foreign to me. He produced a pair of lavender gloves, which were stained with dark brown patches. They looked like ladies' gloves. Again, I shook my head slowly. Barham reached into his pocket, and produced his cigars. He lit one, then placed it in the ashtray beside the tape machine.

'You're sure, sir?' he said, exhaling smoke.

'I'm sure.'

He leant down again and pulled out a dress, again lavender and also badly stained with the brown substance. It was a small dress, short, with plunging back and front, made of stretch material.

'No, I don't recognise this either,' I said, trying to sound helpful and frustrated at once. 'What are all these? Do they have some connection with my wife?'

'The body we found – you know, the one in Baker Street we told you about – was wearing these clothes,' Barham said, picking up his cigar and pushing the dress to one side. He pulled out a pair of shoes, high-heeled and common-looking, also lavender-coloured. They were not stained. He did not seem to need a response from me, so I gave none. Everything from the bag had a label attached to it. He pulled the bag up on to the table, and pulled out three smaller transparent bags, all labelled and tied together with yellow plastic strips. All three contained jewellery.

'I've never seen any of this before, and I'm sure that none of it belonged to my wife,' I said, frustration now more prevalent than co-operation.

Barham didn't seem to notice. 'Well,' he said finally, 'thanks for looking at it. Our forensic boys are looking at the dental records right now, so we should have something to tell you very soon, either way. We do appreciate your co-operation, sir. This is a particularly nasty business.'

This final remark surprised me. Barham was volunteering something, and I had to discover what it was.

'What is?' I asked, a little too quickly.

'Police work, sir,' he said, recovering the power of withheld information. 'Thanks for coming in.'

He got up, and turned to me as he reached the door. 'Can we give you a lift anywhere?'

'No thank you,' I replied, and got up to leave. I glanced again at the array of personal effects on the table, a sad pile of stained clothing that obviously held hidden clues to a crime Barham would not discuss.

We walked back to reception together, and I shook his hand, an involuntary gesture that I regretted immediately.

'We'll be in touch as soon as we have any news,' he said, and turned away, going back to renew his investigation of someone's lavender belongings. I stepped out on to the pavement, and decided I needed to walk home. As I walked towards the King's Road, I realised just how much life had changed. I had no one to tell, and could tell no one, about the things that had happened today. I was utterly alone, and the feeling frightened me, much more than Barham and his blood-stained clothes. The compulsion to talk was strong. Anna would have listened, advised, soothed, and guided. She had taken away some of me when she left, and I needed it back.

FOUR

Sarah was a natural mistress. Men did not want to marry her, they wanted to keep her, secretly, and dress her in exotic and erotic underwear which their wives were too sensible to wear. She was small, dark, and dangerous-looking. She smoked and drank with the boys and the men, and she kept her liaisons discreet. She could infuse the simple act of straightening a man's tie with an intimidating sexual charge. At twenty-six, she was moving into the prime of her magnetism.

She worked on one of the sales desks in the trading room. She was not a graduate, but had worked her way up through the back office, catching the eyes and minds of the senior traders for whom she worked. She was made for sales; her phone manner was immaculate, seducing investors to trade with her when prices might have been better elsewhere. Her voice matched her personality, deep, betraying north-eastern roots, and menacing. She made her numbers every month, and the bank loved her. But, in the same way that she would not easily become a wife, she would not become too senior. Her threat was too great, the sexuality too strong, to gain her access to the glass-panelled offices of power.

The greatest compliment you can pay to a woman is to affect complete immunity to her attraction, and I was immune. In the same way that Anna had passed vital antibodies to our children through her milk, she had passed a resistance and resilience to me that allowed me near danger without fear of infection. The cocoon of life that Anna and I had built was antiseptic, repelling the toxins that lurked beyond the borders of our world.

The first test of my immunity to Sarah had come in Lucho's, almost nine months before Anna disappeared. My desk had made over four million dollars for the bank in a week, some of which would filter its way into my bonus. Lucho's would be another winner; my gold card hung behind the bar with an air of permanence normally reserved for dusty bottles of obscure Italian liqueur or the cigar display box. There was no need to ring Anna to let her know I'd be late and slightly drunk: the long years of marriage had forged an understanding between us, constantly oiled by a large salary and conciliatory presents and bribes.

At forty-three, I was old. By now, I should have had an office, the status of which was determined by the number of carpet tiles it boasted, but I had missed that chance ten years ago, determined to remain a trader. In trading, as in my entire life, everything is immediate: do the deal now, make the money, close the books, and go home. No one ever got fired for making money, but plenty had gone from this bank for making decisions. The trading room insulated all of us from the realities of the commercial marketplace; in our business, fluctuations in the supply of, and demand for, money were our raw materials, fashioned into profits in exactly the same way as a barrow boy operates with apples and oranges.

As quickly as we could produce money, we could spend it. In fact, spending money ostentatiously was almost in the job description. My boss had once hired a private detective to check up on a senior trader who had always bought his clothes from high street stores, had never owned a country retreat, and continued to live in a suburban semi with his dull wife and children. The bank was convinced that he must be financing a drug habit, gambling, or alcoholism. They viewed with cynicism the explanation that he was putting his money into gilts and the building society, 'because this madness can't last forever'.

But the madness had lasted for me, and the prospect of a visit to Lucho's at the end of a week that was no different from a thousand others still excited me. By five o'clock the night-desk traders had arrived, positions had been passed to New York, and we were spilling through the security-controlled doors of the trading room – a barrier that had a metaphysical significance lost to all of us – towards the next comforting womb of our existence, the bar.

Lucho's has been in the City longer than I have,

and has witnessed several lifetimes of the anger, hatred, love and sadness that alcohol induces. The actual bar is long, straight and wooden, darkened by elbows and spilt wine, with a glass rack suspended above it and supported with brass pillars. It is dimly lit, with uncomfortable chairs, and resolutely maintains itself as a drinking and smoking house.

I leaned against the bar and grinned as Ben ordered champagne. Ben was taller than me, younger than me, and cleverer than me. He worked for me. All around us, people drank, shouted, laughed and smoked, a cathartic ritual that suppressed as many emotions as it released. The talk was mainly of deals done, profits made, and competitors stuffed. Later, the subjects would be different, conforming to an unwritten agenda that never changed. I loved it. By Saturday morning, all the words would be forgotten, but I would feel that something important had taken place, that we were building special relationships which added some value to my life.

Ben felt in his inside jacket and pulled out a pale purple business card. He handed it to me, watching my face closely. The card said: 'Madame Lavender invites you to sample her fragrant pleasures at her luxurious apartments. Telephone on 668 1453 to make your special appointment.' Ben laughed; I made a noise and a gesture which suggested disinterested amusement.

'I tell you, she's marvellous,' said Ben. I shook my

head and smiled, affecting a look of bemusement. 'She's old, but she really knows what she's doing,' he continued. 'I thought she might be good for some of our clients,' he added, as if to explain that this was not meant to be a recommendation for me. I put the card in my pocket and looked out again at the collage of faces, suits, briefcases, smoke and drinks. Madame Lavender's proposition was instantly forgotten, and Ben turned away to discuss his great successes, in business and pleasure, with other traders. I stood alone. The adrenalin that drove me through the day was still in me, but now it gave me a different sensation: I wanted to stand and watch, to be a part of it but apart from it. I wasn't tired, and I wasn't ready to return to Anna. For me, this was still work, even though no deals were done and no information or prices exchanged.

I lit a cigar and pulled deeply, letting the ribbons of smoke engulf me. I sipped the champagne, always watching the show, not avoiding direct eye contact but keeping my gaze moving. Jackets were being discarded with a mannered indifference that might suggest a lack of concern for material things. I looked at my watch, and refilled my glass. One of the settlement clerks, a small girl, was crying in a dark corner of the bar. Two of her male colleagues were trying to console her, whilst a nearby group listened avidly as a senior trader talked of his latest car purchase. The caste system in the bar was more elaborate, and indefinable, than at work, but could be discerned by what you drank, whom you talked to, what you wore, and how drunk you got. For me, drinking and smoking were secondary pleasures; I drew my main excitement and intoxication from the studied bonhomie of others, whose professional jealousies and rivalries lay uneasily beneath their pure silk and cotton shirts.

Sarah walked up to me. We knew each other, but the constant osmosis of Anna's protection had guarded me against flying too close to this particular flame. Even in office clothes, sensible wool skirt and jacket with prim white blouse, Sarah could still burn.

'Congratulations. I hear your desk had a very good week.' I could detect the faintest trace of a sentiment something short of unqualified approval in her voice.

'Not bad,' I replied, adopting a tone and stance that suggested, I hoped, nonchalance, experience and knowledge. It was mandatory to behave as if making money was both easy and difficult, important and irrelevant. 'Do you want a glass?' I asked, nodding towards the bottle on the bar.

'Yes, that'd be lovely,' she replied. A barman appeared and reached above his head for a glass from the suspended shelf. I poured the champagne and handed her the glass.

I relit my cigar, giving myself time to consider how the conversation might move forward. Sarah was an attractive threat, who would shortly be producing similar profits to mine, on a much smaller compensation package. But she wasn't yet my equal. The ethics of office deference were delicate, and vitally important.

'How are you getting on?'

She considered my question as if her whole career depended on her reply. Then she laughed quietly. 'Fine,' she said, as if her results had as much significance as her train journey to work. For a second she looked at me in silence, as the circus around us continued, unaware of the small ritual in which we were involved.

'We're planning to go to Covent Garden later for something to eat,' she said. The crisis in our conversation had arrived earlier than I expected. She hadn't asked me to join them, but it was clear this was the question. This was a complication of life that I hated, and had worked hard to avoid. What did she mean? Was I being offered something more than food? If so, did I want it? And, either way, how did I reply?

I settled for the lightly humorous approach. 'This crowd usually finds anything more solid than ice or lemon difficult to handle,' I said, aiming my cigar in the direction of the circus. I hadn't said yes or no, and I had displayed a diffident affection for the cast of players surrounding us.

Sarah drained her glass and lit a cigarette. 'I will definitely need to eat something,' she said, before helping herself to the last of the champagne. 'Cheers.' She raised her glass in front of her nose, never taking her eyes off me.

'Ben's found this new place in Neal Street; knowing him, it's bound to be full of naked women,' she continued, letting me know with her look that this wouldn't bother her. Women in the room had to be strong but not butch, attractive but not pretty, intelligent but not threatening. Sarah broke all the rules.

I had to find a way of saying yes without encouragement, or no without offence. Being a trader doesn't equip you with acute interpersonal skills.

Somebody touched my shoulder. I looked round, and the barman removed his hand. 'There's a call for you,' he said, and passed the phone across the the counter. I turned to smile and nod at Sarah, expecting her to move away. She did not.

'It's Jim. Look, the yen's got its afterburners on in New York. The market's seventy-eighty. What do you want us to do?' Jim was on the early night desk, and often rang me at Lucho's for advice. Suddenly the show around me disappeared, Sarah was no longer a problem, and I was in authority again.

'What's our position?'

'We're ten short at twenty-eight,' Jim replied. I knew he wanted to sit tight, watch the screens, and earn some money out of a promising situation. I drew on the cigar, pretending to think. Sarah watched me.

'OK. Buy five, and sit on the rest. Call me back if anything changes. I'll be here for another hour, I expect. Bye.' This instruction, in a few words, had to send so many messages. I needed to give Jim some latitude for further profit, whilst remaining in control. I wanted Jim, and Sarah, to see me as the complete trader, able to manage a position and make decisions effortlessly. And I had to set a deadline for myself to leave, without answering Sarah's unspoken question.

'Still making money?' she asked as I pushed the phone back across the bar.

'I've got to pay for this champagne somehow,' I said. Sarah did have one thing in common with my daughter: neither was easily impressed by what I did at work.

Ben barged his way towards us. His face was flushed and he was grinning. He put his arm round Sarah, a casual action which shouldn't have had any effect on me, and shouted across us at the barman: 'Another bottle of poo here, chief.' A fresh ice bucket appeared with more champagne.

Ben refilled our glasses. 'Did Sarah tell you,' he asked me, 'we're going to Covent Garden later? Are you coming?' Another decision was laid before me. To buy five million dollars two minutes earlier had been simple, requiring only that I framed the decision in the right style. Now Ben had confronted me with something much more problematic.

I shook my head in a way that left some doubt open. 'I don't think so,' I said. 'Jim just called, and he may need his hand held.'

This was pathetic, and Ben and I both knew it. 'Bollocks. You're coming with us.' In his mind, the issue was settled. I couldn't detect any reaction from Sarah. I couldn't even tell if she liked Ben, or me. I didn't know if that mattered.

Ben now put his arm round me. 'Bloody good week, chief,' he blurted. This was what I enjoyed; there were no hidden messages, no unspoken threats, in Ben's excitement. There was no need for a code, although our behaviour was all coded, because we understood this language. Did Sarah? She smoked and watched us, faintly smiling but, like a language student, appearing to understand more than she could communicate. Another woman, Pippa, joined us, and another glass was produced. Ben spoke again.

'Listen, who are we going to take to the Varsity match?' he asked me. This was a question I liked. Years ago, traders didn't entertain clients – we didn't even have clients, simply competitors to be beaten – but now we were allowed out, and overseas banks would visit us to spend half an hour in the room before entering the maelstrom of life on expenses, with lunches, dinners, parties, clubs, matches and events, all artlessly designed to improve our trading relationship.

'Let's take the Hungarians,' I said. Two burly Magyars were scheduled to visit us during the week of the match, and I knew they would enjoy the spectacle. I had visited them in Budapest, and their hospitality had been spectacular. I had eaten sweet pancakes and drunk their yeasty beer, Tokay which was too good to be exported, and fruit brandies that lit fires in my stomach. We had toured vineyards, and had spent a weekend in a villa on the shore of Lake Balaton. Their traders were sharp, and fiercely competitive, in both trading and drinking.

'Excellent. I'll sort it,' Ben replied. The Varsity

match itself was irrelevant; what mattered was the tide of alcohol, food and women that would engulf them. Ben understood, and would organise suitable entertainment.

Sarah and Pippa were talking in low voices, which betrayed nothing except their lack of interest in our exchange. I waited for them to finish then said to Pippa, 'Making money?' Money was like Rome: all roads led to it. These junior traders could see the wealth that they could create so easily, but not all of them would complete the journey. Pippa would not. But the unwritten code forced her to make light of her difficulties.

'We dropped a hundred thousand today,' she said, shrugging the thought away as she raised her glass to her lips. 'Thank God for the weekend,' she added, and the momentary horror of her losses passed. She was the wounded antelope in the jungle, unable to escape like the rest of us. The talisman of profit had slipped through her fingers.

I looked past her shoulder at the crowd behind her. The girl had stopped crying, and was now sitting too close to a man I vaguely recognised. Talking partners had changed, like an elaborate dance plan, and progress through the agenda continued. Ben had moved away, and Sarah was now looking at me. She seemed to be in my space, the protective wall I had tried to build, and when she spoke her voice was too near to me.

'Where do you live?'

No warning had alerted me to the slap of this

question. Asked by a man, it would have represented nothing more than a conversation filler. Asked by Sarah, it threatened me in ways I couldn't understand.

'Chelsea,' I said.

'I live in Battersea,' Sarah said. 'Whereabouts in Chelsea?'

'Redesdale Street,' I said.

That satisfied her. 'Yes, I know it. The houses there are beautiful.'

'Where in Battersea are you?' I asked, batting away any more discussion of my home territory.

'Oh, I have a flat in a little riverside development. I bought it from a bankrupt, so I did pretty well on the price.' This was a perfunctory reference to money, as if Sarah had perfectly understood the rules of engagement but wasn't too concerned about following them.

I didn't want to talk about the property market; neither did Sarah. Lucho's had become a no-man's-land for us, an oasis that turned out to be a mirage. Sarah spoke again.

'I think they're getting ready to leave. Coming?'

I was in control. When we left Lucho's I went back to the office, unnecessarily, and sat in front of the screens talking to Jim. I called for a taxi on the firm's account and waited in reception. About a dozen people had already gone on to the restaurant, some still clutching bottles, others talking too fast and too loud. Sarah had gone with them.

I thought I felt tired; sitting in the marble-clad hall, brightly lit and completely still, I had no desire to do anything. I opened my briefcase, took out my mobile phone and called Anna. The answering machine picked up the call, and I left a brief message. Then the car arrived.

Sitting in the taxi, I thought of Sarah. I had hardly noticed her physically until tonight, and I was still unsure about the turn of her ankles, the shape of her hips or the colour of her eyes. But her total presence had left a mark on me – not enough to break the skin and wound me, but uncomfortable none the less. As the taxi rattled along the Embankment, I tried hard not to let my mind drift towards physical thoughts. I wasn't sure I liked Sarah.

The car turned into Redesdale Street and stopped outside my house. The outside lamps were on, and I knew that Anna was home. I climbed the steps, opened the front door, and went inside. The smell of fresh pot-pourri and the glow from the apricot walls were reassuring signals that I had successfully moved from one protective lee to another, sheltered from emotion and reality.

FIVE

'You've bought ten at seventy!'

Ben shouted the order at me and I nodded in acknowledgement. The deal was done, the profit already made, and my book was square. I sat down in the expensive swivel chair that senior traders insist on, and watched the screens flash further information at me. My visit to Lucan Place the previous day had been forgotten in the white heat of trading, but now it returned to me, and I resolved to call Barham.

He was there, and was able, if not willing, to talk.

'Have you made any progress?' I asked.

'Yes, sir. Are you calling from work?' The noise of traders shouting, amplified by squawk boxes and intercoms, could not have been mistaken by Barham for the silence of Redesdale Street – but he was a policeman, and obviously assumed nothing.

'Yes, but I can talk,' I replied.

'I think you should come to the station, sir. I'd prefer to talk face to face.' Barham was polite and correct, as always, giving away nothing.

'Is it her?' I asked, ignoring him.

'We need a positive identification before we can decide that. We'd like you to have a look at the body.'

'So you've matched the dental records?'

'As I say, sir, you should really come down and discuss this in person.'

I checked my anger. All around me trades were being done, voices were being raised and information was being shared. On this line, the opposite was happening. I was used to immediate results.

'OK. I can get there at lunchtime.' Drinks with a broker would have to wait. I needed a resolution of this game.

'Good. We'll expect you.' Barham put down the phone.

I didn't know how to prepare for the meeting. I had watched such scenes on television, but imagined it would be different in real life. I tried to picture Anna as a corpse, her life and spirit drained from her. She had to be dead, of course. She would not have walked out on me.

It was five to one when I walked into the station at Lucan Place. The officer at the desk made a call to announce my arrival, and I sat without being asked, feeling as I had when I took important exams or interviews so many years ago. My face was flushed, and my eyes watery. I felt sick, and the smell of the station disagreed with me.

Challis walked in from the street, and was obviously surprised to see me.

46

'Is DI Barham expecting you?'

'Yes.'

That was it. He walked through the side door and disappeared. Very soon afterwards, Barham appeared, unsmiling and serious.

We walked together to the same interview room we had been in the day before, and sat down. Tea was offered and declined. Barham lit a cigar.

'We are conducting a post-mortem on the body we found,' he said, opening the conversation bluntly. 'The dental records suggest that the body is that of your wife.'

The statement drained all feelings from me. The nausea left me; my eyes dried; my face lost its blood. I felt punctured by the words, my shoulders falling forward as if my chest could no longer support their weight. Above all, I felt relief. It was over.

Barham leant forward and looked at me. His tone of voice changed.

'As I said on the phone, we will need you to identify the body. Would you like to wait?'

I looked up at him, moving only my eyes, the muscles in the rest of my body drained of oxygen. My breaths were short and noisy.

'No. Let's do it now.'

Challis and Barham stood behind me. A woman in a white coat stood next to the table, on which there lay a body covered in a white sheet, freshly laundered. Underneath the sheet, probably naked, probably ugly, probably tagged with a cardboard label tied to a toe or ankle, lay Anna. I was cold, and sweated. She was colder.

The room was completely silent. No telephones rang, no water ran from taps or hoses, no one spoke. I wanted to be in a noisy room, full of sound and people and life. I wasn't prepared for this. At an unseen signal from one of the men behind me, the woman leant forward, and pulled the sheet away from the top of the body.

The face was almost unrecognisable. There was bruising across most of it, and the neck was brown and yellow. There was no blood, but many splits in the skin, and large parts were grazed. The hair was lank, and had crusted blood at its roots. I stared at it for what seemed to be a long time, motionless. In those moments, my mind's eye tried to reconcile the image it saw now with the memory it held of Anna the woman, the beautiful wife and mother, and the hiatus this caused delayed my reaction. Then, abruptly and without warning, my body lurched as if it had cracked, and I felt the rising torrent of repressed emotion begin to burst from within me.

'Is this your wife, sir?' Barham asked quietly, his hand resting on my back. 'Take your time.'

I waited until I was sure I could speak without breaking down. 'Yes.'

The sheet was moved over her face again, and I had seen Anna for the last time.

'Tell me what happened.'

I sat in the recovery room with a cup of tea.

Barham was with me. Challis had gone to make some calls.

'The lab boys think she was strangled, and then beaten around the head with a heavy implement. That would explain why there wasn't much blood.'

'Was she . . . violated?'

'There's no evidence to suggest that she was,' Barham replied, which wasn't exactly the answer I was searching for. There was silence. I continued to stare at the floor, holding my teacup and thinking vaguely of Anna. Barham spoke again.

'We still don't know what she was doing there. We've traced the owner of the flat, and we hope to talk to him soon. None of the neighbours know much. I know this must be very hard, sir, but we need you to think again about any possible reason for her to be there.'

'Can you give me the address?'

'Melrose Street. It runs off the south side of Baker Street, towards Marylebone.'

'Will you need me to go there?'

'I think it might be helpful. You might see something there that jogs your memory.'

I thought of Anna's battered face. I thought of Redesdale Street, empty and quiet. The relief I had felt earlier had now given way to grief, and tears began to form in the corners of my eyes. I wanted to cry, and sleep, and scream and, above all, run back to the room next door and hug the bruised body that lay under the sheet.

'Shall we drop you home, sir? We can sort out the

formalities later.' Barham accepted my silence as assent, and he opened the door. Challis was sitting outside, smoking and drinking coffee. He jumped up as we came out, and we walked together along the silent corridor.

The first indication that life was continuing around me was the voice from Challis's radio in the car. Other crimes were being committed or intercepted, fresher felonies that needed their attention. For Barham and Challis, Anna was now a file in their in-tray, a project that would assume and lose priority. Someone was writing her name on the cardboard label attached to her body. They would never see her as I had seen her – a loving, beautiful wife and mother, a half of the whole.

The ground floor of the house consisted of a large double room which ran its entire length. The front half, looking out on to the street, was used as a sitting room, but Anna and I had abandoned it after the children went to boarding school, preferring the warmth of the kitchen or the smaller room we had established directly above it on the first floor. The back half, which had french windows leading on to the small garden, was used as a dining room. There were folding doors between the two areas, but we rarely closed them.

After Challis dropped me at the front door, I went to this room. I sat in an armchair facing the dining area, and looked at the ornaments and decorations that Anna had collected and painstakingly positioned. There was nothing in the room that had come from our single lives; it was as if we had never lived before we married, and the small accruals of those lives had been discarded. I had never liked these rooms, in spite of Anna's best efforts to turn them into comfortable and welcoming spaces.

From the moment I had seen Anna's body, I had not considered the one question Barham would be trying to answer. Anna's death seemed to be the end of things, and further consideration of the circumstances, or the motive, had never crossed my mind. I had simply made no time to think about Anna's death as a crime, as an event that demanded retribution and redress. Now, alone and quiet, I realised that my identification of her body had set in train a new phase of inquiry, pursuit, and discovery. Anna had been killed, brutally. Her life had been harmless – at most inspiring envy in friends and acquaintances. To die alone, beaten and strangled, in a strange environment, couldn't happen to her. But these considerations wouldn't matter to Barham and his colleagues; they needed, and wanted, to find a killer.

I pulled myself out of the comfortable chair and dragged myself down to the kitchen. The light on the answering machine flashed, and I replayed the message. It was Sarah.

'Hi. I heard you had to go to the police. Let me know if I can help, or if you want to see me. Bye.' Her voice was deep and quiet, and reminded me painfully of the warmth I felt in her presence. I had only thought of her in physical terms before now, remembering her smell, her touch, and her sensuality. Stupidly, I now thought about her as a companion and confidante, sharing my pain and easing it. That was not the deal.

I called the office, aware that they would read the story in the evening papers, and spoke to my boss.

'They've found Anna,' I said. Before making him ask the difficult question, I added, 'She's dead.' The words of condolence, offers of assistance and protestations of understanding were lost as I realised what I had accepted and admitted. I thanked him, promised to be in touch, and put the phone down.

I called the office again, and spoke to Sarah.

'Hi, it's me. I got your message. Anna's been found dead.'

I could envisage Sarah pulling hard on a cigarette.

'How are you?' she asked. There didn't seem to be an appropriate answer.

'Numb,' I said at last. That at least was true. I had shed a few tears, but now I simply saw an empty life, well characterised by the huge house around me, with no one to comfort me.

'I'd like to see you tonight,' I continued, and there was a pause in the conversation.

'Is that a good idea?' she answered, obviously keen to avoid the role I wanted her to play.

'Just for an hour or so. You needn't stay – if you don't want to.'

'I'll come round at seven,' she said decisively. 'I'm really sorry; you don't deserve this.'

'OK. See you then.'

Her judgement struck me: I didn't deserve this. I had loved Anna, and we had stayed together. Now she had left me. It wasn't fair. I stood at the work surface, and huge sobs shuddered through me. Anna had no right to be murdered, to be somewhere strange without me, to be lying dead and senseless while I had to carry on. I slumped on to the floor and pulled my knees up to my face, gently rocking myself into deep despair.

Barham was talking.

'This was a particularly vicious murder, and we are very keen to speak to anyone who might have known the victim, or seen anything or anybody strange or unusual in the area.'

The interviewer, a young cub reporter with an American-style perm that made her hair seem sculpted from plasticine, concluded the report with a summary of the facts to date, and some unhealthy speculation. She was standing outside a terrace of flat-fronted houses, one of which was cordoned off with blue and white police tape. I stood before the television screen, still and emotionless.

Barham had told the reporter more than he had told me. Anna had been dead for several days before being discovered, and the police believed she knew her attacker, as there was no sign of forced entry. It was impossible to say whether any valuables had been taken, and they had not established any motive for the killing.

I had to call three people: Nick, Emma, and Anna's mother, Kate. With the media now interested, I needed to give them the facts as I knew them, rather than let them piece it together from second-hand reports. Perversely, I decided to ring Kate first: a strange reasoning within me determined that telling her would be less painful than talking to my children, those babies that Anna and I had created and in whom we had invested so much of ourselves.

The lethargy of despair made it hard to pick up the phone and push the buttons, but I lit a cigar and fought against the pressing instinct for inaction.

She seemed to know it was me, and she seemed to know why I rang. Perhaps she had seen the news, or perhaps she still carried a mother's insight, that extra sense that lets her know of a child's well-being or peril. But however she knew, my call was still the ultimate horror; there was no preparation possible for the news I bore. We talked very quietly, in broken sentences, and we accepted and copied each other's silence. Before hanging up, she promised to come straight away.

I was rubbing my forehead and biting my lip when the doorbell rang, long and insistent. I trudged up to the hall and opened the door. A face I recognised looked at me inquiringly, head cocked to one side in an attempt to appear concerned.

'Hallo. I'm Carole. From next door?' The final sentence was posed as a question, in the hope it would raise some flicker of recognition.

'Yes, of course,' I said vaguely.

'Look, I know it's a very bad time to call, but I just wanted to say that if you need any help, anything at all, please let us know.'

I looked at Carole. She was in her late thirties, with a haircut and clothes that rendered her entirely sexless. She was not going to be found strangled in a flat in central London; she was too sensible and boring for that, and I resented her solidity of character and purpose.

'Thank you. I'm fine at the moment. Just need some peace and quiet.' I tried to make the last remark chatty, but it fell between us as clearly as a barbed wire fence.

'OK. Well, do let us know. Bye.' She turned to leave and walked down my steps, and up hers, back to her protective, and protected, cell. I wondered if she knew Anna; we had certainly never spoken. The visit could have been a genuine gesture of help, but I didn't need the type of help that was on offer. I turned back into the hall and looked at my watch. I had time to shower and change before Sarah would arrive. I had time to call Nick. Anna's death had strangely given me an excess of time. I walked to the kitchen, poured a glass of whisky, and drank it.

As I dialled Nick's number, I watched the images on the television screen and thought of the time that stretched before me. I was still lost in thought when Nick came to the phone. He greeted me with a hesitancy that suggested he already knew why I was calling.

'Hey, Dad,' he said unconvincingly.

'There's no easy way to tell you this, Nick. Your mother . . .' I trailed off, knowing that he knew and unable to find a way of confirming it. The silence that lingered between us was crippling, a testimony to the mutual pain we suffered.

After an age, Nick spoke. 'I'll come down. I'm coming now, Dad.' And that was it; that was all that we needed to say, all that we could say in this most desperate hour.

Deflated, sickened, I slid down the wall and sat on the floor with the bottle and glass, not planning to get drunk, but certainly intending to blunt the edges of my fear of the future.

SIX

The Saturday of Anna's last birthday party had
started like all others. Douglas and I played golf,
although I left later so that Anna and I could share
breakfast together. Anna seemed unchanging, and
unchangeable; her hair was still honey-coloured, falling on to her shoulders with the same thickness as
when we first met, and her face remained beautiful,
clear skin and blue eyes with very small features,
mouth, ears and nose all petite in their most exact
definition. If she had put on weight since we married, I neither noticed it nor cared. When we held
each other, which was really only at weekends, her
body was still warm and welcoming, soft in the right
places and all mine.

At breakfast, Anna displayed no emotion other
than happiness with her presents. I had bought her
a diamond eternity ring, inscribed with her initials
and the date. There were various other presents –
soaps, clothes, perfumes, books, coveted opera tickets
– but the ring obviously struck her as a fresh affirmation of our life together. She held her hand up in

front of her face and twisted it from side to side to catch the morning light in the stones. Our bedroom, where we were having breakfast, was at the back of the house on the first floor, and looked out on to our small garden. When the children were growing up, this had been our big regret: the garden was not big enough, and ball games had to be played in one of the London parks, or at school. I had put up small goalposts for Nick, but he had never used them much, preferring to play football with friends who had bigger gardens. But now, with Emma and Nick gone, we had decided to dig it up and create a special place for us, and work had already started.

When I left Anna she was still lying in bed, inspecting the diamond ring and planning a long soak in the bath. I had not told her about the party that evening; she liked surprises, and I had spent months secretly organising the caterers and the guests. Her mother was coming, and would stay the night with us. Four other couples were invited, two of whom were on second marriages, one of whom would soon no longer be together. We had watched other couples struggle through the lean years, too preoccupied with raising their children to realise that they were drifting apart. By the time they noticed, it was too late. Anna instinctively blamed the men for this: they worked too hard, neglected their wives, had their heads turned by younger women. She would always finish this tirade by remarking on how lucky she was to have me, and that we would survive now the children were grown up.

The morning was perfect for golf; Douglas and I both played well, and we felt invigorated as we stepped into the bar for our whiskies. Douglas produced two fat cigars and we stood silent for a moment, remembering some of the glorious shots we had crafted. Douglas spoke first, and broke the spell.

'Hilary's leaving. She's known about Susie for a long time, and she can't forgive me.'

This was not a surprise, but the breaking of the news was: Douglas and Hilary had agreed to come to the party, and Douglas had told me last week that things were improving between them. Susie was a client of his, a former model whose physical charms Douglas had been unable to resist. The affair soon faded, but the fall-out from it did not.

'Is there no way you can save it?' I asked, more for something to say than out of any belief that it could be saved.

'I honestly don't know if I want to,' Douglas replied. This was the saddest statement he could have made, a confirmation of the mutual dereliction of something they had spent most of their lives building. Involuntarily, I felt smug. I knew Anna would be sympathetic, but would feel the same. We had lasted; we were strong.

'What about the children?' They had two girls, aged thirteen and ten.

Douglas shook his head and shrugged. 'We'll work something out. They already know we're not happy together. I'll find somewhere nearby to live.' He finished his whisky, and ordered more.

I looked at the floor, trying to find the words that

would express a due sense of regret, and encouragement. None came, and I puffed on my cigar. I thought about the party. I wasn't sure I wanted them in our home, a threat to our secure habitat.

If Douglas was looking for a man-to-man chat, he obviously felt we had had it.

'My golf game isn't suffering, anyway,' he said, raising his glass, and smiled. We could now return to the safer ground of men's talk. For another fifteen minutes, we stood discussing our better shots, humbly acknowledging our weaknesses and congratulating each other on our performance. As we carried our clubs back to the car park, Douglas turned to me.

'Looking forward to seeing you and Anna tonight,' he said. 'About eight?'

'That'll be fine. See you then.' A brief shadow passed across my mind, as I wondered how we would greet them, knowing that they had failed to complete the race. Then I climbed in the car, switched on the CD, and slipped back into my Saturday persona.

The caterers, friends of Anna, were scheduled to arrive at six. Because of our extended breakfast, I had told Anna that we would eat at home for lunch, and would go out in the evening. Her mother was due at teatime, and we could leave the house before six, returning on some pretext to present Anna with her surprise party.

Anna was in the kitchen when I returned home. The kitchen was large and white and cluttered with the inconsequential trappings of our existence. I kissed her lightly and sat at the large pine table, which was no longer covered with the patterned vinyl tablecloth we'd considered vital when the children lived with us.

'How was Douglas?' she asked. The question was harmless.

'They're going to break up,' I said, and the shadow reappeared.

Anna was silent; her back to me, she continued to slice tomatoes, with no change in rhythm, no body language that betrayed any reaction.

'Douglas seems fine,' I continued, convinced that a full discussion of his problem would chase away the shadow. 'He thinks he'll move somewhere close, for the children.'

'Do you want a drink?' Anna asked. She moved to the fridge and took out a bottle of Sancerre. She poured two glasses without waiting for my reply. She turned to the table and put both glasses down. Then she sat opposite me.

'How's Hilary?' she said finally.

'I didn't ask, and he didn't say,' I replied, sensing that she knew this.

Anna looked at me as if I were a stranger at the table. She sipped her wine, put the glass down, and got up. She returned to the work surface. The knife continued to slice the tomatoes. Anna's beautiful hands worked carefully, her painted nails glistening with the juice. She finished preparing the salad, crumbling feta cheese over the tomatoes, and placed the plate on the table. She looked at me again.

'Do you want dressing on this?' Her avoidance of the subject was worse than any other reaction; she seemed to be insulating herself against any emotion. Anna was rarely upset by other people's misfortunes, but she normally got involved, either through interest or affection for those concerned.

'Just some balsamic vinegar,' I replied, and she placed the bottle on the table. The new ring glittered on her wedding finger.

'I'm going to lie down,' she said, as she walked towards the stairs outside the kitchen. 'I'll see you later.'

Whatever Anna was thinking, it excluded me. I ate in silence, dreading the rest of the day.

When Anna reappeared, at five, she was beautiful. She was wearing a dress I had not seen before, in rich burgundy with fine gold threads, and her honey-eyed hair was lustrous. She wore a single gold chain – a present from some previous birthday – and black patent shoes. Her make-up was discreet, yet heavier than for the daytime. I remembered why I had fallen for her all those years ago.

Her mother sat at the kitchen table, a dry sherry in front of her. She had arrived an hour before, and had drunk tea with me whilst we waited for Anna to come down. I had warned her that Anna was resting. Kate was excited about the party, the surprise for her girl. She enjoyed the conspiracy. Anna embraced her, they kissed and complimented each other on their appearance, and I poured Anna a glass of sherry before moving upstairs to change.

In our bathroom, I stood in front of the mirror and gazed at myself. I was in good shape – tennis, squash and golf took care of that – and I still had all my hair and my own teeth. The irritation with Anna that I had felt earlier now seemed unreasonable. She was entitled to private thoughts. Couples should have privacy, if not secrecy, from each other. She was not particularly close to Hilary, but might well feel some sorrow for her position.

I showered and changed quickly, and was soon downstairs again, gently guiding them to make sure we left the house before six. I deliberately left my wallet in the kitchen, and slammed shut the front door at five to six. We wandered down Redesdale Street, the summer air still warm. Kate talked too much, asking about Emma and Nick and Anna's birthday presents; Anna smiled and nodded, with the vaguest air of someone not completely engaged in the ritual of small talk. We reached the bar in Sloane Square, sat at a table, and ordered drinks.

The chat between Kate and Anna meandered from topic to topic, and I became a necessary but silent partner. I thought of Cape Cod, and wanted to be there now. We'd bought a single-storey house in a new development five years before. We had decided to take a family holiday in the States on the back of a business trip I had to make, and a colleague rented us his house for two weeks. Almost every state in America thinks it can make the joke, 'If you don't like the weather, wait half an hour,' but on the Cape this holds true. We loved it there, and were perfect prey for the realtor who approached us less than an hour after our check-in at the clubhouse. The realtor promised us steady rental income for the whole year, pointing out the affluence of the area and its resistance to recession. The inference was that old money protected this location from the vagaries of new money. We believed the pitch, signed the papers, and arranged finance. The house quickly became a millstone as the real estate market headed south, and rentals were sporadic and unprofitable. Anna always referred to it as the family folly; Emma had used it once since she went to New York, and we had only had one holiday in it together.

Anna and I were going to the Cape for the last three weeks of the summer, and I couldn't wait to be there. I would play tennis and golf, and read whatever books Anna had bought for me. I knew about Californian wines, and would enjoy choosing the best ones for our meals. Anna liked the change; she would sit on the deck at the back of the house, with a hat protecting her delicate skin, reading endless novels that she had acquired over the last year. We would come back tanned, relaxed and with the confirmatory glow of a happy couple.

We had more drinks, and Kate took on the faint flush of excitement that comes from mixing anticipation and alcohol. Kate and I got on well; she never asked me about work, either through a complete lack of interest or because she was confused by the sheer complexity of what I did. When I started in the dealing room, I remember my father saying to me, 'Tell me what you actually do when you get into work.' He was desperate to understand how his boy was earning a living, perhaps disappointed that I wasn't in what he considered to be a real profession, but proud none the less. He died without ever seeing the real possibilities of trading in money.

I looked at my watch; it was time to move back to the house. We finished our drinks, the girls went to the powder room, and I sat waiting for them. When they returned, I told them I had left my wallet at home, and we should go back to the house to collect it. Anna seemed completely taken in, and we wandered towards Redesdale Street. We reached the front steps, and had little difficulty in persuading Anna to come back in for two minutes. I opened the door to our sitting room, and motioned for Anna to go in. She looked at me strangely, realisation arriving on her face, and she stepped in the room to be confronted by eight smiling friends. They held champagne glasses, and shouted welcomes and congratulations at Anna, a queue forming to embrace her. My girl, my wife, was receiving her due accolades as a successful partner, a beautiful and loving wife, a winner.

Anna's reaction was unexpected. Her eyes watered, the smile on her face transient and fragile, and she seemed to shake slightly. She took a glass of champagne, and looked across at me with a face that said many things I couldn't exactly interpret. Kate hugged her, enjoying the spectacle of her daughter's adoration. I moved to Anna, and kissed her on both cheeks.

'Happy birthday, darling,' I said as I pulled away. 'Surprised?'

The conversation around us shifted into gear again, and I moved from couple to couple, everyone too willing to laugh at the slightest sign of wit. Anna recovered her glow, and the ritual of the dinner party could begin.

I reached Hilary, and put my arm across her shoulder.

'Thanks for coming. It means a lot to us,' I said.

'Doug told you, then?' she asked, and I knew from the tone that she was well on the way to being drunk.

'I'm so sorry,' I said.

'Don't be. Didn't one of the Greek philosophers say that there is nothing so satisfying as seeing your best friend fall off a roof? Enjoy it.' The words were delivered without much venom, as if Hilary had spent much time practising her control.

'No one likes to see old friends split up,' I said, although her comment rang uncomfortably true. 'We love you both. We want to help.'

'Then get me another drink,' she said, and held out her empty glass. I waved to the waitress, smartly dressed in crisp white blouse and black skirt, and the tray of champagne appeared. Hilary took a glass, and drank off the top inch.

'Douglas is weak. He will need your help, the bas-

66

tard. I've given up everything for him, and now I'm going to have my own life. Cheers.' She walked away from me towards Anna, leaving the strength of her mood swirling around me, stingingly close to my skin. She had threatened the force field that Anna and I had built around us, and the very threat was enough. We wouldn't be seeing Hilary again.

The caterers had set the table perfectly, with small nosegays of fresh flowers at each place, the crystal sparkling and the linen crisp and virgin. Anna sat at the head of the table, and we lined up on either side, the french windows open on to the garden. The stream of conversation flowed until the first course arrived, immaculate parcels of salmon mousse wrapped with smoked salmon and tied up with strips of plaited green chives. Wine glasses were emptied and refilled, each tide invigorating the table and driving the evening forward. After the plates had disappeared, Hilary stood up and excused herself. She took the overcareful steps of someone who was aware of their drunkenness, and left the room. Her move came as a punctuation mark in the conversation, Douglas looking at me and then busying himself with his glass. The volume of talk dropped, then rose again, and the exit appeared to be no more than a hyphen.

When Hilary returned no such break occurred. I looked up as she came in, and her eyes betrayed the exertions of nausea. She stood behind one of the guests, Jamie, and faced Douglas.

'You fucking bastard!' she shouted. 'You selfish, weak, arrogant little shit! How you've got the fucking nerve to play this game! You shit! Shit!' She narrowed her eyes, reddened and swollen, and steadied herself on the back of Jamie's chair, preparing for another onslaught or Doug's counter-offensive. The effect on the atmosphere was paralysing. No one moved. The waitress was frozen in mid-delivery of a plate. Everyone waited for the next volley, keen to catch every last detail.

'Where's your bimbo tonight, you two-timing little bastard? Anyone here you fancy? Excluding me, of course. You're nothing but a supercharged prick! Fuck you!' Considering the amount she had drunk – both here and, presumably, before she'd arrived – her control of language, and her tongue, was excellent. Doug's head remained locked in its original position, studying the empty space where his plate was about to be laid. Hilary took another breath, and delivered her next onslaught in a lower tone.

'Don't bother to come home tonight. I've had enough. Find some tart to bury your head in. I'm sure there are plenty of takers.' There was a pause, and I expected Hilary to crack, or leave the room, or build up to another attack. Instead, she walked back to her chair, and sat down, flushed but obviously cleansed and calmed by what she had done. Her movement was the only sign that we were still alive. She picked up her glass, which was empty, and held it out to the waitress.

'Could I have some more wine, please?'

68

Someone cleared their throat, a signal for the next phase of entertainment to begin. Everyone strained to sense what Douglas was doing, and what he might do. Finally, he pulled his napkin from his lap, wiped his mouth, and pushed his chair back.

'Sorry, everyone,' he said. 'I think we'd better go.' He stood up, and turned towards Hilary. 'Come on. We're going. We'll discuss this at home.'

Hilary didn't move. Anna did. She got up from the table, and went over to Doug. She put a gentle hand on his forearm, and they walked out of the dining room. All eyes turned to me.

'More wine, please,' I said to the waitress, and she started moving again. The front door slammed shut, and Anna returned. She went up to Hilary, slid her arms around her shoulders, and whispered in her ear. Hilary stood up and walked out of the room with Anna. As they left, the wine was being replenished, and I got up to follow the girls down to the kitchen. A feeble ripple of talk began behind me. Hilary's fireworks had sobered the drunk, and lowered the voices. The wine would have a lot of work to do to restore the noise.

The scene in the kitchen was arresting. Hilary sat at the table, surrounded by plates of prepared food and empty dishes, a full glass of wine in front of her. Anna stood leaning against a work surface, looking more distressed than Hilary. She stared at me, the iron curtain of womanhood dropping between us.

'I'm taking Hilary home,' she said curtly. 'You're not needed here. Go back to your guests.'

To jump in, to take a blowtorch to the curtain, would have been dangerous. Stupidly, I wanted to help by making sympathetic and understanding gestures, but to Anna I could do neither. I was in the woman's world, and it felt frightening. I simply nodded, held my hands up in self-defence, and left.

Back at the dining-table, food and wine had worked their magic, and the spectre of disharmony had been eaten and drunk away. I spoke before sitting down.

'Anna's going to take Hilary home. Sorry about all this. Right, where's my food?'

A plate was produced, the conversation picked up again, and we made our best effort to ignore the chilly wind that had blown across our lives. Soon we were back to golf, the arts, tabloid scandal, and money. We were comfortable, and it was important to remain unruffled. By the time the port arrived, and we were able to sprawl with analgesic coffee, cigars and mints in the sitting room, the smell of pain had dissipated.

The caterers were gone by one o'clock. I sat at the kitchen table, with the last of the port and a huge cigar, listening to the swirling waters of the dishwasher and waiting for Anna. Hilary was her problem, and she must deal with it at her own pace. At one-thirty I turned off the lights and went to bed. I never heard Anna come in, and I slept well, in spite of the emptiness beside me. I knew Anna was mine, wherever she was. She could never be anything else.

SEVEN

The dryness woke me up. My skin, my eyes, my hair, my tongue, were all too dry. I was lying on my front, partially covered by the bedclothes, still wearing my socks and pants. I moved my eyes slowly towards the clock: it was three-thirty in the morning. I could hear the blood rushing through my ears, and my heartbeat reverberated painfully through my whole body. Carefully, I turned my head to see if Sarah was lying next to me. She wasn't.

I slithered out of bed on to the floor, steadying myself and my stomach on all fours before crawling towards the bathroom. I pushed open the door; the light was on, although I didn't need it. I wrapped myself round the bowl of the lavatory, and heaved and retched, desperately trying to exorcise the spirit inside me. My stomach was empty, even of bile and phlegm, and the violent contractions merely transferred the centre of my heartbeat to my forehead. My eyes watered and bulged, and I lay on my haunches, arms around the bowl, in a cataleptic stupor. The roaring of blood through my ears increased, blocking any reasonable thought.

Tears of effort dribbled down my cheeks, and my nose leaked, but the dryness stayed within me. After an age, I hauled myself on to my knees and reached the nearest water supply, the bidet. I ran the cold tap, and let the water spray over me. I kept my head still, the persistent beat of my heart the only indication that I was still alive. I stood up, shakily and unconvincingly, and moved to the basin. I rested my whole body weight with my hands on the rim, my head stiffly slumped forward, and waited for the next wave of nausea. Nothing came.

I stumbled back to the bed and fell on to it. I felt as if the muscles of my body were not long enough to stretch over the bones, causing me to contract and shrivel. I shivered, not the shivering of cold but the uncontrolled shaking of physical and mental agony. My eyes stung when open, and my eyelids felt too small to cover the bulging eyeballs. Every physical routine – the heartbeat, the blood stream, the air passage – was magnified to replace the normal senses, which I had lost the use of. Monochrome kaleidoscopic patterns swirled on the insides of my eyelids, eventually hypnotising me into the dusk of uneasy sleep.

By five-thirty I was standing in the shower, the water finding no purchase on my parched skin. The motions of early morning preparation each required a new effort, as if I was learning the disciplines for the first time. After shaving, I put on a dressing-gown and walked downstairs, sliding my shoulder along the wall for support. I put my head round the door of the sitting room and turned on the light. There was no evidence that I had been there the night before; the cushions were straight, and the still air betrayed only the faintest trace of cigar smoke. I moved downstairs to the kitchen. Everything was in its place. The table was clear, the work surfaces clean, and a bottle of Scotch, half-full, stood in its usual place. There was a note propped against the answering machine.

> Ring me if you ever wake up!
> Love S xoxoxo

Coffee may cure a hangover, but only if you have the courage to swallow it. I made tea, English Breakfast, and hoped that it would reach my stomach by osmosis, not keen to sip and feel it pass from mouth to gullet to the pounding maelstrom in my midriff. Sarah's note had encouraged me; she couldn't be too cross with me. The relief I felt about this would have surprised and confused me if I had been feeling well enough to understand those emotions.

Sitting at the table, looking at the challenge of the liquid in front of me, I was feeling brave enough to try to remember what had happened. The conscious part of my mind battled with the subconscious, which was determined to jettison any memory of the last twelve hours. The human brain has the ability to administer anaesthetic for the mental agonies of drunkenness, and now I was too

73

weak to fight against it. I walked to the phone, and called Sarah.

'Hi.' She sounded alert, and cheerful. 'How are you feeling?'

'I'm alive,' I said huskily, the dryness of my throat betraying itself. 'What happened?' I waited for the reply with the same anticipation I might have felt for an exam result, wanting and yet not wanting to know.

'Do you remember anything?'

I shook my head, the left side of my face twitching. 'Nothing.'

'You were pretty pissed when I arrived. You rambled on for about an hour, and drank a lot more. I sat and listened. You said some pretty crazy things.'

'I'm sorry. I don't know what made me do it.'

'That's OK. I got an early night. You were unconscious by nine o'clock.'

'Thanks. Thanks for everything.' My conversation was limited to thanks and regrets and apologies.

'Just let me know if you need anything. I'm not going to come round with your family there.'

Her words broke through the blood roar that still ran across my eardrums, releasing suspended emotion like a lance in a boil. The muscles that had lain so taut against my frame relaxed. But what I wanted to say was still trapped between my brain and tongue.

'Thanks. I'll call you – soon.'

'OK. Bye.' She was gone, and so was much of the pain.

How do you lose touch with your children? Emma was in a foreign country, physically and emotionally. Had I driven her there? She lived in Manhattan, working as an assistant to a publisher whose daughter she had been at school with.

Emma's ambition seemed to be to put distance between us and her – or me and her. By the time she announced her decision, Anna and I had picked up the basics of the new age of parenting: positive encouragement, financial support, the security of a safety net – offering without dissent the key to the cage of childhood. She flew away without a backward glance.

Sometimes she called home, always when I was at work. The magic bridge that links father and daughter had not disintegrated – it had never been built. Even as a child, she never asked for physical comfort from me. Nick could be very demonstrative, hugging and kissing freely when he wasn't ranting and fighting, but Emma stayed aloof. Nick had two worlds, home and school, but Emma had one, and I wasn't part of it. To say I had lost touch with her was wrong: I had never been in touch.

I could only remember Emma's childhood by looking at photos. There were a thousand scraps of memory about Nick's early years – the first words, the first bike, the first day at school – but Emma had kept all this from me. It had never struck me, or worried me; I had a son and daughter, and they were different. I loved them both. Before Emma's birth, Anna and I had talked about our fear of rationing love, which we believed to be a finite commodity. I reasoned that children were like separate parts of a garden, needing different nutrients and attention but no less loved because of that. And the love was always there, available and ready to be tapped. Emma never drew from the reserves I had for her.

The dull drone of the transatlantic dial tone was muted; it rang four times before a sleepy voice answered.

'Emma, it's Dad.'

There was an immediate change in her tone. 'What's wrong? Have they found Mum?' She was awake now, on the defensive, electrified by three words from me.

'I'm sorry, baby. Mum is dead.' The confession coiled its way through the black space between us, a vague echo on the line cruelly replaying the words.

'What do you mean? How? How did it happen?' Frantic now, and obviously moving into a better position to hear the details and absorb the impact of the punched information, Emma talked too fast for the line and echo to keep up.

'Someone killed her. They don't know who. I only just found out,' I lied.

Emma went silent, the line between us hissing gently, waiting for the next violent blow.

'How? How? Why?' she called across the abyss.

'Listen. I'll call the airline, and book you on a

flight. I'll see if I can get you on Concorde. Just get packed, and I'll call you back.' I paused, but she said nothing. 'I'm so sorry, baby. Let's get you home.'

Emma wanted more information, but it was hard enough to talk to her face to face, let alone across the bloodless wires and darkness. I rang off, hating myself for realising that she had not stopped to ask how I was, something Nick had instinctively done.

The rushing waves of blood continued to hiss, like the phone line but pulsed. I called the airline, and got a flight booked on Concorde. Then I called her back. If she had been crying, she was determined not to let me know.

'Dad, tell me more. What happened?'

'Honestly, there isn't much to tell. She was found in a strange flat. No one knows why she was there. The police are doing everything they can.'

'Who could do this to her? Everyone loved her.'

'I know, I know. I can't accept it myself. Just come home and we'll sort everything out.' This was a paternal promise that was made to be broken, and accepted by both as such. There was more silence than distance between us. I promised to meet her at Heathrow, and we hung up.

As I stood in the shower, trying for the second time to wash away the ache that I felt, the phone rang. I stood at the bedside table, dripping and naked, and listened to Challis speak.

'We will need you to visit the flat with us, sir. Could we do that today?'

I explained about the imminent arrivals of family, unable to tell him when I might be free. He understood but still wanted a commitment from me. I agreed that he should send a car now, confident that Kate and Nick would not arrive before lunchtime.

He went on. 'We need to conduct a post-mortem before releasing the, er, your wife's body,' he said. 'Have you made any arrangements?'

The attendant formalities of death had completely escaped me. I didn't even know what Anna would have wanted as a funeral. 'No, not yet,' I replied.

'Well, let us know and we'll try to fit in with whatever you decide.' He spoke as if we were arranging for a car to be serviced. I thanked him, and hung up.

I went back into the bathroom, and brushed my teeth for the third time, still unsuccessful in overcoming the stench and taste of stale whisky. The dead face of Anna, bruised and divorced from her life, flashed in my mind. I didn't want to stand still. Action, activity, noise, friendship, even the company of policemen, would be preferable to the dead and deadening atmosphere in this house. Looking out of the bedroom window, I saw that the garden too seemed to be dying, mourning the loss of spirit, or a spirit, inside. The feeble autumn sun, white through a grey membrane of thin cloud, was sucking life away, pulling moisture and vigour from the air around me, and the house, and the garden.

I dressed, and got ready for my police escort.

EIGHT

Making love to Sarah didn't feel like infidelity. The passionate hours we spent together fulfilled two people's needs. No one got hurt, and we knew we could control and manage the consequences of our physical desires. In the moments when we lay together, I felt no regret or remorse, and I never thought of Anna. This was a private deal, offer and acceptance of sexual ecstasy, and Anna was not a party to our contract.

In bed, Sarah exceeded the promise that she held out to all men. The act of intercourse was a religion for her, the rituals keenly observed and fully executed. Each part of her body was available and willing to yield to pleasure, and her smooth architecture yearned to be admired and touched. Her nipples were the sensitive barometers of her lust; at rest, they were small and dark and crinkled, but aroused, they burst into flower, full and black and proudly stiff. They were the beacons of our hunger for each other, reference points on the map of her body that I returned to again and again with mouth and fingers. The violent clattering of our bones together beat out our desperate cravings in a rhythmic tattoo.

To arrive at Sarah's bed, to travel the road to her private Damascus, had involved no lies or subterfuge. Everything about Sarah was direct – her attention, her threat, her needs, and her approach. Standing in Lucho's, aware of the unspoken voltage that had built up between us, she leant across to me, her face close to mine.

'I want you to fuck me,' she said in her low, determined voice.

I looked down at the floor, then looked into her eyes, searching for something. There was no reply needed, or asked for. This was her way, her culture. Offer and acceptance, all in one.

'Now?' I asked, the question surprising me with its intent.

'Now. Let's go.'

A door had opened, just when it seemed that I would travel along the corridor of my life with no diversions, breaks or pauses. There was no agony, no first or second thoughts – simply a look, a feeling, an understanding, and an agreement.

The taxi ride was silent, our contract needing no words of affirmation or token gestures of affection. Once in the flat, Sarah wrapped her taut body around me, a deep embrace that covered tongues and lips and legs and arms, as if she needed to be inside me. I held her under her buttocks, the heat of her burning through to my skin, the tension in her body threatening to snap her. She climbed off me, holding me by the hand and pulling me towards a darkened room. Shoes dropped off, buttons slipped, zips released, and we stood again, the fury of our passion locking us together.

The dark moist crevice of her buttocks opened as she embraced me with her legs, and I ran my hand through the warmth of hair and dampness, fingertips eagerly sensing her excitement. Her head rested on my shoulder as I dipped my fingers deeply, her arms stiffly immobile as she let me discover hidden treasures. We fell on the bed together, and she relaxed, leaning to turn on a dim light before pushing me on to my back. Her face rubbed against my chest, her dark hair falling to cover her expression, as she slowly kissed a deviant route down across my stomach, reaching her target with flicks of the tongue whilst her hands followed different paths to the same destination. I pulled her head towards mine, from a fear of too much pleasure, and we kissed again, Sarah now astride me, rubbing her moisture down me. She sat up, pushing her hands hard against my chest, and raised herself whilst I ran my hands behind her thighs, stroking them until I could wait no longer and entered her. Warmth turning to searing heat, Sarah eased down until she sat upright, repeating the movement with her fingertips on my stomach. The large black nipples transfixed me as her rhythm took hold, and my hands rested limply on her thighs. She leaned back and stopped her movement, holding me inside her as her head pushed away from me, her stomach concave and tightened, the clear neck tensed with imminence.

Her legs drew in to my sides and she collapsed back on to me, our faces now together, as she began the long strokes of final passion, measured and perfected as I clasped her buttocks, my fingers feeling the point at which we joined. The silent ecstasy was broken by her order – 'Now!' – and her head pressed hard into my neck as the terminal wave of climax rolled shuddering through us.

Still tightly linked, we lay as one, the dew of passion cooling beneath my fingers as I ran them down her spine. Sarah gently kissed my face, then looked at me.

'We needed that,' she said. She kissed my mouth, then slid off me. Her hand rested on my chest, and the disappearance of her warmth, the boilerhouse of her sensuality, made me shiver.

'Do you have to go?' she asked, before I had even thought it.

I took her hand, and turned towards her.

'Only if you want me to,' I replied.

'Not yet,' she replied, and I was lost to her.

'In the end, all men are bastards,' Sarah said.

We were lying on the bed, a sheet over us, basking in the post-coital twilight until passion returned.

'Look at you,' she continued. 'Here you are, screwing me, cheating on your wife, and planning to get away with it.' The remark had no sting in it. 'But women know it. We're all wise to you. As long as you work on the premiss that all men are total bastards, you won't be disappointed.'

That was it; Sarah had given me her philosophy, directly and succinctly. There seemed to be little point in disputing or discussing it.

'Your nipples are like burnt champagne corks,' I said, leaning over under the sheet and gently kissing the nearer one. I cupped the breast under my hand, concentrating my mouth on the held flesh, and Sarah pressed my head in towards her. Moving from one small breast to the other, I licked and sucked while Sarah used her fingers for herself. The force and speed with which she came surprised me. As she relaxed, I pressed myself against her, sideways on. Then she pulled me across her, astride her stomach, and she brought her hands down my chest and stomach, slowly caressing then pumping as I leant forward to hold her shoulders. I gripped her hard and tightened round her, every muscle popping as I reached release. Sarah looked up at me, and smiled.

'How lovely. A pearl necklace. Just what I always wanted,' she laughed.

I walked along the Embankment from Battersea Bridge, the night air cooling my mind. The traffic on the river picks up at night, long cargo boats trailing stealthily, their look-outs passive on the bow, their wake the merest whispers on the water. I leant against the river wall and lit a cigar. I knew that I should be feeling different, and searched in vain for guilt, remorse and sickness.

Now I had it all. Until tonight, I hadn't known

about the deep hunger of sex, the gnawing appetite that drains the mind and soul and flesh until it feeds on other bodies. Anna hadn't fed this: neither she nor I even knew it existed. Our lovemaking was gentle and even-paced, a literal exposition of the term. Sarah had love somewhere, but kept it far away from the crunching, tight and sweaty contract of her bed.

I strolled towards Albert Bridge, a pastel confection of icing and lights. The parting gift of Sarah's warm soft skin under my hands stayed with me. Two men, very drunk, performed a three-legged dance as they leant against each other and swayed along the pavement towards me. They were laughing, a different joy from mine, but we were all infected by some powerful stimulant that made the muscles weak and the soul sing.

I reached the door of my home, the same as every other night. The house was quiet and dark. I turned on lights, and went down to the kitchen, carrying some mail that must have arrived by second post. I poured a Scotch and water, and listened to the sounds of the house at rest. I walked up to the bedroom and looked at the empty bed, undisturbed as Anna would have left it that morning. I opened drawers and cupboards, visited every room for signs of life. I found myself at the kitchen again, and sat with my drink. I listened to the message I had left for Anna on the machine. It was real; Anna wasn't there. I finished my drink, then called the police.

NINE

That summer was a shining, shimmering season. Every early morning held the promise of finer weather, the sky quite cloudless and the streets still damp from light night showers; the evenings were long and lazy, as if the sun resented dipping away from sight.

That summer promised and delivered many joys. Nick was excited by the prospect of university, the potential for escape into a further stage of his maturity, whilst Emma was impatiently planning her own life and future. Anna and I were well aware of what this presaged, of lonely nights and tidy rooms, of quiet times when we wanted noise, but we secretly harboured our own excitement, for them as well as us. Change hurts, but the bruises are temporary; we had been preparing for this moment, telling each other and ourselves of the need for new horizons, and we all felt a delicious tingling on our skin as we considered the mysteries that lay ahead.

My office life seemed to reflect this mood of evolution, revolution almost: just after Easter I'd been promoted to the secretive and powerful Asset and Liability Committee – known by the acronym ALCO – which met weekly to consider the bank's exposures to markets and players, and formulated trading and positioning strategies. The thrill of being at the heart of the treasury machine was heightened by the new way in which I was treated by others: secretaries delivered huge packages of facts and figures, full of sensitivity analyses and yield curve charts which I was supposed to understand and digest, whilst even Ben seemed quite impressed by my elevated status, a feeling which manifested itself in the huge drinking session we had to celebrate my promotion, sponsored by Ben and attended by all the usual suspects. Sarah remained casual, her coolness like a lump of melting ice slithering down my spine, that questioning look of hers acting as a thermostat lest my self-esteem become overheated.

At a special weekend off-site meeting held in a Surrey hotel, ALCO decided to refurbish the dealing room. We pored over numbers, watched presentations from excited sales representatives of software and hardware vendors as they sought to prise additional funds from us, and studied the ramifications of the upheaval. Architects advised us on the ergonomics, interior designers flashed colour charts and swatches in front of us, and financial controllers dazzled us with forecasts of budgets and projected income streams. To me this was a thrill every bit as stimulating as the actual trading; now I was at the centre, making decisions that would endure long after the yen had dropped or the Mark had strengthened. At last I was being asked for my opinion, and it felt good.

It was hard to explain this to Anna. 'I thought you had no interest in management,' she had said when I first told her the news of my promotion.

'This isn't management *per se*, it's recognition,' I said. 'The bank is saying I've done a good job, and here is my reward. It's almost symbolic.'

'Then why are you so excited?'

'Because someone else is finally confirming what we've always believed. Someone whose opinion I value is telling us that I have more to give, and this is the best way of getting it.'

Anna shrugged and smiled at me wistfully, then put her hand on my shoulder and kissed me. 'If that's what it takes to please you, then I'm happy for you. It's just . . .'

'What?'

'Nothing,' she said frustratingly. 'Forget it.'

'No, what? I want to know what you think. It's important.'

'I'd always thought that you wanted to be a dealer for ever. I thought you were completely happy with what you were doing. It just seems as if this is a step in a different direction, away from your beloved trading room and into the executive suite.'

Anna had always affected a complete lack of interest in the mechanics and politics of my business life. She congratulated me when I'd done well, commiserated when I hadn't, and left the rest to me.

87

She never tried to offer advice, never sought to be involved – and yet what she said now was perceptive and revealed an understanding of my motivation that I'd never realised she had.

'Maybe I haven't explained it very well,' I said, still a little surprised by the sharpness of her observation.

'Try me.'

'Moving up to ALCO won't change a thing, not in practical terms. It simply sends a message, to me and the other traders, about my competence. But I'm not going to leave the room, and I'm not going to lose touch with the markets, which is what I love.'

'Your first love,' she said, almost teasingly. I laughed as if to recognise that she was joking, although a doubt remained.

'At work, sure. Nothing can beat going into that room every morning and testing yourself again – giving yourself eight hours to beat the market and the other players, and to come out unscathed, ready for another battle the next day. I'd never get that buzz with anything else.'

'And can you go on with it? Will that buzz last for ever, like you hope?'

'What you're really asking me is what I want to do when I grow up, isn't it? My hope is that I never have to answer that question. I know you don't think much of my work, but it's what makes me happy. We must all seem very silly to you, standing there shouting at each other and watching the wealth of nations flashing across our screens. But it's like a drug, and I don't fancy cold turkey yet.' I didn't want to sound annoyed with her, but she was blunting the edge of my triumph.

'To be perfectly honest I don't think anything about your work. Of course I like what it's given us, and I'm eternally grateful to you and the bank for the opportunities we've had. But I haven't sat down and analysed its merits. Do you want me to?'

'Anna, for God's sake, let's not make something out of this that isn't there. Nothing's going to change. The money will still be there, the bonuses will still roll in, and we'll have the same life. Just be happy for me – for us – that I'm doing a job I love and that I'm earning the respect of my peers.'

'I am,' she said. 'I don't mean to sound negative. I suppose we're just in the middle of so many changes. Emma and Nick are about to leave the nest, and that's making me unsettled. And here you are, suddenly taking a step up the corporate ladder which I don't really understand. I'm trying to put some order into everything, that's all.'

She sounded vulnerable then, and it was uncomfortable. I'd always depended on Anna as my anchor, holding fast whatever the weather was like above, and I didn't want her to show signs of premature corrosion. With this admission of doubt she was undermining me, and I couldn't afford to have the balance of our lives disturbed by Anna's trepidation. As much for me as for her, I needed to smooth out these worrying wrinkles.

'I know,' I said soothingly. 'We're all a little

anxious. But it's all going to turn out fine, I promise.'

She looked at me in a certain way, and it took some time to put my finger on what it meant: the look was like the one that children give you when they finally discover that you're not infallible, that you're no longer the fount of all knowledge and wisdom, and that you can be just as wrong as the next man. I'd never seen that look from Anna before.

There are few things, I'm told, that are more stressful than a family holiday. In part, the stress comes from the sudden leap from doing lots to doing nothing: one minute you're a busy executive, shepherding millions from one account to another, the next you're just another tripper, herded on to a charter flight and indistinguishable from all the other grockles. You lose your status and your identity as you pass through Customs and into the departure lounge, weighed down with your trashy novels and new sunglasses. There's nothing by which you can set yourself apart; you're suddenly in with the great unwashed.

We'd had our share of disastrous holidays, and we'd always promised to take more time next year. When I got my bonus that year, paid in February, I went straight to the travel agent and bought four first-class tickets to Boston for the summer; Anna and I had agreed to spend a month in the Cape, with Nick and Emma free to stay with us or move around as it suited them. We knew it would be our last family holiday, and we were determined not to ruin it by trying too hard. The children – even as they were now, almost fully grown and very independent, they were still children to us – needed their space, and the modern parents we'd become would give them all they required.

That summer . . . June had been the biggest month of all. Amidst the wreckage of the dealing room, with grubby telephone engineers pulling massive skeins of wiring from the floor and cutting them with seeming abandon, I had my first million-dollar day. Traders will tell you that making a million in a day depends more on luck than judgement; but the traders who say that have probably never done it for themselves. There were only four people in the room who had done it, and we all knew who they were. I'd been close, and then had lost it all when New York opened. But one bright and blistering day in June, when Moscow still played the currency markets in a big way and engendered major panic in every London trading room when they called, I caught myself with a huge position from the Red Man and traded my way out profitably. I watched my screen as the deals were entered, and I knew I was making a fortune. I sat very still as the profit figure escalated.

By four-fifteen I knew I'd made it; Ben knew it too, and was dying to make an announcement, but I asked him not to. I wanted to savour the moment for myself, before it was diminished and subsumed in the culture of a business that never lingers on past achievement or history that is only seconds old.

And I will always remember those precious seconds when only I knew what I had done; in fact, I still get a little thrill when I recall it, even now when it seems such a long way off in the past.

My success was duly noted and forgotten, but it made me feel I'd earnt my holiday. I traded lightly for the rest of the summer, letting Ben do much of the work as I began to wind down for the break. By late July many of the senior traders had already left the room, most of them bound for exotic destinations which they advertised broadly as a badge of their seniority. On my final day we had the mandatory sunshine drinks in Lucho's, and I lectured Ben a little about the markets and what was expected of him. I went home early, still slightly drunk from lunch, and watched as Anna finalised the packing and brought order to the chaos of our preparations.

We took an early morning flight, getting into Boston in the afternoon and driving straight up to the Cape. We were tired and fractious in the car, so no one said too much, each of us nurturing different hopes and concerns for the month ahead. The thing I wanted most was to spend some time with Nick and Emma – quality time, I suppose they'd call it nowadays – when I could finally, unequivocally demonstrate my love and support, and show them that I wasn't merely the person who paid for their clothes and subsidised their social life, but a father who cared for them and their future happiness. In the final scene of this latest act in a never-ending drama, I wanted us to be that elusive, illusory nuclear family, however ill-equipped I might be to play my part.

Much to my surprise, it seemed that the children too had longed for this to happen. We swam, played tennis, sunbathed, walked, dined out, but most of all we talked, of everything and nothing, on all the subjects we could think of. Often I would be accompanied on one of my long beach walks by one or both of the children; sometimes we'd have little to say, and the pleasure would simply be in being together, in doing something together, however trivial. On other walks we would chatter and laugh incessantly. And all the time I felt that this was highly therapeutic, and that a greater good would permeate us all as a result.

Did Anna pick this up? More often than not she chose to stay behind and read her book or lie in the sun, and I chose to interpret this as a sign that she understood my wishes and was tactfully pulling back to allow me the time and space I needed. Whatever the true reasons for her behaviour, I loved her all the more for it. Like the instinctive habits of a family of birds, it appeared that my role was to stay with the fledglings in their final hours before they flew the nest, that the mother's work was done and she now devolved responsibility to me.

We'd had a tacit understanding that the family would spend the last few days together before returning home; both Nick and Emma wanted to go off for ten days and see some more of New England, and we loaded them up with money and pointed

93

them in the right direction. But when the time came for them to go they seemed almost reluctant, giving the impression that they were really only going because it was expected of them. I liked this, but never said so. It proved to me that we could still rub along together, and that our unit was a place where they wanted to be, despite all the attractions of freedom and independence.

On the first night Anna and I were alone we decided to eat on the deck and watch the sunset. Suddenly there was a lot of room in the house, and a lot of space between the two of us. In such a short time we had grown used to the children's clutter and noise, and the absence of these diversions was painfully poignant. We sat facing each other in silence. Behind Anna the sky was the colour of crushed apricots as the sun melted into it. The meal over, she drew breath and shivered.

'Do you want a sweater?' I asked.

'No, I'm fine. It's not the chill anyway.'

'I know what you mean,' I said. 'It's like someone just walked on your grave.'

'Do you know how guilty they feel?'

'How do you mean?' I asked, puzzled by the question.

'I've told them you don't do it on purpose, but they can't really work it out, either of them.'

'Do what?'

'I truly believe you don't know, do you? Emma and Nick have had the most wonderful time up here. They were both dreading it, if you must know. They begged me to let them off coming, but I held the party line and told them that it would probably be the last time we'd ever go away together, and that you wanted them to come, and not to think about themselves all the time. But they were not happy.'

This shocked me. I'd had not the faintest hint that there was any resentment about the holiday, and they had been such good company that I was still unconvinced by Anna's propaganda. 'They've made a pretty good job of hiding their true feelings, I must say. They've been incredibly well behaved. Are you saying this was all an act to keep me sweet?'

'No. They were genuine enough. You saw how unenthusiastic they were about leaving. Oh no, they've had a fantastic time. And that's the problem, isn't it?'

'This is a problem?' I couldn't fathom the depths of Anna's mind. 'Why so?'

She sipped her wine and tossed her beautiful hair to one side; she was still the jewel that outshone all others, even making a perfect sunset seem dull in comparison. 'There's never really a good time to talk about things like this, is there? And we don't talk too much nowadays anyway. We've lost the knack, I suppose. We used to talk a lot, but then the children and work got in the way, and suddenly here we are, alone together, and there's so much to catch up on that we don't know where to start. It's no one's fault – that's how life is. You look up from what you're doing and it's shot past you without you even noticing it.'

'What's got into you? I thought everything was pretty wonderful at the moment.'

'Oh it is, it is,' she sighed. 'I'm always reminding myself of how much luckier we are than Doug and Hilary, or all the others for that matter. But we could have had even more, you know. We did once.'

'Do you mind if I ask what?'

'When the children came along, nothing much changed for you. Oh, I know you've been a good father, and they've turned out really well, but you've never had to deal with the changes that I faced. That's biology for you. We lost so much of ourselves, and our relationship, in bringing them up that it's a daunting task to see how we'll ever recover it. I know you don't see it like that, because you're a man and it's different for you and you're not to blame for that. But I do still need us, just you and me, like it was. Do you see that?' It was a literal cry in the dark, as dusk finally gave way to night.

My logical mind tried to set this all in order. 'We seem to be having two conversations here. This started with a discussion about the children, and we haven't finished that yet, have we?'

'No, it's one conversation. Emma and Nick can't work you out. To them, you're a benign but distant influence. You've always been there, but they're not quite sure of how to approach you. Sometimes they've been terrified of you – irrational, I know, but they're children – and sometimes they've loved you to distraction but can't get close to you. The problem for them is the same as it is for me – nothing changes you. You are a constant, which should be good, but not if it means you never adapt or slow down or speed up. You've always been the same – children, promotions, wealth, poverty, whatever, you're the same as you always were. Life doesn't keep pace with you, and neither do we.'

'And that makes you feel guilty?'

'Only in the sense that they've loved being with you here, and have had a whale of a time. Now they wonder, quite reasonably, if it might always have been like this if only they'd tried harder. They're the ones who feel that they haven't invested enough in the relationship. And I know exactly how they feel. God, the anguish I've suffered from thinking that everything's my fault, the times I've said to myself "if only". But a little bit of it has to be your responsibility too. We can't all be perfect all the time.'

Pressed to describe my emotions at this point, I would probably say that I felt completely over-whelmed by a lack of comprehension. My own reading of my performance as a father was so totally at odds with Anna's that I could never hope to reconcile the two. Yes, I'd been consistent, but no, I'd never made that a creed by which I slavishly abided; the accusation, that I was somehow too perfect for them, was so far-fetched that it defied denial. I was speechless.

Anna continued, obviously aware of the impact she'd made. 'You're a lovely man, and I love you more now than I did the day we were married. But it hasn't always been easy to live with you. I'm not asking you to change. I don't even know if I want you to. But for their sake, not mine, I think you need to know the pressure they've been under, and how much that's all been brought to a head by this holiday. They've never really spent any time with you until now – at least I've had the advantage of knowing you before they came along. It's been a tough revelation for them, especially when they're just thinking about setting out on their own.'

We sat there for a long time in the dark, listening to the bug-zapper as flies were fried on it. I felt a little fried myself, singed and stinging; this was not what I had wanted, or expected, to hear. We went to bed separately that night, Anna disappearing first as I finished the bottle of wine and reflected on what had been unveiled. And I knew, as I drained my glass and sat in the curls of translucent smoke from my cigar, that there was not one single thing I could do to change it.

TEN

London is not a city. It is an agglomeration of tribes and hamlets, carelessly thrown together and forced to share space and facilities in spite of their discrete identities and values. The Chelsea natives know and understand little of the Baker Street citizens, their habits and routines and needs and desires. The drive to Melrose Street took us through foreign fiefdoms, the casual disdain of my police escorts protecting us from unknown evils.

89A was a basement flat; Challis and Barham stood at the railings which ran in front of the house, discussing some issue which they dropped as soon as I approached them.

'Good morning, sir,' Barham said. 'Very good of you to come.'

I nodded. A uniformed officer stood at the top of the steps to the flat, and moved aside as we walked towards him. Challis went down first, then me, then Barham. We reached the front door, painted off-white with a panel of frosted glass. Challis played with some keys whilst Barham spoke.

'It's only fair to warn you, sir. What you see inside may shock you.'

'Let's get this over with, shall we?' I replied, impatient with Barham's condescension.

Challis opened the door, and we all walked in.

Where there might once have been a lobby had been knocked down to open up a large room, painted in the same off-white as the door. The carpet was brown and old, and the furniture was utilitarian and ugly: a white self-assembly wardrobe, a small glass and wrought iron coffee table, a brown velour arm-chair, and a kitchen chair. Three doors led off this room, and all were open. I could see a kitchen, with a stand-alone unit and a very old gas cooker and sink. Another door led to a bathroom, although I could only see the flimsy plastic curtain of a shower unit. The third door was ajar, but I could not see inside.

Standing in the main room, there was nothing to suggest that anyone lived there. The usual papers and ornaments were missing, the worthless collections of unwanted mail and unread magazines. Incongruously, a new telephone and answering machine sat on the floor. Barham and Challis watched me as I looked around, seeking some sign that Anna had ever settled here voluntarily. I walked towards the third door and pushed it open.

The room was small, with only enough space for a double bed, a nightstand, and a wardrobe. On the nightstand was a small lamp with a tasselled shade. The bed had been stripped, revealing a stained mattress with striped rep. Above the bed, two mirrored

100

plates had been screwed to the ceiling, and another large sheet of mirror was propped against a wall. The window had been covered with a thick grey blanket.

One door of the wardrobe was open. Inside, there were several wire hangers. On one hanger, there was a short black dress with a white pinafore attached to it; on another, a white uniform that might have been a nurse's. At the bottom of the wardrobe there were three pairs of shoes, all high-heeled, and a pair of long black leather boots. There were lengths of rope coiled on the floor, and four or five sections of bamboo cane.

I moved to the nightstand and opened the drawer, aware still of the eyes following me. There were at least twenty condoms, a tube of lubricant jelly, two new plastic shakers of talc, and a full bottle of clear oil.

I pushed the drawer closed very slowly, and stood up fully to face Barham and Challis.

'This is a whore's bedroom,' I said.

'Exactly, sir,' Barham replied, with Challis never taking his stare from me.

'So what relevance has this to my wife's death?'

Barham began to leave the bedroom, and I followed him. When we stood in the main room, he replied.

'We've contacted the owner of the flat. He rented it out for cash; no questions asked, rent always paid in full in advance, every month. He has identified your wife as the tenant.'

'What exactly are you suggesting?'

'We're not suggesting anything, sir. Neighbours have confirmed that there was a steady flow of male visitors to this flat. When we found your wife's body, there was over four hundred pounds in the kitchen cupboard. There's something else you should hear.'

He nodded to Challis, who moved over to the phone and pressed a button on the answering machine. There was silence, then a recorded message.

'Hi. I'm busy at the moment, but if you leave your first name and number, I can call you back. Alternatively, ring again in an hour.'

The message ended; the voice was mannered and low, but unmistakable.

'Would you say that that was your wife's voice, sir?' Barham asked.

My skin was bursting in an effort to control the shaking, racking sobs that wanted to escape. The normal rhythm of my blood stream disappeared and violent spots of heat exploded inside my cheeks.

'It sounds like her.' The voice inside me rattled and scratched its way out.

'We think your wife was here pretty regularly over the last eighteen months. We have several witnesses who can confirm that she came here, and the chemist round the corner has positively identified her. It gives me no pleasure to tell you this, but I think you'll have to accept the fact that your wife used this flat to entertain men for profit.'

Barham's flat tone, and the finality of his delivery, denied any further debate. My head dropped, the muscles weakening as blood failed to bring adequate oxygen, the keystone of my body slyly removed to bring internal collapse. No questions could be asked, no reasoning could be applied. Barham seemed satisfied.

'You remember the clothes we showed you at the station, sir? Your wife was wearing those when she was murdered. They were like a trademark. We've found some calling cards she must have used. Called herself Madame Lavender.'

Barham's words were narcotic. As he spoke, I could feel the heaviness drop over me and I wanted to lie down, to sleep forever.

'She had been dead for a week before she was discovered. It took us some time to match up your report of her being missing with this murder. You can understand why. We think she was strangled with a length of rope taken from the wardrobe. She was hit about the face after she was dead, although we haven't found the implement that was used. There was one wound on her scalp, which she received when falling to the floor. There were no fingerprints other than hers in the flat.'

With the same effort and emotion as he might have used to turn out a light, Barham had summed up the final hour of Anna's life. He gave me no guidance as to what should happen next. We sat alone in our interview room at Lucan Place, hunched over the table with a shared interest but different objectives.

'There's no reason to suppose that she knew her killer, although most victims do. She was playing a very dangerous game. Oddly, there weren't any signs of a struggle; either the killer tidied up afterwards, or your wife gave up the fight.'

Barham was punching the information into me, pausing to affirm assimilation, then moving on to the next blow. Each thud of data painlessly swept across me, as if delivered through a cushion of numbness.

'We shall need to ask you some questions – simply routine – and we would like to have a little look round your house, just to make sure we haven't missed anything obvious.'

'When can I take Anna home?' The question cracked and croaked as it came out of me.

'We're finished with her. I'm expecting the results of the post-mortem this afternoon, although I'm not hopeful it'll tell me anything. As soon as you're ready.'

'Thanks. Could I go home now?'

'Of course. I'll get one of my men to take you.'

Barham got up and walked to the door. Then he played his usual trick, turning towards me just as he was about to go out.

'We will catch him. It may take some time, but you have my assurance that we will catch him.'

This was not the braggadocio of a maverick vigilante, but a calm statement of intent from a level-headed, methodical plod. His manner, this room, the whole deal, frightened me, and I remembered just how lonely fear is. Barham raised his eyebrows in a silent farewell, and left me with his valedictory still resonating well beyond my ears.

Time and grief are kissing cousins. They have worked out a deal to make sure that neither runs on too fast in front, holding each other's hand and lingering and loitering with no intent.

I had visited another world and come back by ten-thirty. In the time I'd been away, the natives had continued without me, post, papers and milk all bearing witness to the thrumming monotony of life at its lowest, the constant flow of the barest essentials streaming up and through my front door.

Nick and Kate had both called to let me know they were on their way. I had a plan for Kate: she would deal with food and shelter, base requirements that I couldn't deny but couldn't order. Nick would be a problem; his very presence would pierce the carapace of self-protecting gloom I cowered under. Gloom was better than despair, or grief, or madness, all of which seemed readily available.

Burning Anna's body would help to close the chapter; on the car journey back, I chose cremation as a suitable means of laying the ghost and breaking with the past. I made the arrangements as soon as I got in, and booked caterers for the wake. Then I waited. I thought of going out; I thought of work; I thought of Sarah. I thought of anything that sprang to mind and distracted me from thinking about Anna, her beaten face, her secret life, her life and liveliness, and my place in it.

Homes are never silent – water runs, pipes sing,

105

radiators crackle, fridges hum – but this house was still, as if it felt the absence of a need to pump and gush and throb and buzz. The vital organs of domestic life had stopped in memory of Anna. In this sepulchral stillness, my body reminded me of last night's excess, the corporal pulsation of heat, light and power pounding through my ears and stomach.

Sarah had said, 'You said some pretty crazy things.' What were those crazy things? I winced and ached at the danger of unknown indiscretions. I got up, and climbed the long stairs to my bed, collapsing, shuddering, shrinking into restless sleep.

Two people were talking, their voices low and the silences between exchanges long. Water was running. Strange noises, the sounds of kitchen life, snaked up the stairwell. I pulled back the bedclothes, turning on to my side in preparation for the effort of standing. Two-thirty; the light outside was milky, and the room needed air. I pulled myself up and opened a window. The garden was an oasis of sorrow, the dead heads of roses silently stiff and awaiting execution.

'I've brought you coffee,' a voice said behind me as I stared from the window.

I turned to face Kate, neatly dressed in powder-blue twin-set, with a darker blue skirt and a silk scarf. She put the coffee down on the bedside table, and walked over to me. We hugged, but I could feel no nascent welling of sorrow from within her. She was calm, and steady.

'I must have dropped off,' I said. 'I'm so sorry I wasn't around to meet you.'

'Don't worry about that. Nick was already here, so he let me in.'

'How is he?'

'The same as all of us, I think. Completely stunned.' She was right. The hammer blows of Barham's revelations had cumulatively shocked, hurt and stunned, and we teetered on the edge of punch-drunkenness. Kate's eyes were clear, no reddening to display her inner grief, and she seemed no different from when I had seen her last, at Anna's birthday party.

Kate and Anna had argued furiously after that party; Kate had surprised me with her vehemence, and her appraisal of life and love. She felt that Hilary was spoilt and senseless, failing to see that Douglas too was watching his life slip away faster than he could control. Men have needs, of reassurance, tenderness, uncomplicated physical affection, she had said, and if Douglas couldn't find that with Hilary, it was inevitable he would search for it elsewhere. Anna was horrified: in Kate's credo, she saw the threat of broken lives and misery, a journey wasted. But there was something else: Kate and Anna shared some secret knowledge that divided them, unmentioned but unmistakable. Their row was too intense, their interest in the fortunes of two strangers too strong, and I couldn't understand it.

One night, lying in bed, I asked Anna to explain.

'Men are so stupid,' she said, closing her book. 'You

don't understand, do you? Daddy fucked everything that moved. Mummy just watched it, always knowing but never questioning. He screwed friends, clients, strangers, even our daily, and they both pretended it was normal. To you, he may have seemed a quiet, boring little provincial solicitor. Maybe he thought that about himself, and sex was his way of proving otherwise. He was a selfish prick, and Douglas is no better.'

Now Kate stood in my arms, not a frail and beaten woman, damaged by her husband's priapic wanderings, but a strong, sensible lady, wise with age in a way old people rarely achieve. Perhaps her wisdom came from knowing when to close her eyes and mind.

'I'd better shower and change,' I said as our embrace broke up. 'Emma's arriving at Heathrow at six.'

Nick was not as I remembered him. He was larger, tougher, louder than in my imagination. We hugged each other, and it seemed my arms could no longer envelop him as they had before.

The niceties of small talk, of catching up and building back the bridges of familiarity, were hard to find. There were silences between us that we didn't care to fill, gaps in our life that Anna might have filled. Was that her role? Was she the grout between the tiles, the layer in the cake? Anna was the catalyst that held us together, we who had nothing much in common except blood and grief.

Nick wanted to be out, and I had no reason for

him to stay. He wanted to walk in the King's Road and visit friends, his desire for action and activity precisely matching mine. I gave him money, and he went. Kate took herself off to her bedroom, and slept. Once again, I sat alone and watched the slothful seconds ticking by.

I was pleased when the phone rang. It was Barham.

'How are you bearing up?' he asked, a genuine concern in his voice.

'Fine. The family is here.'

'Oh. Can you talk?'

'Yes, of course. What is it?'

'I wanted to let you know something that I couldn't tell you earlier. It's about the post-mortem.'

'What? Have you found something?' Life was pounding back into me, uncomfortably revving the motor.

'Well, not evidence, but something . . . something you should know.' Barham was having difficulty with this conversation. 'Your wife,' he began, and then hesitated, drawing breath or pulling on a cigar, or standing up or sitting down.

'What?' I asked impatiently.

'She was HIV-positive,' he said, in a stilted voice.

'I see,' I groaned, but I hardly did.

ELEVEN

'Now I'm free to sleep with anyone I want to; that's a freedom I intend to cherish.'

Hilary was sitting opposite me, looking fresh and attractive in a way that would hardly have seemed possible just a fortnight before, when she had left scorch-marks on Douglas at Anna's birthday party. I'd resolved never to see her again; now I was having lunch with her. She had called me at work, apologetic and seductive, and had convinced me that she wanted to remain friends.

We were eating in a stylish restaurant in Broadgate, all light wood and light food, where the waiters were prettier than the waitresses and neither chewed their fingernails. Most people appeared to be eating huge mountains of leaves, devoid of dressing or meat or cheese or anything that might have calories, cholesterol or taste. In an extravagant gesture, Hilary and I had ordered fettucine with mushrooms and a bottle of white wine. Hilary was now attacking the latter as if it were near to its sell-by date, fearful that it might turn sour, or evaporate, if not immediately slooshed down.

Douglas and I were still golf partners, but his state of mind was not conducive to either good golf or good companionship. In frequent breaches of etiquette, he would swear or hit the ground with his club, and he no longer recognised and remarked upon some of the better shots that his partner occasionally played. Once at the nineteenth hole, he would drink his whisky quickly, not in an effort to get away sooner, but so that he could have more. In a way that only men can, he had turned bitter against Hilary, feeling her lack of understanding and compassion was at the root of their problems, never accepting that his indiscretions were anything but a manifestation of the poor state of the marriage. Douglas had become a bore, and bores are really impossible to shake off.

On the other hand, Hilary was born again, reconstituted as a youthful, interesting and attractive individual, seemingly untroubled by recent events and determined to take advantage of her opportunities. Her new-found liberation extended to her tongue; she could hardly draw breath in between her talking and her drinking.

'I spent a week at a health spa,' she said, 'and left Douglas to look after the children. That week sorted me out; I slept, and cried, and thought a lot, about what I wanted from life, and how I would get it. That's why I wanted to see you.'

'Well, of course, anything I can do, I'd be more than happy to . . .' the words trailed off as a small thought crossed my mind, impure and unkind.

'I do need your advice,' Hilary said, moving my mind back on to purer tracks. I hoped that any relief I felt was not apparent.

The waiter arrived with our main course, fettucine flecked with saffron artfully twisted to form a perfect mount in the centre of a bed of creamy mushrooms. I leant over to Hilary. 'I bet the chef is really pleased that someone's ordered something normal, something that he has to cook rather than grow.'

Hilary laughed, raised her glass, and drank its contents. I looked at the bottle standing in the perspex cooler, and was amazed to see it was empty.

'Do you want some more?' I asked, tilting the empty bottle at her.

'Why not?'

The waiter, who still hovered prettily beside us, took the bottle and left us. Hilary was acting sober, and it was none of my business if she drank too much. As she stressed, she was free. We began eating, and Hilary started talking again.

'I want to go back to work. Like Anna, I gave everything up when I got married, and I always missed it. But I have no idea where to start, or whether I'd be any use to anyone. I wondered what you thought.'

What did I think? What did I know? Hilary would be a great personal assistant for someone who wanted charm, maturity, good legs and dress sense. Were she not Hilary, I would have snapped her up. This I told her.

I think she blushed, although it might have been

colouring brought on by the tide of wine she was swallowing. 'But I don't know anything about word processors, or computers, or anything like that.'

'That you can learn. I wouldn't worry too much about it.'

This pleased her, and she finished another glass of wine. Her pasta lay uneaten, pushed about half-heartedly with her fork. The waiter materialised as I put my fork down.

'Was everything all right?' he asked.

'Oh, lovely, thank you,' said Hilary, 'I'm just not terribly hungry.'

'Would you care for something else?'

Hilary and I looked at each other, both shaking our heads.

'I'd like a cappuccino, and a sambuca,' Hilary said to him.

'Just an espresso for me, please,' I said, trying not to sound sanctimonious.

'Does Anna want to go back to work?'

'No. Or at least, she's never said she does.'

'I probably shouldn't say this, but that night, when we were talking, it felt as if she was the one in trouble, not me.' Hilary's vaguely glassy stare fixed on me. A small ripple passed through my chest, very fleeting, and very disconcerting.

'What do you mean?' I asked, against my better judgement.

'Oh, I don't know, just a feeling really. As if everything I was going through was somehow hurting her. I'm probably completely wrong. I do hope so. You

114

both seem so happy together.'

'We are,' I said, perhaps a little too eagerly. 'I don't think anyone enjoys seeing their friends in trouble, in spite of what you believe. It may have hurt her, but she's happy. We both are.'

Hilary smiled with her mouth, but her eyes remained emotionless. 'Do you have to get back soon?' she asked.

'I should do, but there's no great hurry.'

The sambuca had an immediate effect on her.

'Could you slip away for an hour or so?'

My head was clear; I had sipped at my wine, and I was in complete control. But the proposition just laid before me had flipped a switch in my brain, and my eyesight and hearing started to fail me. Peripheral vision disappeared; previously clear voices now sounded like slowly rewinding tape; and even the edges of Hilary, straight ahead, became blurred. This was probably what it felt like when you were hit full on the temple.

'No commitment; just a good old-fashioned fuck,' she explained.

'Hilary,' I began, somewhat unoriginally although the very remembrance of her name was something of a triumph, 'this is very flattering, but . . .' I opened my hands and raised them off the table as if to show the emptiness of my heart.

Hilary should have been very embarrassed; I certainly was. But she was defiant. 'That's quite all right. Forget it. I only asked because I'd like some company this afternoon, and I know you aren't exactly overwhelmed with sex and companionship. But if you can't accept that, I quite understand.'

Although Hilary was obviously drunk, and her words made no sense, I was magnetically drawn into the argument that she wanted.

'Hilary, I don't know what you mean. I'm sorry that I don't – I *can't* spend the afternoon with you but, as you say, let's just forget it.' This was crazy; I was apologising to her. It didn't work.

'You feel smug because I've – we've – failed. But you have no right. Your marriage is completely hollow. I don't see any love there at all. You're simply following a path that was drawn for you, regardless of whether it makes sense or not. Watch out, because I don't think Anna is quite as committed as you.'

I had to ask her what the hell she meant, when I should have got up and left.

'Have you ever asked her if she's happy? Do you know what she's thinking and feeling? Have you ever considered what she wants out of life?'

'She wants the same as me. We've built our lives together. We're after the same things.'

Hilary smiled, a baring of teeth that indicated knowledge and contempt. 'You really know nothing at all. Anna's interests are very different to yours. So are her needs. You're just too pig-headed to see that.'

I had had enough. I caught the waiter's eye, and made the motion for the bill. We sat silently, my face tingling with anger and shame.

'Anna feels neglected, taken for granted, used up. She's given you children, she's made a home for you, she's always there for you, and what does she get in return? She feels worthless. Believe me, I know, because that's how it felt with Doug. With me, I need to get my brain in gear, although sex is important too. With Anna, it's the opposite.'

'Christ, what are you saying, Hilary?' Now my face was scalded with her fire-throwing.

'Anna is a bored housewife. What do you think she does all day? Why do you think she's never there when you phone? Are you so stupid?'

The bill arrived, and I produced a credit card without even looking at the total. Tears, of rage or horror or both, were stupidly blurring my vision. I got up, and put my napkin down on the table. 'Hilary, you are very drunk and you're out of order. Let's pretend we never had this conversation.'

'You still don't see, do you? You can't make it go away. You're to blame. Anna's searching for something that you won't, or can't, give her.'

'Goodbye, Hilary. Please don't bother to call me again. I really don't think we have much in common.'

'I'll drink to that. You're just like Douglas: pig-headed, self-centred, self-satisfied, and completely and utterly wrong. I'm trying to help you, to save what you've got. Don't be too proud and stupid to ignore it.'

I collected my credit card and walked out of the restaurant, determined that I would never see Hilary again.

Ben was standing, shouting an order across the room, one shoulder crooked as he held the phone to his ear, while his hands fluttered in front of the green and orange screens. The usual afternoon rush, when New York entered the market, had begun, and traders dropped sandwiches, hurried back from lunch, and forgot the real world for another three hours of frantic money-shovelling.

I hung my jacket over the back of my chair and sat down, checking our position and our profit before turning to Ben.

'We're ten long at sixty-five. New York's bullish about the trade figures, so we might just wait.'

I felt as if I had unwittingly disturbed a wasps' nest, thousands of little stings all over me, right in my hair, inside my ears, everywhere. Ben's report to me was good, but no use. I couldn't concentrate on this, this work, while life interfered. One would have to wait, take its place in the queue. After two minutes in my chair, I knew which came first.

'Ben, I have to go out. Cover for me. Stay long, or square up. For God's sake don't go short.' Redundant advice was rarely given, and never heeded, in the trading room, and Ben barely moved his head as I walked out of the room and into reality.

I pulled my phone out of my case and called home. There was no reply, simply the answering machine's dreary message. I looked at my watch: three-thirty, and no one home. I ran out of the building, and jumped into a waiting cab.

'Redesdale Street, please.'

I fumbled with my keys, perhaps unaccustomed to

using them in daylight. Eventually I pushed open the front door, and stepped inside. I resisted an urge to call out, and walked down the stairs to the kitchen. The table was bare and clean, and the sink and draining-board were empty and dry. The light on the answering machine flashed quietly and patiently.

I ran up the stairs, past the sitting room and up to the first floor, still wanting to shout, even to hear my echo rather than believe I was completely alone. Our bedroom door was closed. I lightly rested my fingers on the handle, closed my eyes, breathed hard, and pushed.

The room was dark, the curtains drawn to block out the fragile afternoon light. The door to the bathroom was closed. I looked from it to the bed, my head having to work to force my line of vision around to it. On the bed lay Anna, shoeless but clothed, still and noiseless. Unknown chemicals in my body reacted to this shock, and I tensed involuntarily. She looked dead, especially in this lowering half-light, and I reached to touch her, half-expecting coldness on her hand. It was cool, but it was the cool of sleep, and I breathed out very loudly through my nostrils.

I sat on the side of the bed, elbows on my knees, screwing up my face in an effort to suppress the shame I felt. Beside me slept Anna, my Anna, innocent and loving, unaware of stupid hurtful lies casually related and tipped with poison. I wanted to hug her, to tell her how much I loved her and needed her. I wanted to make love to her, to demonstrate to her the passion I still felt for her, and I stood up and undressed, throwing clothes carelessly over Anna's chair. I lay down beside her, anxious not to wake her, and slowly stroked her face and hair, feeling a guilty excitement. I kissed her cheek, hardly touching her with my lips, and moved her hand against me.

Anna's eyes flickered open, and she looked at me with dreamy puzzlement. The hand that I had moved towards me stayed still, and she rolled over on her side.

'What are you doing here?' she asked hazily.

'Just a little surprise for you,' I said, smiling to hide my embarrassment.

'Not so little,' she replied, and she pushed me on to my back. She was wearing a cream silk blouse and a tan skirt, and she stood up to pull them off. Then she took off her bra, leaving on lace-trimmed white knickers.

'I have the curse,' she explained, as she lay beside me, pushing herself against my side. We were lovers again, stealing this moment from the schedules we had built around us to defend against unknown enemies, and I knew that Anna was still mine, completely mine.

TWELVE

It always surprised me to find the car clean, free of the flotsam of family life. For so many years I had cleared out half-eaten biscuits, rejected sweets, discarded wrappers, straws, juice boxes, marbles, books, hair grips, socks, hankies, tissues and crumbs, that they had become an expected and accepted part of the car décor. Even now, as I climbed in to collect Emma, it seemed strange not to see a favourite scrap of sheet or muslin or blanket tossed on to the back seat, to see the black leather upholstery still pristine and unmuddied.

I turned on the radio, very frightened to be locked in this metal tomb with only my thoughts. Whatever interest there had been in Anna was quickly waning: the story went cold as fast as her body, and there was no mention of her on the news. I drove towards Hammersmith, a greasy flimsy rain falling against the windscreen. What had shocked me most was Barham's obvious shock; he had struggled to articulate the information, even in the hideous babble of police talk, and he'd clearly chosen not to confront me with it but to pass it over electronic lines, a little as if this might reduce the risk of infection from the words themselves. But that shock had soon turned to fear, to that darkest fear in which you're never quite sure what it is you're afraid of, and that fear had made me weak and indecisive, unable to manage Barham's information rationally. I was too frightened to confront it, too confused to acknowledge it, so it lay within me like a poisonous goitre.

Now Barham and I shared secrets that maybe even Anna didn't know. My family, her family, would never need or want to hear about such secrets, the memory of Anna as mother and daughter too strong and dear to crack apart with the sordid details of her soiled existence. That Anna should be dead before her time was agony enough; Kate and Nick and Emma needed no more pain from further revelation.

And this was my essential dilemma: for every piece of information that Barham uncovered, for every lead he pursued and every shred of evidence he inspected, he inflicted further pain on Anna's family as victims. His pursuit of truth and justice, however laudable it seemed, simply burned a deeper scar on all of us, prolonging the suffering we'd already endured from her death. His investigative successes rained down on us like poisoned darts, exposing us to yet more hurt when what we really wanted was to mourn and grieve in peace.

I switched off the radio and punched out Sarah's number on the car phone. I imagined her at her desk, smoking and laughing and pushing her beautiful dark hair away from her face. She answered after several rings.

'It's me,' I said. 'I'm on my way to collect Emma.'

'How are you doing?'

'Rough. I'd like to see you. And I promise I'll stay sober.'

'That might be boring. You're pretty entertaining when you're pissed.'

'What are you doing tonight?'

'Nothing, but I thought your family was there.'

'I could get away. They're all grown up.' I heard myself starting to sound desperate, with a voice that asked for too much. If Sarah noticed, she ignored it.

'Come round at nine,' she said gently. 'Look after yourself.'

My voice had really overstretched itself, and now it cracked and stumbled as I tried to say what I felt. It wouldn't work, and I merely bit my bottom lip hard, urging the tears back down their ducts.

'Oh – gotta go,' Sarah said in a completely changed manner, switching instantly from pleasure to business as she moved from one call to another. I shut off the phone, and concentrated on the glacial progress of traffic towards Heathrow.

Emma was tired, from crying and travel, and her eyes were smudged with grief. She had hugged me in a new way, not as a daughter but as an equal, giving as much as she took out of the embrace. But, even in each other's arms with a single sorrow to bind us, there was a chasm of emptiness between us, and all our best efforts of synthesis could not span it.

It was lonelier in the car with her than it had been coming to get her. Emma's presence merely emphasised the loss of Anna, the absence of a partner, the blown-out shell of life that lay ahead. Emma pretended to doze, and perhaps she really did drop off. When we arrived back at the house, she protested exhaustion and disappeared to her room. Nick and Kate were in the kitchen.

'Would you like something to eat?' Kate asked me, and I realised I'd had nothing all day. The hangover had finally abated, and I was ready to handle solids.

'I'd love something – whatever you and Nick are having. Have you got a drink?'

I poured wine for Kate, and a beer for Nick. I took a small Scotch, with a lot of mineral water, and sat at the table whilst Kate moved efficiently between fridge, oven and sink.

'How's Emma handling it?' Nick asked.

'Your guess is as good as mine. She slept all the way back. She won't say much to me, I shouldn't think.'

Kate put some cutlery on the table, and looked at me as she straightened herself. 'This is your chance. You can mend the fences. She really needs support and love, and only you can give it to her.'

I sipped my drink, and a weariness I hadn't felt before enveloped me. What Kate said was quite right: now I could start again with Emma, offering that store of love that was specially reserved for her, fresh and untarnished by time or experience. Emma would fight it, protecting herself from getting too close, using Anna's death as a shield, and it would be tempting to give up and accept my failure as final. But who else needed my love, now Anna was gone?

Nick spoke. 'Do you mind if I see some friends tonight?'

I shook my head in compliance. 'Go ahead. I'm afraid there's nothing much happening to keep you here. Actually, I've got to go out myself.'

As I handed Nick a sheaf of money, the reflex reaction of a father who feels irrational guilt and inadequacy, Kate produced supper, and we ate together, the three of us chewing silently, digesting food and thoughts privately, each of us fearing that conversation would lead to unseemly displays of grieving, which were better saved for darkened moments in our beds.

Nick squeezed my shoulders before he left, a gentle affirmation of his continued concern and love, and Kate and I drank coffee while I smoked a cigar and she fiddled unproductively with a tapestry, suppressed tears refracting the clear sight she needed and wanted. At quarter to nine, I got up and put my jacket on.

'I have to go out, Kate. Don't wait up for me. I may be quite late.'

As I looked down at her she broke, one large breath caught mid-stream and then a muffled wail of agony and despair, tears that had waited too long to be shed now coursing down her cheeks. I knelt beside her, still sitting at the kitchen table, and put my arm round her. Strangely, her submission had made me stronger, more robust, as if I could suffer through her as proxy.

'You go,' she said. 'I'll be fine. Honestly. Off you go.'

I kissed her, stroked her grey hair, and left the house, but the ordure of grief came with me.

Stunning Sarah, sensual Sarah, sheathed in a white body suit and jet black leggings, a skin waiting to be peeled to reveal long-dreamt-of pleasures, was waiting with a cigarette and a scotch. We kissed, one single reaction to separate lusts, the kiss intense enough to start the heaters of desire, the fires down below. I pulled back and watched her lick her lips.

'Do you want something?' she asked, her body never moving, her eyes locked with mine, her voice a gravelly growl tempered by alcohol and craving.

'Scotch,' I replied, and she pulled away reluctantly. As she reached the galley kitchen, she called over her shoulder.

'How are things at home?'

'A vale of tears. No one's saying very much. Everyone's still coming to terms with it.'

'And you?'

'I'm waiting for it to hit me. I want to keep moving, to try and avoid it.'

'Is that why you're here?'

'I'm here to see you. I wanted to be with you.'

The Scotch arrived with Sarah close behind it. 'Sit down.' She opened her hand at a leather and metal chair that was as uncomfortable as it looked. There were hard surfaces everywhere, except on Sarah herself, as if she had specifically assembled a tough and unforgiving habitat which would bruise or pierce her softness at the slightest chance. It was a very masculine room, black and white, sharp and stark.

She sat opposite me, legs tucked up under her, toenails glossed with clear varnish, somehow sexier than vivid red. We sipped drinks, and I lit a cigar.

'We haven't talked much,' Sarah observed, cutting to the quick of our relationship in a single comment.

'What's going on at work?'

'The usual. Shouting, drinking, dealing – I think Ben is doing well, in all those categories.'

'Has anyone said anything about me?'

'Nothing worth repeating. You know them – attention spans of goldfish. They're busy worrying about something else by now.'

'What do you think?' I couldn't believe I'd asked her this; I didn't even know that I cared what she thought.

Sarah lit a cigarette, slowly pulling in large lungfuls of smoke. She pulled her legs in tighter underneath her, then pushed her hair back. 'You're strong. You'll survive.'

The judgement was made, and I had passed. Wasn't that the ultimate accolade, to be seen as a survivor, bloodied but unbowed? The verdict of Sarah meant more to me than I had thought possible. And now the ache, the sweet agony of love and desire and sadness, swept from my scalp through my flesh and bones, and my throat closed uncomfortably, as if to separate the head and the heart.

Sarah slipped off her seat and came over to me, kneeling with her arms crossed over my thighs, her chin resting on her hands. She looked up at me. 'I wish I wasn't so fond of you. I don't want to see you like this.'

I leant forward, and put my hands around her head. 'I'm going to be fine.' I pulled her up gently, and we kissed again, a soft-lipped kiss that felt a lot like love. Now the central heater moved upwards, from the loins towards the heart, starting a heat much more likely to scald and scar irreparably.

'I have to go,' I said close to her face.

She looked down, examining a hand without a wedding ring. 'Of course. Call me when you can.'

I stood up and drained my glass. Sarah clung to me, her head against my chest, pressed tight in as if she felt she might fuse with me, and I brought my arms down to hold her around her waist. She felt very small, and very tense, and I wanted to engulf her within my embrace, to shield her from danger and fear and grief.

'Go on then, bugger off,' she said, but she didn't break the spell.

The table lamp in the hall was on, and I looked at myself briefly in the gilded mirror as I walked past.

I couldn't see anything different about my face, or my look: there were no contusions, or extra lines, or swellings, nothing to suggest the constant rain of hammering blows that Anna's death, and life, had unleashed. My shoulders remained unhunched, the body open for another slamming punch of evidence from police investigations.

Behind the half-closed door of the sitting room I could see a light; I stepped inside quietly, and saw Emma sitting on a large blue and cream sofa, feet tucked up exactly as Sarah's had been earlier. She was in silk pyjamas, and her long brown hair was tied back with a black velvet band.

'Hi. How are you?'

'I couldn't sleep,' she said. 'I wanted to sit in here, with Mum's things.'

'We never sat in here. We hated it. It was too big just for us.'

'Actually, Mum really liked it. You hated it, so it never got used. But all her favourite things, her memories, are in here.'

Emma's face was tight with the exertion of showing no emotion towards me, and her eyes might have been closed, so flat were the surfaces, as if she could consciously shutter them to stop me seeing into her mind.

I sat down next to her, and held her hand. 'Emma, don't do this.'

'What? Don't do what?'

'We're all sad. We should be close together, not fighting each other. Don't you see that?'

Her face remained a mask. She sighed, but nothing but breath was released.

'Who's fighting? It always takes time to get comfortable again, and this makes it especially difficult. Right now, I can only think about Mummy.'

'I know that. Just remember that I'm always here, available, if you need me. I am still your dad.'

She looked at me and smiled, the weak movement of a deeply sad face, and the brown eyes dared not blink, in case they spilled treacherous tears or the movement of the lids disturbed their shuttered blankness. 'I just need time. It hurts too much at the moment,' she said at last, and a tiny crack seemed to form on her passive face. I squeezed her hand, kissed it, and got up.

'Can I get you anything? I'm going downstairs.'

'No thanks. Nothing.'

'Don't stay up too late, poppet,' I said, and left.

Kate's tapestry lay on the kitchen table; she had cleared everything else away, leaving nothing in the dishwasher but cleaning everything by hand. She had closed the yellow blind over the front window, something Anna never did, and the room looked strangely constricted by it.

I drank the first Scotch very quickly, and poured another, larger one. I pulled out a notepad and pencil, and began scribbling a list of things to do and people to call. But nothing would come; I couldn't busy myself with the details of life, life after death, and I pushed the paper away, preferring to brood and drift with the unhurried passage of bereavement.

Emma sat upstairs, lonely and alone but unable to let me in and take some of the pain away. Nick might still be out, searching for comfort through noise and action, while Kate's inner eye saw and felt things that I would never know, and wept tears that I would never see.

I popped my head round the door of the sitting room on my way to bed, and saw Emma sleeping on the sofa. Her eyes were swollen, and balls of used tissues surrounded her. I went up to her room to get her duvet, and saw that she had placed a photo of Anna and her on the chest of drawers. I had taken the photo in Isabella Plantation, and they stood surrounded by bright azaleas and rhododendrons, their faces close together and their smiles symmetrically perfect. The love they had for each other was out of my reach, and seeing the photo hurt and burnt me.

I took the duvet and a pillow down to Emma, and managed to rearrange her without waking her. I kissed her very lightly, switched off the light, and went up to my bedroom. Kate had closed the curtains and one lamp was already on. I undressed, standing in front of the mirror on Anna's dressing table, then pulled open the three drawers of the table. The central one held brushes and compacts and lipsticks and powders; the two outer ones were filled with jewellery boxes, mostly empty, and punched cards of pills.

I looked in her wardrobe, the mirror inside the

door reflecting my nakedness, and felt each dress, limp and lifeless without Anna's warmth and vitality inside it, and crouched to look at her shoes, neatly filed and each with a tree inside it. On the shelves beside the hanging space were Anna's underclothes. Some I recognised, and I held them to my mouth and nose, inhaling the vaguest scent of Anna's life. Some were new; there were camisoles, and teddies, and a dozen pairs of stockings, waiting for the soft caress of Anna's skin, that skin that now stood cold and bruised and stiff, exposed and mottled, never again excited or exciting.

I pulled out everything new: all the lace and silk and cotton, still wrapped or with the smell of newness, and I began to rip it all to shreds, methodically at first but then becoming frenzied, using my teeth to unpick stitches, each garment reduced to tatters of frayed material lying on the floor and bed. I was sweating when I finished, and I reached back into the wardrobe to pull out one of Anna's petticoats. As I did so, a small sachet fell to the floor, a bag of fabric tied at the neck with pale purple ribbon. I picked it up, smelt the unmistakable perfume of dried lavender, and tossed it back on to the shelf. Then I lay on the bed, wrapping the petticoat around me, its hem across my face, and the levee I had so carefully built collapsed, the flood tide of tears washing it away.

THIRTEEN

Marty Weinstein was thirty-eight, with tightly curled black hair and a complexion the colour and texture of chilled semolina. His dandruff was free-range, falling where it may, a micro-snowstorm announcing his impending arrival. It was hard to sympathise with Marty: living the expatriate life in London, he was cosseted by the bank, spoon-fed gulps of money which his two ex-wives devoured like baby cuckoos. He spoke the hard-edged language of international business, as understood from the borders of the East River on Manhattan, and he hated and despised London and Londoners. Marty was my boss.

We tried to be friends, but it didn't work. Anna and I entertained him in Redesdale Street: he arrived late without apology, ate nothing, made no small or big talk, and left without thanks. In displaying this complete lack of grace or charisma, Marty was consciously building an image and a wall. He wanted the world to see him as uncaring, hard, and untouchable: in business he felt this would be an asset, and in his personal life it allowed him to abdicate his duties as a human being. He was, in every sense, the perfect trader.

It was the perverse nature of the bank, like any major organisation whose ambitions have far outreached their managers' ability to realise them, to promote people with a particular skill or aptitude into positions where they would never need to exercise or demonstrate that acuity. In fact, the bank could almost guarantee that a promotion would lead to a diminution of effectiveness for the manager concerned, who would eventually be fired for incompetence.

Thus was Marty made director of trading, in charge of thirty-five highly-paid, highly-strung, egotistical, back-stabbing dealers, requiring the diplomacy and patience he so patently lacked, drowning him in the constant drip of paperwork, removing him from the trading room, and asking him to acquire the gloss of senior management that he had fought so long to scratch off others.

I was going to call Marty to keep him in touch with developments, but his secretary had beaten me to it, summoning me to his office. It felt odd to be in a suit, even odder to be going in to the office without the daily mission to make money driving me forward. To get to Marty's office, I had to walk through the room. I flashed my card at the security panel, a little red dot flickering at the centre of it, but the usual click of the door unlocking didn't happen. I tried again, without success. I picked up the internal phone on the wall and called Marty's number. His secretary answered.

'Alison, I can't get the door to open. I'm just outside the room, street-side.'

'OK, I'll come and get you.' Through the plate glass side panel I could see the rows of trading positions, screens resting upon screens, every vista designed to pump more information into you. Alison appeared at the other side of the door and pulled it open.

'Sorry about that,' she said, genuinely enough. Alison was either too dim or too clever to be intimidated by Marty, and she worked for him with the same quiet resignation as she had for his predecessor, who had been reshuffled out of a job.

'Marty's just on the phone, but he said you should go straight in,' she continued. We walked together across the room, a narrow passage between the ranks of flashing desks and baying traders. Most ignored me; I looked over to Sarah's desk, but her chair was empty, an electric blue tunic hanging open over the back of it.

Marty's office was in the middle of a row of rooms, some for private meetings, others housing senior managers and traders, all of them looking out through glass walls to the trading floor. I could see Marty in his leather Pullman chair, back to the door, feet up on the black lacquer credenza, barking into the phone. I walked in and raised a hand as he looked up; he neither acknowledged my presence nor made any suggestion that I should sit down, which I did. He was in no hurry to finish his conversation, which involved some negotiation of a deal to bring a trader in from Milan. Alison put her head round the door.

'Would you like coffee?'

'Please – white, no sugar.'

Marty put a thumb up, the first sign that he was aware of other life within his office. As the coffee arrived, he began the usual tirade which ended many of his conversations. 'I don't give a flying fuck what he expects. He has to take this package, or go fuck himself. Don't present this bullshit to me again. It isn't my problem. Just get him over here.'

Another notch on his gun barrel, Marty was ready to talk to me. 'You Brits, you just have no idea,' he said. He got up, and walked to the glass wall, leaning against it and watching the frantic activity outside. Alison had closed the door, but the blinds for the wall remained tied up, allowing us to see out, and them to see in.

Marty turned, still leaning on the glass. 'So, there's some pretty bad shit around,' he said. 'What are you going to do?'

'After the funeral, I want to go away for a few days. I'll need to sort out some things at home, and then I'll be ready for work again.'

Marty walked past me, round his desk, and slumped into his chair. He sighed, entirely for my benefit, to demonstrate the demands and pulls on him and the effort needed to be so important. He picked up a paper clip, unbent one part of it, and used it to clean under his fingernails. As he dug, he spoke.

'Let's get one thing straight. As of now, you no longer work for us.'

He paused, letting his words percolate in the silence, and composing himself for the expected reaction.

'Why? What's happened?' I asked quietly, genuinely surprised by this.

Marty's soapy complexion remained constant, but he sprang forward on to his elbows, the paper clip flying across the desk. 'Jesus fuck, where are you living? Get real. One: you are the prime suspect in a murder case involving your wife. Two: your wife was running a whoring business on the side, something we don't think much of here. Three: whilst all this is going on, you're pronging one of your colleagues. I'd say that adds up to a major lack of professionalism. What would you say?'

Heat and blood and anger rushed to my head and mouth a long way ahead of reason and calm and consideration. Marty had just articulated a thought that no one else had – that I was suspected of murdering my wife – and the way in which he said it, almost gleefully, was offensive and repulsive. There had been no intimation of this from Barham, or anyone else associated with the case, and I couldn't let it pass unchallenged.

'Where the fucking hell have you got that idea from?' I shouted. 'My wife has been murdered. The police don't know who did it. Neither do I, and you certainly don't. As for your other two allegations, you'd better back those up with proof, or withdraw them.'

Marty enjoyed listening to this, if only because it gave him the opportunity to deliver a speech he had obviously been rehearsing.

'The police were here this morning, some guy called Barham. He knows about you and Sarah, and he asked a lot of questions about your work, your behaviour, that sort of stuff. It sounded to me like they are looking very closely at everything you're up to. And I don't want that kind of shit in my office.' Now he sat back again, his hands behind his head, revealing huge patches of sweat under his arms. He smoothed the back of his hair, releasing a fresh swirl of scurf, and looked at me as he savoured this moment, an obvious high spot for him.

I was still furious, but I managed to control my breathing enough to speak more evenly than before. 'Everything you say is conjecture and speculation,' I said after a sip of coffee, 'and I don't see that you have the right to sit in judgement based on nothing but supposition. Barham is merely being thorough; I'm Anna's husband, for Christ's sake. He's bound to be interested in me. It doesn't make me guilty.'

'But it makes you smell bad. And you can't go around shafting women in the office, especially at a time like this, and hope to get away with it. My guess is, you're really screwed up. Take a long vacation, and get yourself a shrink.' The considered advice of Marty, delivered in his adenoidal drawl, fell some way short of what I wanted.

For a fleeting instant I considered up-ending his desk, tearing up the office and physically attacking him. The idea seemed attractive, but instead I sat still, gripping the arms of my chair until my knuckles were white and cold. Silence worked in my favour.

'We don't want to humiliate you. There's two years' salary waiting for you, tax-free, if you resign and sign a confidentiality agreement. We'll keep on making your pension contributions, and you can keep the car, and the cheap loans. Just sign, and get the fuck out of my face.'

He pushed a document across the desk, two pages of closely typed information, restricting liabilities and promising secrecy, the consideration for this package of money and chattels that they would never miss and had already written off. The instinct was to hold out for more, to mention my advisers, to bluff and raise the stakes, but the trader inside me told me to take the profit, close the deal, and move on. I pulled out my pen and signed the letter. Alison was suddenly standing next to me, taking the letter to be photocopied, whilst Marty swivelled round in his chair and pressed a speed-dial button on his phone. The meeting was finished.

The walk back with Alison through the room was painful. I looked straight ahead, the colleagues of yesterday now strangers, the flickering screens sending blank blurs of garbled information. The worst feeling came when I glanced across for Sarah, expecting stares of alienation and maybe some regret, but finding nothing, no eyes meeting mine, the traders already on their next deal, my existence of no more value than last week's prices. Sarah's chair remained empty, the jacket still in place. Alison opened the door, and I stepped out into the vacuum that was the rest of my life.

FOURTEEN

'God's tears,' Kate said.

The rain was not that satisfying sheet of liquid screws that drill towards the ground, but a feeble pallid blur that looked unable to reach or wet the earth. We stood at the window, early by far for the cars that would take us to the funeral.

'I'm going back tomorrow. I'm no use to you here; in fact, I'm just in your way. I want to get back to my home, and put all this behind me. You do understand, don't you?'

'Of course. But you know you're welcome to stay; it's really no trouble.' This at least was honest: Kate's presence, and her sense, had made the last few days bearable. I dreaded her leaving.

'What will you do now?'

The question, such a simple one, had never been asked of me before, not in any way that suggested there were alternatives, or doubts, or decisions. I settled for the truth, or my version of it.

'I don't know. I'd sell this place, but you know what the market's like. I want to get away. I might try and persuade Nick to come on holiday with me.'

'What about Emma?'

'She'll be back to New York like a shot. She doesn't want to hang around with me.'

Kate leant her head to one side, still facing out to watch the drizzle's dilatory descent, and considered this. 'Have you asked her?' she said, having given due thought to the proper arrangement and pitch of the question.

'Should I?'

'You're her father. You decide.'

The conversation matched the weather: indeterminate, passing through shades of grey, no direct attack, simply a slow process of erosion. Emma was in the kitchen now; I could go down to her, ask her. I stood still.

A car pulled up outside the house – not a black one, not one I'd ordered, but one I knew. One door opened, and the passenger got out. I walked out of the sitting room and opened the front door.

'Is this a bad time?'

'No worse than any other,' I said, more brightly than I'd intended. 'Come in – we were just making coffee.'

'So what makes you so sure?'

We sat at the kitchen table, a cafetière between us, a jug of milk and a bowl of brown sugar at our side, and two streams of smoke dispersing into the air above us.

'Everything fits. We have separate positive identifications, putting him in Melrose Street the day you reported her missing. He's even admitted he knew her, and had visited her, although he claims he didn't see her that day. But his fingerprints have been found on the money – you know I told you we found a load of cash in the kitchen – and he's a known attacker. He got a suspended sentence for assault on a tom – er, a prostitute – a few years back. It's him.'

Barham seemed excited, perhaps because the apprehension of this man had seemed so unlikely, so remote, just days before. Now he had his suspect, his prime suspect. My dread of further revelations about Anna was tempered by an instinctive curiosity, and I wanted Barham to tell me more.

'How did you find him?'

'We did house-to-house in the area, and found a lady who spent most of her days watching the comings and goings at your ... the flat. She'd been at her window the morning it happened – before she went shopping, so it seems – so we took her down to the station, she looked at some photos, and picked him out. Saw him hanging around, like they all do, saw him go in, saw him leave.'

'The ultimate neighbourhood watch,' I said, and we both managed a smile. Barham was careful not to smile more broadly than me, in deference to my grief.

A thought crossed my mind, and I decided to take advantage of Barham's unnatural openness. 'Was he the only man she saw that day?'

'That morning, yes. As I say, she wasn't around

later, but I'm pretty confident we've got our man.'

Barham and I were both satisfied with that. As I refilled our cups, I said to him: 'Would you like something a little stronger? Just to celebrate your success?'

He looked at his watch, me, and the bottle of malt that was directly in his line of vision over my shoulder. 'Just a very small one. Cheers.'

I poured two glasses, offered water which he declined, and sat down again. 'What happens next?'

'We're questioning him. We're pretty confident we'll be able to charge him tonight or first thing tomorrow. We'll let you know, whatever happens.'

'I appreciate that. You've been very understanding. Thanks.' I lifted my glass in salute to him, and we drank together. His discovery might be the final chapter of this affair, a signal that Anna's memory could soon rest in peace, and a small knot in my stomach unwound, not yet completely loose, but a great deal more comfortable.

There was food for fifty. Caterers know what to serve at wakes, delicacies that divert attention from death and its consideration, wedges of precious food that suppress the need to talk about the subject in question. Jugs of funereal black velvet and bright Buck's fizz were emptied and filled, discreet indulgence at a difficult time. Affirmations of undying love for Anna, and me, and meaningless offers of help, as if I had lost a limb, were laid before me as a rite and my right.

There were unfamiliar faces, but I had expected that. I had not expected that no one would want me to talk, that everyone would spend two minutes with me, speaking at me, sure of my mute misery, and would move away, distancing themselves from the interface with death before they could catch the snap of its cold breath.

A small woman with fuzzy auburn hair, tied back with a black bow, moved towards me. Her face was natural, no make-up and some broken veins in the cheeks, and she was at least a foot shorter than me. She didn't smile as she approached, the first sign that she was different.

When she got near enough, she put her hand on my forearm, resting it there gently. She looked directly into my eyes. 'I knew it would happen,' she said, with a finality that made me believe her.

'What?'

'Anna. I just knew it.'

Although I hate small talk, and had heard enough that day to last for ever, this plunge into deeper waters was equally uncomfortable. I looked down past her eyes, at her skinny body and her faded black dress, a dress she might have worn every day. The hand on my arm was contradictory: it was beautiful, the flesh covering the tendons well, the fingers long and the nails unpainted but perfectly filed. I took a large swig of black velvet.

'I need to talk to you about Anna. It's very important.'

'I'm not sure I quite understand. I'm afraid I don't

know who you are. Were you a friend of Anna's?'

'Of course. You're quite right. I'll wait until your other guests have gone. See you later.' She moved away, out of the room and probably out of the house. I didn't like her, and I couldn't imagine what Anna had been doing being friendly with someone like her.

Douglas was next in the queue, and he put his arm round my shoulder, squeezing tight before releasing me and patting me on the back. 'I won't ask you how you're doing,' he said.

'Nor I you,' I replied.

'Have you noticed how nobody ever gets pissed at these things, no matter how much they have to drink?' he said.

'I'm not really much of an expert. I've only been to a couple.'

'In my line of work, you're always going to them. Death is very good for business.'

'Now you mention it, I do need to talk to you. Anna's affairs need to be sorted out. I'll make an appointment.'

'Don't bother to come to the office. I'll come over here one evening. We can get a curry and go through the whole thing.'

'Excellent. Give me a call, and we'll arrange it.'

'Done.'

Now there was silence between us, as the most important things in our lives had both disappeared and we didn't know what else to talk about. Douglas looked at his watch.

'I'd better get back. Time is money, my boy,' he said

in a heavy parody of a Jewish accent, unnecessary as he was Jewish.

I smiled, and cupped my hand round his upper arm. 'Thanks for coming. I hope I made it financially viable.'

'You will, my boy, you will.' He saluted me and left. I was once again at the mercy of the mourners, and I looked for liquid support.

When the last monochrome matron had gone, and the last grief nostrum had been delivered, I slumped on to the sofa in the sitting room. I had graduated to Scotch, and my scalp was beginning to tingle with the effects of four hours of steady alcohol intake. Downstairs I could hear the caterers clearing up. Nick and Emma had left with some friends, Kate was upstairs packing, and I was left to do whatever I was meant to do.

The door from the hall opened, and I looked up expecting to see Kate. Instead, I saw the strange woman I had talked to earlier, whose name I still didn't know, and whom I still didn't like. I half sat up, too surprised to react with any words.

'Good. Everyone's gone. Now we can talk.' I didn't want to talk, but I suspected she didn't anticipate much talking from me either. If so, she was right: I said nothing.

'You have sadness in your eyes, but there's something else too.' This was not a good start.

'I'm terribly sorry, but it has been a stressful day and I'm quite tired. Could this wait?'

'Did your wife ever mention me to you? I'm Gwyneth – Gwyneth Strong.' As she said this, she sat down next to me on the sofa, far too close to me. She smelt strongly of rose essence, an unpleasant waxy smell.

'No, she never did. Are you . . . related?'

'Oh no. I was Anna's spiritual adviser.' Her look challenged me; she was obviously used to ridicule, insults and plain amazement, and she was keen to see my reaction.

'I see.'

'Well, you probably don't. Men normally find this type of thing threatening, so they make fun of it. Anyway, Anna had been coming to see me for several years.'

An image of Anna in a room bathed in a reddish glow, draped in swirling Oriental fabrics, studying the tarot cards as this little woman turned them over, came to mind. It seemed unlikely.

'You probably have this notion of crystal balls and tea leaves and tarot cards,' she said unnervingly.

'No, not at all,' I protested, shaking my head at the sheer lunacy of the idea. 'But I'm not entirely sure . . .'

'Anna needed to get in touch with her feelings. She wanted to express them, and to find release from her frustrations.'

'And how did you help her?' There was a lingering schoolboyish smutty connotation to the word 'frustration', and I wanted to be quite sure that this was misplaced.

'At first, kinetics, then phrenology, and polarity therapy.'

It had been a stupid question, and now I had the problem of asking another one.

'What exactly does that involve?'

'Your wife had great emotional turmoil, and she found difficulty in dealing with it. She came to me for help; I could interpret her feelings through the use of various techniques, and allow her to express herself.'

'You say she'd been coming to you for some time?'

'Oh yes, every week for nearly three years. And I tried to warn her that she was vulnerable, but she never listened.'

'What do you mean, vulnerable?'

'Her feelings were almost bound to lead her to take some desperate action, a cry for help if you like, and I felt that this would lead to danger. I was right.'

I finished my drink and looked at her. It was hard to know whether she was a total fraud, or someone blessed with remarkable insight. I walked over to the bottle of Scotch, offering her one which she refused with a wave of her delicate hands.

'Can you tell me some more about these feelings?'

'Didn't she?' the woman said accusingly, knowing the answer.

'I don't know. We talked about many things. I knew her inside out.'

'I don't think she'd have come to me if you'd been listening.' This was said more sympathetically, as if it was only natural that I should be so useless. 'Your wife needed constant stimulation, both mentally and physically. When the children left home, she felt empty, and she felt that you saw her real work in life completed. You sent the children away, but you never offered to replace them with anything.'

I wasn't going to argue with her, in spite of the trash she was talking. All my blood sugar appeared to have been used in absorbing the Scotch, and I was barely able to move.

'Anna needed you to demonstrate your continuing love, not with rings and flowers and dresses, but by being with her. She resented your work, the hours you kept, the way you would disappear at the weekends to play golf rather than be with her. She felt unwanted.'

Now I had to ask her. She was building up to it anyway, so I thought I could steer the conversation towards it. 'Did she tell you . . . did you know . . . ?' I failed to get the right words in the right order, and she looked at me steadily, as if she would not help.

'As I said, it was obvious she would do something desperate. I thought she wanted a lover, but that was wrong. She did, but the lover was you. That was why she came to me: she was terrified that her feelings would show to you, and you would walk away, avoiding problems like you normally do.'

This was promising; I was getting some free spiritual advice. I continued to sit impassively, taking my spiritual input in healthy swigs.

'She'd watched her father, and knew what men are capable of. Although she resented her mother's complicity, she was heading in exactly the same direction. I honestly believe she would have preferred you to beat her than to show her the indifference you did. She was prepared to pay any price to keep you – even death, as it turned out.'

Suddenly this amusing side-show had turned sinister. The little woman sitting next to me was enumerating the sorrows of a life that I thought I knew so well, that I thought was partly mine and, although I had not been aware of this dark side, I could believe it existed. She changed pitch.

'And what about you? I can see that you've been upset, but there's much more behind those eyes. Why don't you tell me?' This was not the prurient interest of a lonely busybody, not in the way she asked the question and touched my hand, but I instinctively recoiled from the idea.

'Mine's a simple story. The problem's with my future, not my past.' As I said this, it sounded overlyrical, and I blamed the Scotch, which had not yet thickened my tongue sufficiently to prevent such foolish talk.

She was watching me, not in judgement, but as if she could see right through the skin and bone and muscle, to the core of my soul. It was an unpleasant feeling, but I was too weary to move out of her gaze.

'You'll probably never have a better opportunity to work these things out,' she said. 'You're low now, and you can let all your darkest thoughts run free. Talking to someone will help to get them into perspective.'

'I don't have any dark thoughts,' I protested.

'Everyone does. It's just that some people, like Anna, are brave enough to admit it, and face up to them. You should do the same.'

I looked round the room for support, but we were completely alone. Gwyneth didn't look at me with the mannered expression of ersatz sorrow, but studied me with fixed interest and an uncomfortable understanding of exactly what I was thinking. I didn't like it one little bit.

'Let me make you an offer,' she said finally. 'You can come and see me, or call me, at any time of day or night. Whenever you're ready to talk, I'll be ready to listen. You have much to tell, and you'll need to tell it to someone sooner or later.' She laid the back of her hand very gently against my cheek, in an action that was not sexual but was highly sensual, and her knowing stare drilled through me again. She got up, and turned to leave.

'You can't hold back the tide forever,' she said, and then she drifted silently out of the room. My cheek still tingled from that small touch, and my nose still carried the scent of her; a chill pulse ran right through me, and I drank quickly to try to ignore it.

FIFTEEN

It was a strange phenomenon: no matter how much I loved or liked someone, I always became much happier in their company when I knew they were about to leave me. My conversation was more animated, my senses more acute, when our time together was nearly at an end.

The four of us sat at the breakfast table, and I seemed to be the only one who had slept well, the only one with any appetite. Nick sat opposite me, his dressing-gown hardly covering his body, Emma next to him, already dressed in a shapeless grey track suit, and Kate beside me, quiet, immaculate, lost in private thoughts.

Gwyneth's therapy had done the trick: I felt energetic, and much of the mental sloth of the last week had lifted from me. She'd suggested that I go back, but I couldn't see that I would need to do that.

I turned to Kate. 'Are you sure you won't stay? It would be no trouble, and I'd love to have you.'

'That's very kind, but I must go. Life has to go on, to get back to normal.'

Nick spoke. 'I'm going back today. You don't need me here, do you, Dad?'

'Well, I don't need you, but I'd certainly like you to stay a bit longer. I've hardly had a chance to talk to you.' There was a touch too much petulance in my reply, but it was wasted on him.

'I've already missed a week of term. I should get back.'

'OK. Let's do a deal. I'll buy you a drink in the Surprise at lunchtime, then you can be on your way. Deal?'

'Fine.' Nick dropped his napkin on to the table, and left to go upstairs.

I looked at Emma, impassive as ever, the conversation having washed past her.

'Are you staying with me for a bit longer?'

Her eyes moved, but nothing else. She was still suffering, unable to deal with her loss as we had dealt with ours. 'I was thinking of flying back tomorrow afternoon.'

This pleased me; I didn't want to spend Sunday on my own, and I could take her to the airport, whiling away Sunday evening driving back and eating out somewhere. 'Great. Let's go out for dinner tonight.'

'OK. Sounds good,' she said. It was her turn to leave. Kate and I were alone, although she could have been in another room, another world, for all the company she was providing.

'What did that policeman want?' she asked me suddenly.

'Just routine. One or two loose ends he was tidying up.'

'It's just . . . I know it sounds funny, but I thought there was something odd about him, as if he knew things and he wanted you to know that he knew, but he wouldn't tell you what they were.'

'That sounds a little deep for me. He's just a plod, doing his job. Nice, but not particularly intelligent.'

'Hmm, you may be right,' Kate said in a tone which suggested she thought I wasn't.

'Do they know who did it?'

'Not that I know of,' I replied.

'I think that's what I saw in his face: he knows, but isn't saying until he's sure.'

'What time is your taxi coming?'

Kate looked at her watch. 'In fifteen minutes. I'd better get ready.' She didn't move. 'Anna and I had few secrets, whether we liked it or not. She loved you a great deal, possibly more than you deserved or realised. If she did things that hurt you, it was to bring you back to her. I don't know what was going on between you, but I do know that you owe it to her to stay close to Nick and Emma – especially Emma. She's feeling very lonely, and very threatened. You must look after her.' Kate put her hand on mine, patted it, and then got up. 'Don't let everything fall to pieces. You've got to take control.'

I stood up to face her, and then hugged her loosely. I was very surprised to realise that I was weeping.

It is the inalienable prerogative of every father to

believe that their son, however successful or wealthy, cannot afford a round of drinks in the pub. In fact, it is highly offensive of children, whatever age, to suggest otherwise. Nick had never threatened to offend me in this way.

We reached the Surprise at midday, the professional drinkers already installed and warming up. Nick took a pint of best, and I had a large gin and tonic. We stood at the bar, two men out together, ready to talk about everything and nothing. But the talk wouldn't flow like the drink. We were both wary, unwilling to say the wrong thing and spoil the relationship that we thought was so valuable.

I didn't want him to see me as a father, more a friend in whom he could confide. But if he had confidences, he wasn't ready to share them with me. He spoke at last.

'What will you do now?'

The question was not becoming any easier to answer. 'That's one reason I wanted to have a drink with you. I've decided to give up my job – there doesn't appear to be much point slogging my guts out like that any more. And the house is really far too big just for me. So I'm going to be taking a long hard look at what I want to do.'

'Have you spoken to Emma about selling the house?'

'Not yet.'

'You should. She's likely to be pretty upset.'

'What about you? What do you think?'

'I don't know. I've liked it more since I've been at Durham. But I understand if you want to get rid of it. Anyway, you've got to do what you want. You've spent your whole life worrying about other people. Emma and I will be fine. Just keep on sending the money.' Nick and I both laughed at this last remark.

This was big talk from my little boy. Imperceptibly, he was letting go of so much, smiling as he did it, drinking beer and rearranging his hair, completely undisturbed by the losses he was building up.

'I'll probably go on a long holiday before I make any decisions. I'd like to lie on the beach, play some golf, perhaps even learn to sail. I do want to escape from the house.'

'Wish I could come with you.'

'Why don't you, Nick? I'd love you to come. We'd have a great time.'

'I just can't do it. My work is backed up as it is, and I've too many commitments.'

Opened and closed, the opportunity had gone. I felt sad, but not angry. He had his own life, and he had started living it, successfully and painlessly weaned.

I ordered another round of drinks, and we thought about how we should open the next engagement. I decided to start.

'You know I'll never be able to replace your mother. She was a very special woman.'

'I don't want you to replace her,' Nick replied. 'Although I'll always miss her like hell, I don't need another mother. I haven't got over her death – I won't do for a long time – but life has to go on. For you, too.'

We both drank, looking at each other over the rims

of our glasses. Nick spoke again. 'Do the police know exactly what happened?'

'No. Neither they, nor I, have the faintest idea why she was there. I wonder if she was suffering from amnesia. But there doesn't appear to be much progress with their enquiries. They don't know where to start.'

'You will let me know what's going on, won't you?'

'Of course.' Media attention and interest had waned long before the full details of Anna's death had come to light, and Nick seemed oblivious of the sordid reality of the case. Crisis over, I finished my drink and pulled on my cigar, the smoke useful in hiding my confusion. I looked at my watch. 'Time for another?'

The cool calmness of the house was refreshing, the first time since Anna's disappearance that I had enjoyed returning to it. I sensed that Emma was not there, and I went downstairs and turned on the television for the sports programme. Anna and I had put a large television in the first-floor sitting room, but I preferred to sit down here.

The answering machine was flashing. There were three messages.

'It's Gwyneth. I hope you'll come and see me soon. I did so enjoy our chat. Call me. Bye.'

'It's Kate. Just to let you know I got back safely. Love to you all. Speak to you soon.'

'It's Sarah. You can't do this to me. I think I have a right to know what's going on. Please call me.'

I knew I wouldn't see Gwyneth again. The more I remembered of our evening together, the more my stomach churned. She had caught me at the bottom of the pit, and now I was on my way up and out. She had had a passing value, but was no longer necessary.

I wondered if I would ever talk to Kate again. If I didn't call her, it was unlikely she would call me. She had unsettled me with her knowledge, and her certainty, and now the link was broken I wasn't keen to keep in touch.

I couldn't call Sarah, but she didn't know that. The ache inside me had not subsided from our last meeting, sitting amongst the lunchtime lovers in Finsbury Circus. After my exit interview with Marty, I had wandered from the bank across Broadgate and into the square. It was too early to go into The Pavilion, the bar that overlooked the pristine bowling green, so I sat on a bench and rested, mind and muscles collapsing after the clenched tension of the last hour. The image of Sarah's empty chair nagged at me, and I got up and walked over to a phone booth, determined to reach her.

Ring my bell and enter Hell.

Madam Stern is bound to please.

School mistress gives bottom marks to naughty boys.

The booth was festooned with coloured calling cards, most promising violence or domination of some kind. I plucked them all out from behind the metal strips, and put them into my jacket pocket.

159

Then I called Sarah's line. She answered.

'Oh Christ, what the hell is going on?'

'Are you OK? I didn't see you when I came in.'

'They yanked me out of there. I had to sit with Personnel until they were sure you were out of the building. What the fuck's going on?'

'Marty fired me. He concocted some crap about the police, and you. He paid me off, so I'll be OK for money.'

'Where are you now?'

'London Wall. I've just been sitting in Finsbury Circus.'

'Can I come and see you?'

'I'd love you to. By The Pavilion?'

'I'll be there in ten,' she said, and hung up.

We sat together on a bench, the early lunchers unwrapping their sandwiches around us, the winos uncurling themselves from their bundles of blankets.

Sarah was very beautiful, the pallor of shock suiting her, contrasting with her dark hair and eyes. She smoked rapidly.

'The police questioned me. They wanted to know all about us. They've taken the tapes on our phone lines, yours and mine. Marty was really loving it.'

'What did they ask you?'

'How long had we been together, had you ever discussed Anna, what sort of person were you, that kind of stuff. They seemed to know a lot already. They're very interested in you. Marty's not kidding.'

'I don't think they are. They're just doing their job. They have to be thorough.'

Sarah's dark eyes stared into mine, wanting something more from me, perhaps even expecting it. 'Are you sure?'

'Positive. But I have to protect you from all this. Maybe it's better if we don't see each other for a few days, let things calm down a bit.'

'You're not telling me everything. Something's wrong, I know it is. Why can't you tell me, why won't you tell me?' I had never seen Sarah so animated, so distressed, and it harmed me. I held both her hands with mine.

'There's nothing to tell. We just have to be patient, and a little bit careful. You'll see.'

Sarah pursed her lips in a feeble attempt at a smile, and lit another cigarette. Then she looked straight at me. 'Christ knows why I should trust you. After all, you're a man and a trader. That's two strikes against you.' She kissed me full on the mouth, then got up.

'Call me when you're ready.'

'I will, I promise.'

Emma had not asked me what I intended to do now.

Either she didn't care, or she felt it was none of her business, or she realised that I hadn't got a good answer. We sat on comfortable chairs, the restaurant already buzzing with Saturday night fever. She had made an effort to look good, but I found the blackness of her clothes off-putting, as if it was a barrier between me and her feelings.

We talked about Manhattan, and the life she had

made for herself. I was surprised at how well we were getting on.

'Do you ever make it up to the Cape?' I asked her.

'Yes, we went up about a month ago.' The flush that came to her cheeks as she said this suggested that the admission was a mistake.

'Great. How is everything up there?'

'The house is fine. It's clean, and all the appliances are working. I was just there for the weekend.'

'Good weather?' I couldn't get round to it directly, so I had to show interest in other things first.

'Some. It rained at first, then cleared up.'

'Who did you go with?'

Emma took her wine as I was asking the question, ready to hide her embarrassment. It didn't work very well; the glass stayed too long at her mouth, and her redness blotched her throat. 'Just a friend. No one you know.'

'Sorry. I didn't mean to intrude.'

'That's fine. I should be glad you're interested. It's just so . . . weird to be talking to you about my life. You've been so remote.'

'I haven't wanted to be. I've always been here, ready when you needed me. It just seemed you never did.'

'Oh Dad,' Emma sighed, 'you can't just hope that things will work themselves out. You have to do something about it. You let me go to New York. You can't then say it's my fault we don't talk.'

'I didn't let you go. I had no right to stop you, and I wanted to support you in whatever you decided to

do. I hate not having you close to us ... to home.'
'Us' was a word I would have to learn to drop from my vocabulary.

'Well, it seemed like you were letting me go without a second thought.'

'Let's not argue about it. There was an obvious misunderstanding. I thought you'd be much crosser if I objected to your going. I was wrong, and I'm sorry. How's the food?'

The joy of taking out my beautiful daughter for a meal in Chelsea was only slightly abated by her vegetarianism. Much of the pleasure of eating disappeared with the knowledge that your partner was going to crunch her way through a pile of colourful tasteless vegetables, disapprovingly watching as I savoured rare flesh.

'Great. I'm glad we came out. The house is oppressive. It's as if it's in mourning. Will you sell it?'

'I'm not sure I could, even if I wanted to. There are three others for sale, and they've been on the market for ages. I'm in no hurry.'

'I wouldn't care if you did. It meant something to me when you were both in it, but now it's just another house.'

I put my cutlery down, drank some more wine, then leant over towards her. 'I was thinking of coming over to the States. Not immediately, but soon. I thought I might come and see you, and we could go up to the Cape.'

The reaction was a little quick. 'That'd be lovely,

but you couldn't stay with me. There's not enough room.'

'I didn't think you'd want me cramping your style,' I replied. 'I'd stay in a hotel. But we could have some fun.'

'Fantastic. Let's do it. Just give me a bit of warning.' I tried to imagine Emma with a boyfriend – I didn't try to imagine her with a girlfriend – and I smiled at her.

'What?' she asked, seeing me grinning foolishly.

'Nothing really. I'm just thinking about how much you've grown up, how much I've missed, how pleased I am that we're here now.'

She smiled too. It was a smile I couldn't have paid for, a smile I had waited too many years to see. The gulf between us looked much smaller, almost jumpable. She was still my baby.

SIXTEEN

Manhattan is brutal. The brutality is in the earth beneath the cement, seeping up with the radon: this is the city of brutal contrasts, black and white, rich and poor, hot and cold, gross and skinny, bludgeoning you like the raw rough fist of a navvy, relentless through day and night, twenty-four-hour GBH. To compromise, to look for the grey, is to face the fist head on, unprotected. The rhythm of the streets scans to the thwack of losers falling back, hit by the wall of right and wrong, do or die, dog eat dog.

To reach this splintering, splintered island you must pay your sop to Cerberus, the multi-headed toll booths at the Triboro Bridge or the midtown tunnel swallowing coins and tokens as you hit the Styxian currents that wash you towards Hades-by-the-Sea. Your personal Charon, the New York cabbie, cruises on these waters in deafmute mode, speaking nothing of the evils he sees and hears. A cab drive from JFK can cost you twenty-five dollars, or your life.

The Lexington House Hotel squats beneath the

shining sinewy superstructures success and money built, a brownstone anomaly amongst steel and glass and wealth. This is the midtown hotel you stay at if you're not on company expenses – the cockroaches are friendly, the staff less so. On Lexington and 39th, it boasts one coffee shop, two elevators, and a handful of Puerto Rican staff eager to assimilate you into the charming lifestyle of native New Yorkers.

I climbed out of the cab, safely delivered to the edge of the underworld, and the trunk clunked open automatically, the driver firmly wedged behind his steering wheel. The Lexington House Hotel doorman pulled my luggage out, ran to the front door, and heaved all three cases across the floor towards the front desk, an exercise which rendered redundant the cleaner's need to polish and buff the next morning. I slid in behind my cases and stood at the desk, while the doorman waited for his reward for such a well-aimed delivery. But I knew this hotel, and I knew I could wait, too. A woman appeared behind the desk, chewing gum, and looked at me in surprise, as if to say, 'What would you be wanting in a dump like this?'

'I'd like to check in, please,' answering the unasked question.

The gum clicked in her mouth. 'Surely. Do you have a reservation?'

I produced my passport, and handed it to her. She tapped something into a computer, hitting the same key a dozen times, still chewing and clicking.

'You're all set. I just need an imprint of your credit

card. Room 441. Do you need any help with your luggage?'

For all the emotion she showed in delivering this welcome, she might have been reading it for the first time off a cue card. But she had achieved something magical: the doorman had become the bellhop, and he stood ready to carry my bags, or hurl them, to the elevator. I glanced at his name badge. It said 'Lenny', but he might have stolen it, so I decided to nod at him, and we walked to the elevator, 'Lenny', the bags and I. He pushed the button, and a pair of sliding doors parted. The room inside would just about accommodate me and the cases. I peeled off a five dollar bill and gave it to Lenny. He grinned, and went back to work as the doorman. It was clearly a tough life for him, holding down two jobs.

The room had air-conditioning – a window that opened – and an en-suite bathroom tiled from floor to ceiling in pumice, separated from the main room by a sliding door that no longer slid. There was a chair, a table, a wardrobe and a bed, all within one pace of the door. I pulled the covers back from the bed, checking the sheets for stains and hairs, and was pleased to find none. The room was perfect. From it, I could hear the hum of life below, the muted car horns that echoed along the canyons of skyscrapers, the searing screams of emergency vehicles, and the angry whistles of bicycle couriers as they wrong-wayed along the streets and avenues. There was no barrier between me and life, and the blunt bitter breath of Manhattan streamed through the window and door. I fell on the bed, the luxurious wave of illicit, stolen sleep breaking over me.

Anna at the edge of my dream, dressed as she had been when I last saw her, something not quite right, pinching at my mind as it tried to relax, Anna saying something that was just out of earshot, a vague noise a million miles away, in someone else's dream, a beating thrum inside me, Anna moving backwards, spiralling away . . .

The noise came inside, no longer in a dream, but real and in the room, shaking me awake. I was sweating, and the sleep was still in my body, heavy and cramped. I was very hungry. I smelt bad and looked awful, but this was New York, so I didn't bother to shower and change. I sprayed some after-shave around me, flattened my hair, and walked out of the room. The light from the hallway lamps was barely strong enough to reach the floor, and I decided to take the stairs, three flights to shake off the excess of sleep.

The foyer was deserted, and the coffee shop that led off it was long closed. I dropped my key into the box on the front desk, then walked out into the muscular Manhattan night. Over the road from the hotel, there was a Tex-Mex bar, South of the Border, built into a new office block. I wondered whether I wanted a frozen margarita now, or after some dinner. I looked at my watch, as if that would tell me. It was ten-thirty, but grazing is a full-time occupation in New York, so I could get food any time. On the next block, there was a well-lit deli, the fruit display outside immaculate, row upon row of pristine oranges, apples, grapefruit, nectarines, all challenging you to take one and ruin the perfect symmetry of the arrangement. There were pre-packed fruit salads, with three kinds of melon and fat black grapes, all resting in mountains of crushed ice.

A gloomy Japanese restaurant seemed to be doing good business next door, but I wanted American food, big and brash and unsubtle. I hailed a cab, jumped in, and immediately forgot my manners.

'Good evening,' I said. The cabbie was impassive.

'Carnegie Hall, please.' The cab lurched away, and we zig-zagged cross- and uptown, the radio softly heard through the perspex shield separating the driver and me, some baseball game that didn't sound very exciting.

In any other city, the volume of traffic and people on the sidewalks would have qualified as rush hour, but here the rush hour never began and never ended: Manhattan was the rush, the blood stream of people in relentless pursuit of money, power and pleasure, preferably delivered in one package.

I paid the cabbie, and stepped out towards the Carnegie deli. As usual, there was a dribble of people waiting to get inside, and I joined the queue. Inside, I could see the counter staff taking orders, slicing meat, shouting at each other, intimidating punters who hesitated or changed their minds. I got a seat, squeezed in beside two large men, both drinking sodas and attacking vast sandwiches. I knew what I wanted when the lady came to take my order.

'Reuben and diet Coke, please.' No hesitation, a direct command, just as they wanted it.

'You want the Reuben juicy?' This was the coronary option.

'Please.'

I had nothing to read and plenty to think about, and I watched as locals fed their faces with piles of baloney and Swiss and pastrami and raw onion crammed between fat slices of speciality breads, mayo oozing from the corners, mutant dill pickles a foot long and waxed containers of coleslaw standing ready at their elbows. The feeding was furious, platters of fries and extra salads arriving at frequent intervals, but the chomping of jaws was no obstacle to conversation, the talk of sports and wives and husbands and lovers filtering through the mounds of fodder.

My sandwich arrived, a monstrous mountain of hot pastrami and sauerkraut between thick toasted slices of rye, the juices drenching the plate. This is why Americans have big mouths: there was no easy way to start, to make the first impression, and my opening bite merely caught a steaming escaping slither of meat. I felt the diners were watching me, judging my performance and my credibility as a native, the Reuben test their mandatory exam for the Manhattan tribe.

This was serious work, and I applied every muscle in my face to do a good job. Around me, the talk and chewing continued, the men beside me discussing and debating, and then it hit me. In this human zoo, feeding time in full flow, I was the only single, the only specimen without a mate. At every table there were friends and lovers, workmates and colleagues, carelessly sharing the moments together, whilst I sat with Reuben, quiet and alone – and I wanted to talk. I wanted to understand baseball, to make informed comments on the latest art-house movie, to listen as a partner to someone's cares and woes, to talk and be talked to. The juice was going cold, the soda was going flat, and the food wasn't filling me up.

If there is a God, He was sitting at my table that night. He felt the ache, saw the emptiness, and decided to act. I walked back from the deli, along Central Park South and down Fifth, a thousand windows lit to show their wealth of wares or partners dining, the city full of light and warmth. I reached the hotel, and the girl at reception greeted me.

'Hi. Howyadoin'?'

'Fine, thanks. Room 441, please.'

She reached behind, the piece of colourless gum still gently chewed and clicking, and pulled out my key from its slot. She also produced a folded slip of paper.

'Thanks. Good night.'

'Good night.'

I walked to the elevator, and unfolded the paper.

'MESSAGE,' it read. 'While you were out, Sarah rang. Please call her.'

I read it twice while the elevator arrived, and

twice more on the way up. Sarah rang. Sarah rang. I knew the pain in my heart was not from the Reuben, but had been delivered across telephone lines, silently and stealthily. I wanted her here, I wanted the smell and touch of her, and I understood that I wanted to make love to her, to honour her and to value her.

The call took an age to arrange – at least thirty seconds – and then the fizzy sound of the ringing tone reached my ear, through to my brain, and then my heart. I thought of the phone in her flat, and I thought of her in the shower, or eating her breakfast, and then I heard an answer.

'Hello.'

I jumped in too quickly. 'Sarah, it's me.'

'I'm afraid I'm not able to take your call at the moment, but leave a message after the tone, and I'll get back to you.'

Such agony, not sweet but sour, to hear her voice and not to hear her. The machine beeped at me.

'Sorry I missed you. I was just having dinner. You can call me when you get in, or I'll try again tomorrow.'

'Wait, wait, I'm here,' Sarah said, and I lost my voice and control completely. 'I was just in the bathroom,' she said, filling the space that was mine to talk in. I was still silent. 'Are you OK? You must be exhausted.'

'I'm fine. How are you? You should be on your way to work.'

'Don't worry about that. I just thought I should

call, see you're OK.' A pause, then she spoke again. 'I miss you already.'

The wires hissed between us, as if to soften the hard edges of all emotion, and I struggled to find something neutral to say. I couldn't find it, and I didn't trust my voice.

Sarah was oblivious of this. 'You'd better get some sleep. Will you call me tomorrow?'

'Which tomorrow? Yours or mine?' I asked.

'Either. Both.'

'Yes . . . yes, I'll call you. Sorry I'm so quiet. I'm really tired.'

'Go to bed, and enjoy it. Just take your time. And be a good boy. New York's full of naughtiness.'

'I'll try,' I said, and the little nasal laugh probably didn't span the wires. I didn't want to hang up. Sarah didn't want to hang up.

'OK. Talk to you soon. Sleep well.' She said the words slowly, and avoided the terminal words that would cut us off.

'Yup. Sarah . . .' Her name was suspended in the ether, waiting to be joined by something I knew I should say, but couldn't.

'I know,' she said. 'Me too.' And the line went dead.

I sat on the edge of the bed, holding the receiver against my face. I wanted to call her back, and say those things that were there, right at the front of my mind and body, but I didn't. I stood up and walked to the window, a fine mist in my eyes and no thought of sleep. I remembered the bottle of duty-free Scotch I had bought, and retrieved it. There was a glass in the bathroom, and I rinsed it under the tap.

I sat at the table and thought about writing a letter. There was no notepaper, and I couldn't find my pen. I doubted if I could find the eloquence to string three words together, and it was only three words that I wanted to write. I drank a glass of Scotch, and tensed myself against the coming dread of dark solitude, when the lights are out and there is nothing to protect you from thoughts and wishes and fears and dreams. I poured another drink, and moved over to the bed, propping myself against the puny pillows. I left the light on, and I must have drifted off like that.

SEVENTEEN

Breakfast in America needs strength and persever-
ance, not just in the eating but in the ordering. By
ten in the morning the businessmen had left the
coffee shop, and I took my place at the counter. A
dark-skinned girl with heavy eye make-up and
beautiful teeth approached. She poured a coffee
without bidding, and produced a small jug of cream.

'Howyadoin'?' she asked, and by now I knew that
the question needed no reply. The laminated menu
lay in front of me, four sides of variations on the
theme of excess eating. I knew I should have something light and healthy, but I never found that
section.

'Can I have orange juice, eggs and bacon with
country fries, and some toast with grape jelly?'

She scribbled the order on her pad. 'You want the
eggs easy over?'

'Please.' She was satisfied with this, and marched
off to deliver the order. She was wearing a light
brown work dress, with a white pinafore, and had
the regulation sneakers and white sports socks. She

wiped the counter and rearranged settings, and chewed some gum that I could see was pink. I would have liked to talk to her, but I didn't know where to start. She came back towards me.

'You from Australia?' she asked.

'Er, no, England actually.'

'Oh God, I love you English. Say something to me. I love your accent.'

'Have you ever been to England?' I managed in my best intonations.

'God, no, but I'd love to go. I wanna see your Queen, and all that stuff. You from London?'

'Yes, I live there.'

'No kidding. You here on business?' I, too, loved her accent, the way she truncated sentences to cut out the superfluous.

'No, I'm just visiting my daughter. She lives here.'

'No kidding. Where?'

'On Murray Hill.' This impressed her, although I felt she would have been impressed if I'd have said Emma was living in Hell's Kitchen.

'That's a bit different to London, I bet,' she said. Another client arrived at the counter, and she poured him coffee, the interruption to our conversation only temporary.

'I think so,' I replied, when she returned.

'Well, you just enjoy yourself, OK? You want anything, you let me know.'

'Thanks.'

She had managed to sound completely sincere, offering help and friendship, directly and without the slightest trace of falsehood. The food arrived. 'You're all set,' she said, and she laid the plates in front of me. 'Enjoy.'

I did. The bacon was crisp, the eggs fresh, and the country fries browned and steaming. My mug was never allowed to get even half-empty before she was back to top it up. It was impossible to read the papers and concentrate on the food, and her. Around me, customers ordered, and she accepted their poor manners, their grunts and nods, as if they meant nothing to her, inured to the brash curt manner of people in a hurry, rushing to do deals and talk money.

Out on the street, life raced by, men in dark suits with white shirts and red ties, women in dark suits with white blouses and red cravats, the uniforms of midtown trade, missionaries with a single aim; and I was a stranger in their land, no longer sharing their mission. My clothes betrayed me, and my eyes lacked focus, the light of money no longer burning inside. I was looking into a tunnel from outside, watching them as they hurtled towards the pinpoint of light at the other end, the eternal flame of wealth and success that they pursued both day and night.

'You need anything?' the waitress asked.

'No thanks, I'm done,' I replied, and I wiped my mouth.

'More coffee?'

'I couldn't, thanks.'

'You want the check?'

'Please.'

I paid the bill, and left her a good tip.

She smiled. 'You have a nice day. See ya.'

Then I left my dark-skinned friend, and went back to my room. I brushed my teeth, pulled on my jacket, and went out, eager to fill the space and the aimless time ahead.

On Lex, a black man was walking slowly, a huge white wooden cross carried over one shoulder, his arm looped over it. His hair was dirty, and he wore a mac and no trousers. He carried a shopping bag in his free hand, and his dead eyes glared at the ground. He talked to himself, very softly, and I was the only person watching him, the only person who appeared to see him. He walked right past me, and by his smell I knew he was no mirage, the stench of urine strong, but I turned to watch him as he drifted away, the white cross visible for many blocks. I shook my head and smiled. Welcome to New York.

Emma's office was on Avenue of the Americas, near to Central Park. The building was twenty years old, and lacked the gloss of other more recent towers. The reception area was dull, a small marble-faced desk with a fat security guard and some grubby leather chairs in front of the corridor to the elevators.

When I'd decided to come to the States, I'd called her, and we'd arranged lunch. This was the cautious, prudent start to our conciliation; she wanted to meet me on her turf, to be in charge, the short lunch

178

in business hours designed to take things slowly. I announced my arrival to the guard.

'Will you be going up?' he asked. Although I hoped she'd show me round, I didn't know, and I shrugged.

'I'll call her,' he said. 'Take a seat.'

I knew I'd made my first mistake when I heard him speak.

'Your father's in reception.' I could imagine Emma, the confidence of independence pricked by Daddy turning up.

The guard put the phone down. 'She'll come down.'

My armpits were warm, and my hands trembled. She'd be angry, cross that even the security guard knew she had a father. I watched the lunchers as they filed in and out of the elevators, clutching brown bags and soda cans. No sign of Emma, but I knew she'd take her time.

Then she arrived, but I hardly recognised her. Gone was the pallor of bereavement, the looseness of the face, the blackness of her clothes; her hair was neatly pulled back, tight against her scalp, and she wore a red-striped blouse with a ruffled collar, a short blue skirt, blue tights, and flat black shoes with gold trimmings, almost like slippers. She was walking with another woman, talking all the time until she reached me. The woman said, 'Later', and Emma was left with me. Then she surprised me. She put her arms round me, and squeezed tight. 'You made it then. When did you get in?'

'Last night.'

'Where are you staying?'

'The Lexington House.' She made a face. 'It's cheap.'

'Come on, let's go and eat.' She let go of me, and we walked out into the sunshine.

'Where are we going?' I asked.

'Alfredo's. It's Italian. I know you like pasta.' This was a good start. We walked briskly, and reached the entrance to a gleaming skyscraper on stilts. It took a minute to adjust to the light and coolness inside, and we went down an escalator, across a concourse, and into the restaurant. A smiling woman led us to our table, and took our orders for drinks, a beer for me, water for her.

'So. Tell me everything. What's going on in London?'

'Same as usual. Rain, England doing badly at cricket, the government ruining everything. I'm not missing it yet.'

'How are you?' She seemed to be interested in my answer.

'Recovering. I shan't stay here long. I want to get up to the Cape.'

'Oh, here's something that'll interest you. Nick called me. Some kind of record – the first time he's ever called.'

'Why? Is anything wrong?'

'You won't believe me, but he's worried about you. He thinks you're keeping it all inside you. He wanted to know what I thought.' She smiled, hoping that a smile might temper the impact of what she said.

I looked at the menu while I thought of a reply.

180

'We all carry our sadness in different ways. I'm learning to live with it, just as you and Nick are. I just need some time to think things through.'

'But you're not going to crack up, are you, Daddy?' This was an order, not a question.

'No, baby, I'm not going to crack up.' I smiled back, and held her hand across the table. 'As long as I have you and Nick, I'll be fine. Honestly.'

'Good.' The lecture was over. 'Let's order.'

I let Emma take charge, and I listened to her as she discussed Manhattan, her assurance strong as she told me where to eat, what galleries to visit, where to walk, cleverly emphasising her power of knowledge over me. I remembered when we visited her at boarding school, and she had shown Anna and me round the buildings, using school terminology without explanation, a conscious effort to let us know that she understood this private world of hers, and we were the visitors, the strangers, the unwashed infidel.

'Will you stay for the weekend?'

'I thought I'd rent a car, and drive up on Sunday,' I said. I think I saw relief on her face, but it wasn't clear.

'I'd love to come with you, but I'm really snowed under here,' she said easily.

'I'll be there some time. You could always visit me later.' The pasta arrived, forestalling any need for her to reply.

Sitting with my daughter, lunching together, the smallest talk of greatest value, I felt refreshed. We were two regular people, no eyes upon us to question our status, just observing the common routines, and the feeling buzzed through me and sparked at the nerve-endings. I had two more beers, and let Emma excite me with her companionship.

I ordered an espresso, and she had some tea, looking at her watch to remind me that this was a time-tabled meeting in her life, on her terms. I needed to go very slowly.

'Will you have time to see me again this week?'

There was no hesitation in her answer. 'Of course. There's a great restaurant just opened on Columbus. We could go there one evening, if you like.'

The disappointment that I felt was tiny, but it still hurt. She wasn't ready to let me judge her home life, and I knew I shouldn't ask.

'Sounds great. When?'

'Tomorrow night? I could get a table at, say, nine. Is that OK?'

'Perfect. I think my diary is free.' We laughed together.

'Dad, I really have to run. I have a meeting at two-thirty.'

'Don't worry, I'll get the bill.' For one frightening moment, I thought she might object, insist on going Dutch, but she let it pass. We rose together, and she kissed me.

'I'll call you this evening to arrange things,' she said. 'Be good.'

'I'll try,' I said, and she left, determined, confident, and all grown-up, and I sat down at the table, no

longer anxious at being a single swimmer in the sea
of life around me.

I sat in my room with a glass of Scotch and a pile
of postcards. In a reflex action I had bought a dozen,
and now I looked at them and realised that I didn't
want to write to anybody – except Sarah. The room
was cool, but it was dark and oppressive, and I was
feeling lethargic. I lay down and thought of Sarah,
the thrill of talking to her wearing off as I turned
over the decisions that I had made before coming to
the States.

I'd pretty much decided to cut loose, and make a
fresh start in New York. I had plenty of contacts in
Manhattan, and Boston, who would be only too
pleased to give me a job, and I had already called
several to tell them I'd be over. I told Barham that
I was going away, and he seemed interested, but not
concerned. He took details of where I'd stay, and
promised to call if he had any news for me. He didn't
mention his suspect, but I took this to mean that
there was nothing further to report and didn't ask
him for any news. I'd left the house keys with Carole,
the neighbour, telling her that I'd be back in a month
or so. She was friendly, and promised support again,
and I was polite.

I'd hoped that the distance between Sarah and me
would soon blunt the sharpness of our feelings, but
her call, and my boyish reaction to it, had thrown
that into question. I wanted to leave everything
behind – belongings, memories, emotions – but

Sarah's scent had followed me, lingering in my mind and my baggage. I wanted her to feel abandoned, and move on to the next man, but she was frustratingly persistent, in a way I liked and hated at once. I couldn't start a new life with her; there was too much she might already know of my past, and I could endanger her in ways she didn't understand. Anna had seen to that.

Now the past seemed over, Sarah the only link with what had gone before. I wanted to re-join the race here, fresh and clean, unencumbered and unjudged. Emma was here, but she could deal with that: she'd proved her independence, and I respected it. We could be friends, and I had no desire for anything more. Nick had been colder than I'd hoped in London, and he was drifting away, his life leading to a separate end from mine. There seemed no point in fighting to hold on to the little I had left. But Sarah . . . the gravity, the forceful pull that she exerted, was stronger than I'd bargained for.

I was tired, and I wanted to float off into black dreamless stupor. I climbed on to the bed and closed my eyes, shutting the eyelids hard to squeeze out the dangerous thoughts. It worked; I passed out.

I was soaking. My shirt was drenched, my neck wet, my whole body sticky, and I was shivering. My head ached, throbbing on one side and then the other. The sheets I had climbed under felt as cold and heavy as metal. I rolled over, and my joints creaked in noisy complaint. A little patch on one side of my chin, where the beard grows thickest, was itching furiously. I tried to sit up, but the feverish pain prevented me. The inside of my mouth tasted of coins, and my gullet was constricted.

I scratched my face, then let my hand fall limply back to my side. I needed a drink of water, but couldn't see how I was going to get to the bathroom. Weakly, slowly, I picked up the phone by the bed and called room service.

'Yallow,' a male voice shouted at me.

'Please – room 441 – some iced water and Tylenol. Quick as you can.'

'You OK?'

'Not so good. Quick – please.'

'On its way, sir.'

I dropped the phone back on to its cradle and shivered, a tremor that ran from my toenails right to my jaw, where it stayed. I couldn't remember ever having felt like this before. The patch on my face was burning in its irritation, and I scratched some more, looking at my fingernails for blood or pus.

Room service knocked, then unlocked the door. It was Lenny.

'Hey, you look like shit.' He put the tray down on the nightstand and poured me a glass of water, the clinking of ice rattling my eardrums uncomfortably. I took the glass, resting on one shaking elbow, and sipped. He slipped me two tablets, and I swallowed them down, the cold water feeling good until it hit my stomach.

'You want me to get a doctor?'

'No!' I said as strongly as I could. 'No doctor. I need to rest. It's just a chill.'

'You take it easy, man. You need anything?'

'I'm all set. Thanks.'

'Sure. Take it easy.' Lenny backed away, then left the room, silently closing the warped door.

I collapsed, and fell into that restless half-consciousness that seems like death, shaking and shivering and aching everywhere.

It was still light outside, so I hadn't been out for long. The tablets had made a little headway, and I finished the pitcher of water, the ice nearly all gone. I called Sarah.

'You sound awful,' she said.

'I think I've picked up a chill. It's nothing serious.' I scratched my face again.

'Can you get to a doctor?'

'They can't do anything. I'll be fine after a good night's sleep. I've got some pills. I just wanted to call to say goodnight.'

'That's nice,' she said, the low laziness of her voice soothing and cooling. 'You sure you haven't caught anything from those wild New York dolls?'

I snorted out a little grunt, the joke unwittingly ironic. 'Haven't had the chance. I saw Emma at lunchtime. She's getting on well.'

'Go to bed, and get warm,' Sarah said softly. 'Let's talk tomorrow.'

'OK. I'm going. You know, I really . . . miss you. A lot.'

'Me too. Oh! I have some news that might speed your recovery.'

'What?'

'Marty. He got fired today. He's already gone. They're bringing in a new guy from Frankfurt. I thought you'd be pleased.'

'Sweet, sweet justice. Goodnight, Sarah. I'll call you tomorrow.'

'Get better soon. I need you healthy.'

I don't know whether it was the pills or Sarah, or her news, but I was sure something had made me feel a lot better.

EIGHTEEN

Hampton Ebling Junior had his office on the twenty-second floor. As befitted a senior vice-president, it was a corner office overlooking Park Avenue, with a view that ran all the way down to the Pan Am building, which straddles Park in the low forties. Ham was sitting in his plush burgundy chair, facing out to watch the noiseless scene below, as his secretary brought me into his office.

'Mr Ebling,' the secretary said.

He turned round, a Dictaphone in his hand, and jumped up from his seat, tossing the machine on to his desk. 'Why, there you are, you old dog,' he shouted. He came round his desk, and put a thick muscular arm around me.

'Ham, good to see you,' I managed to say in between bear-like squeezes.

'When did you get in?'

'Sunday night.'

'Great. Where are you staying?'

'Oh, a small hotel on Lex. It's good.'

'Excellent.' Ham stood gripping my right hand. He

was at least six foot four, and had the bigness of a man that height, but no more. His hair was thick on top, golden brown, and cut above the ears. He had the ruggedness of face that came from all free time spent in boats, on horses, and skiing, and he had the old-fashioned manners of a Bostonian. Ham and I had known each other for twenty years; he had come on a temporary secondment to London, and we had ripped up the town together. He had met Anna, who loved him, and we had stayed in close contact.

'Take a seat. Lorraine will be getting coffee. Cigar?' He had a large silver box on the desk, which he pushed towards me. Ham was senior enough to ignore the rules on smoking in the office.

'No, I won't at the moment.' I was still feeling weak from my fever; the idea of a fat cigar didn't appeal.

'Well, you old dog, what brings you here?'

This was the first time I would have to explain the events of the last few weeks, and I'd been practising. 'Anna died last month. As you know, my daughter Emma lives here, so I came out to spend some time with her. Then I'm going up to the Cape. It's a kind of enforced holiday.' I laughed, but Ham's face was stonily serious.

'I am so terribly, terribly sorry. You know how fond I was of her. God, you must be devastated.'

'I'm coming to terms with it. Being close to my children helps.'

'Was her death expected?' The question was asked slowly, gently.

'No. It was a shock to all of us.'

'God, if there's anything I can do, you just holler. Would you like to come stay with us?' Ham had a huge colonial farmhouse in Westchester County, fifty miles north of Manhattan. His wife, Gayle, rattled around in the place with their only child, Hampton III. I had stayed there before, the hospitality was warm and genuine, and his offer was tempting.

'That's kind of you, Ham. Can I get myself sorted out, and then I may well take you up on your offer? How are Gayle and Hamlet?'

'They're great. Fit as fiddles. But, look, I'm serious. Come and stay with us. We would really love to have you come visit with us.'

The charm, the sincerity, the concern, all overwhelmed me.

'OK. I definitely will. As soon as I've got things cleared up.'

Coffee arrived, and Lorraine poured. We sat at an arrangement of sofas and armchairs at the other end of Ham's office, which was large enough for some serious cricket practice.

'So, you still working for that lousy bank?' We smiled.

'Actually, no. With everything that's gone on, I felt I needed a clean break. That's one of the reasons I came to see you. I'm thinking about settling down here.'

'That'd be fantastic. Have you got a job lined up?'

'Not yet. I was wondering if you knew of anything likely.'

Ham steepled his large hands in front of his face, his elbows resting on the arms of his chair. He thought for a long time. I looked around the office. There were pennants from college, family photos in gilded frames, souvenirs from past marketing campaigns, a model of the boat Ham owned, a battered football helmet, and lucite tombstones from important deals. Ham was comfortable in this office.

Finally he spoke. 'You'll probably hate this idea, but we're looking for someone. It's kind of a rainmaker deal, you know, bring the business in, make things happen. You'd be ideal.'

'When do I start?' I really didn't know how to react.

'Hey, look, if you're interested, I can line up some discussions, get the ball rolling. It'd be neat. Whattya say?' So simple, so direct, this kindness from Ham was the salve I needed, and it tingled exquisitely on my scalp.

'Let's try. I'd be very interested.'

'Leave it to me. Give Lorraine your number, and we'll get it all fixed. Shake on it, partner.' His hand extended, covering mine, and we shook vigorously. 'More coffee?'

The after-effect of Ham's tonic was painful. I was shaking, whether from excitement or exhaustion I didn't know, but I wanted to keep talking, to keep hearing kindnesses and companionship. I was sitting in the coffee-shop, my friend behind the counter. I had a large mug of coffee in front of me.

'What's your name?' I asked her as she breezed

past on her way to refill another mug.

'Louise.' The way she said it made it into one syllable, 'Wheeze'. It was nearing lunchtime, and she was busy, but she still made enough time to smile and show her beautiful teeth. I thought she was gorgeous.

'Well, Louise, you make the best coffee in New York.'

'So they say,' she replied laughing, and scuttled off to fetch another order.

I watched the first of the lunchtime rush arrive, earnest and focused, money on their minds, and I vaguely hoped that soon I would join them in their headlong hurtling towards the citadel of wealth. I wanted to sit on the twenty-second floor, and watch the yellow cabs flow back and forth, and talk the language of commerce. I didn't want to be a stranger.

'You gonna eat?' Louise asked.

'After your breakfasts, I don't feel hungry for a day after,' I replied, and she smiled.

'The special's good today. Chicken à la King. It's the only thing the cook knows how to do.'

'Maybe later.'

I looked up as she moved away, and turned to watch the other diners. The tables were filling up fast, twos and threes and fours of business people. I was about to turn back to my coffee when I realised what I'd seen. My stomach told me first, a huge, single churn as it got the message from my optic nerves.

Though he had his back to me, I recognised him

none the less. The blue-suited shoulders gave him away. They were covered in a fine dusting of flakes. Above, the curly-haired head jerked as he empha-sised his points to the woman opposite him. From this distance, it was impossible to hear what he was saying but, even from this angle, his body language showed aggression and rudeness and incivility. It was Marty.

Sometimes your body works well ahead of your mind, and I was already slipping off my stool towards him before I checked myself. I stood up, pulled out a five dollar bill, and laid it on the counter.

'Thanks, Louise. Catch you later.' I pointed to the money, then put my head down and made it to the door unseen.

I sat in my room and opened the envelope that had been delivered by Lenny. Lorraine had been very efficient.

Mr Ebling has asked that you meet with the following senior officers:

Scott Hines, EVP and Head of Transaction Banking.
Barry Baronius, SVP and Head of Client Service.
Walt Gramlich, SVP and Head of Worldwide Sales and Marketing.
Mary Jo Garber, VP and Head of Divisional Human Resources.

Please arrive at the main desk at 9.30 a.m. and ask for me.

I'd not expected things to move so quickly. The appointments were for the next Monday, and I had to decide whether to go to the Cape now, and come back, or simply delay the trip. Realistically, I didn't think I would have the strength to drive both ways in a couple of days, so I resolved to stay in Manhattan. I called Emma.

'Are we still on for tonight?'

'I was just about to call you. Nine o'clock, Caramba, Columbus Avenue. Do you need directions?'

'No, I'm sure I'll find it. I'll see you then.'

'Is everything OK? You sound tired.'

'Couldn't be better. Looking forward to it. Bye.'

I had bought some cream from a pharmacy for my face, and I went into the bathroom to look at the damage. The patch was no bigger than before, but no smaller. Around the edges the skin was flaking badly, and the centre was red and slightly raised, but the surface was not broken or weeping. I rubbed on a large dollop of cream, the coldness a shock, and washed my hands. I had six hours before meeting Emma, and I wanted to walk in the streams of the city, but I had to rest first. I slipped off my clothes and climbed into bed. I would call Sarah when I woke. That thought helped to relax me, and I went out like a light.

The urgent immediacy of the telephone bell frightens

the dreamer, clamouring through the gentle rhythm of slumber, and I woke with a start. The orange light on the corner of the cradle flickered in time with the ringing, emphasising the obligation to pick it up.

'Hello?'

'Hi. It's me.' The voice was quiet and low, distant in a way that was different.

I sat up against the headboard and switched the phone to my other ear. 'How are you?' I asked.

'Not so good. They've let me go.'

'What do you mean? Who?' I was being pretty thick.

'I lost my job. The new guy – Ernst Muller – he sacked a whole group of us. I just can't believe it.'

'Hang on. How did this happen? He's only been there five minutes.'

'I know, I know. They've been planning this for some time. Marty was just the first. Ten of us went this morning. Muller's the hatchet man.'

My sensitivity deserted me. 'Did you get a package?'

'Oh yes, it's pretty good, but I've got no job. It could take years to find something else.'

'No it won't. You're good, so good. You'll find something easily.'

'I wish. I've spent today just sitting here, wondering how I'm going to get it together. I really need you.'

'Do you want me to come back?' It was an offer lightly made.

'No, for God's sake don't do that. I just needed to

talk to you, to let you know. I'll be fine. I've got my cigarettes, and I've got a bottle of wine.'

'Marty's turned up here. I saw him in the coffee-shop at lunchtime. The proverbial bad penny.'

'Did you speak to him?'

'No. I managed to stop myself before I went over and punched him.'

'Anyway, how are you getting on?'

'Good. I'm seeing Emma tonight. She's taking me to some hot spot on Columbus. I'll probably double the average age on arrival.'

'But you'll be the sexiest man there, too.'

In forty-three years, that was one adjective I'd never heard used to describe me, and I could feel myself blushing. That didn't happen too much, either. Sarah must have felt the heat down the phone.

'Come back soon, won't you?' she said, and I think she really meant it. Then I lost myself.

'Better still, why don't you come over here? There's nothing to keep you there, and you could use a break. Come up to the Cape. You'd love it.'

There was a lot of silence, and a lot of rustling as she rearranged herself and pulled on her cigarette. Then she spoke, that low growl that promised everything a healthy male could ever want. 'Are you sure you mean that?' And her words echoed on the line.

'I'm sure.'

'Then I'm coming. I have to go and pack now. I'll call you when everything's settled. You . . . bye.' The phone went dead, and the receiver slipped in my hand as the sweat ran free. But this time I had a very different kind of fever, and I think I liked it.

I had a bourbon in front of me, full of ice and with a short striped straw in the glass. I stirred the drink lazily, pulled out the straw and sucked it, and watched. I was sitting at a table laid for four, my back to the wall which was painted toothpaste green. There was a great deal of stained pine, the colour of comb honey, and the chairs were dark grey metal with inadequate cushioning. The lights were too bright, the music too loud, and I hated it.

The clock above the bar said it was ten past nine. I wasn't the oldest person there, but I was the only one wearing a tie and jacket. The bourbon tasted sweet, and I crunched on some foul Chinese crackers from a bowl in front of me. I was hungry, and my walk from the hotel had left me pretty tired. The two women next to me had shaved heads and wore tight leather and studded belts, and looked into each other's eyes intensely as they talked.

Emma's lateness was probably simple etiquette, the kind that decreed that you never got anywhere on time. This was a social grace I had never learnt, or understood. I banged my left hand on the table, and it clicked. I looked down and realised that I had never taken off my wedding ring. It was a simple band of gold, bevelled at the edges, and its presence troubled me. I couldn't decide whether to take it off. I couldn't even decide if it really mattered. I tapped the table again, liked the sound it made, and left it on.

As the clock reached the quarter, Emma walked in, sandwiched between two young men. The one in front waved at friends, and went over to their table. I waved at Emma, and she grinned and walked towards me. The man behind her followed. Emma looked flushed, as if she had been hurrying. The man behind seemed in no hurry at all.

I stood up to greet her, and we hugged and kissed. As we did so, I could see that the man was still behind her. We disengaged, and Emma turned to the man.

'Dad, I want you to meet Henry.'

In a thousand books and films, the father never likes the daughter's boyfriends. It's true: life imitates art. Henry stood there, a sullen, part-shaven, black-clad rake, greasy hair tied back in a little pony tail. I thought a handshake might be inappropriate, but the instinctive reaction still jerked my right arm forward. He took it, and shook my hand warmly.

'Good evening, sir. It's very good to meet you.' I would have been less surprised if he'd broken wind, or merely grunted. Physically, and mentally, I was disarmed by him. He let my hand go, and we moved to sit down.

'I was truly sorry to hear about your loss,' he said, as he held the chair for Emma. 'I know this must be a very difficult time for you.'

'Thank you, Henry.' I looked at Emma, a strong smile on her face and the flush still evident.

'Henry is a writer,' she said to fill the gap. 'We're going to publish his first novel.' She seemed very proud of this; he was not so sure. He put his hands up, the palms facing me. They looked grubby.

'I'm sure your father doesn't want to hear about my scribblings,' he said. 'Shall we get a drink?' He caught a waiter's attention, and ordered a spritzer for Emma, and two bourbons.

'Emma doesn't like me drinking hard liquor, but you'll support me, won't you?' he said lightly, completely at ease.

'As long as it helps the writing,' I said.

'Actually, it doesn't, but that's just our secret, OK?'

'How are you feeling now, Dad? You sounded awful earlier.'

'Oh, it was nothing, just a chill.'

'Yes, you have a cold sore,' Emma helpfully reminded me. It wasn't throbbing too much. 'Do you have some cream for it? It looks bad.' Now it started to throb.

'Emma, I can take care of it.' I finished the first glass of bourbon, and turned to Henry. 'So tell me about your book.' I tried not to sound pejorative, but it was a challenge.

'It sounds pretentious when I explain it. Simply put, it's the study of a man who loses all his material wealth and possessions, very much a man of the Reagan era, and what he does, and how his moral code changes, in the nineties.'

I wondered if he had put it simply because he felt I wouldn't understand it otherwise, but I let this pass. 'What happens to him, in the end?'

'I hope you'll buy the book and find out.' We all laughed at this high wit, especially Emma. 'Sorry –

I only said that for my publisher's benefit.' Another round of laughter at this priceless remark.

'Actually,' he continued, 'I'm pretty cynical, despite my tender years. I don't think that much has changed. People still chase after money at the cost of everything else. That's why I was so impressed when Em told me that you were dropping out of the race. That takes real courage.'

I wasn't able to put my finger on the exact sentiment I felt after this panegyric, coming as it did from a boy with an infrequent acquaintance with shampoo and soap, and who called my daughter Em, a name she had despised all through her earlier years.

'I'm not sure I share your cynicism. Certainly the events of the last few weeks have made me think again about my values, and maybe they'll change my whole outlook.' I decided that my news about Ham's offer could be deferred.

'Well, I hope you're right, sir. But a wholesale change of morals won't help my book sales any!' This was sharp repartee, greeted with more polite smiles.

The drinks and the menus arrived, and Emma enthused about the food. I wanted a steak, but this wasn't that type of restaurant. I longed to be sitting in front of Louise, who probably could have recommended the coffee-shop steak.

We ordered, Henry asking for small changes to every item he wanted, but the waiter took this in his stride. Perhaps this was another social grace I had failed to grasp.

'Em tells me you're off to the Cape. I hope you have luck with the weather. Still, if you don't like it, you can always wait half an hour.'

'Coming from England, I can tell you that the weather is the last thing on my mind. We've had an awful summer.'

'Yes, an island climate has its drawbacks.' I was grateful for his meteorological opinion.

The restaurant had its redeeming features. The service was very quick, and the portions were very small. I felt we might finish before ten o'clock.

'Do you write full-time?' I asked Henry.

'God, I wish. No, I work part-time as an AIDS counsellor. Sadly, that's a growing profession.' Henry and Emma looked very sad.

'You must see some terrible things,' I said casually.

'I think ignorance is the worst part of it. There is a great fear of AIDS, and that's obviously a good thing. But the ignorance about it – and the prejudice – is difficult to fight. You probably know how difficult it is to contract AIDS, but a lot of people out there are frightened of touching sufferers, or even being in the same room as them. It's not like leprosy. What's really needed is counselling for the people who *don't* have AIDS. They're the ones who need the education and advice.'

'If it's so difficult to catch, why is it so prevalent?'

'It isn't so much prevalent, as prominent. It's a very high-profile condition, emotionally and politically. It's hard to be objective about it. That's the most difficult part of my job – to be non-judgemental.'

Henry and Emma looked at each other lovingly, and goose-pimples exploded over my skin. He put his hand casually on hers, squeezing it before stroking it. The mere thought, let alone the sight, of Henry pawing her, was making the meal hard to swallow. He seemed entirely oblivious of this, at ease in front of me, rudely trying to put me at ease. But I did want to go on with this conversation; Henry had valuable information that could set my mind at rest. Through clenched teeth, I continued.

'Is it really that hard to contract? The way the media has it, you'd think everyone was at risk.'

'Far from it. For so-called straight heterosexuals who practise safe sex, the risk is practically zero. I hate to say this, but the medical profession has a lot to answer for. They are putting the fear of God into everyone – prophesying a plague that isn't too likely to occur, if you ask me.'

'Speaking of God, do you think it's divine retribution?'

'I don't know enough about the way He operates to give you a good answer to that. I've tried to rationalise it, but I can't. I just try to help the best I can.'

He had given me enough comfort to help me relax, and I leant back in my seat in relief. The plates were empty, and were swiftly removed. The waiter, who had kindly introduced himself as Bruce, offered us desserts and coffee. We all skipped pudding. Henry leant over to me.

'Would you like an armagnac? They have a very good list here.'

I didn't want him to do this, to be my friend and

ally, but I did want an armagnac. We ordered two large ones, and Emma murmured not a word of admonition. She had said very little all evening, but now she talked.

'Henry and I are going away this weekend; we're going to Chicago. Henry's from there.'

'People always laugh when I tell them Chicago is my favourite American city,' I said.

'Well, it looks much better to me from here. But it's kinda fun for a weekend.'

'I find mid-westerners very civilised after New York.'

'That's for sure. But being there permanently is the pits.'

We drained the golden drops of brandy, and Emma looked at her watch.

'Dad, I'm sorry, but we have to go. I promised to drop in on a party for a writer. I hope you don't mind.'

Henry leant over to me again. 'I have to tell you, I'd prefer to sit and talk with you some more, and make an impact on that armagnac. But she must be obeyed.'

He took Emma's hand, and they looked into each other's eyes with the full force of love. It hurt, but they didn't notice.

Henry pulled out his wallet from his back pocket, and I waved a hand at him. The gesture was enough. He put it back.

'Sir, it's been a pleasure meeting you. Em had told me about your strength, and I've had the honour to see it for myself. I hope we can meet again – and next time, the brandies are on me.'

He held out a grubby hand, which was uninviting but demanded attention. Emma glowed as we said our goodbyes, and she hugged me tightly.

'Goodnight, Daddy. I love you so much.'

'I love you too, baby. Take care of yourself.'

When they had left, and I ordered another brandy, I wondered if Bruce noticed the tiniest tears in the corners of my eyes.

NINETEEN

'Bottom line, we're looking for vertical integration to upside revenue potential from incremental business opportunities. We have to lever off our primary market capability, cascade those centres of excellence all the way through the hierarchy, and manage the pipeline more effectively.'

I was looking at Scott's eyes, but not into them. I was thinking of Sarah, who was probably sitting at the coffee-shop counter, chatting to Louise or reading the *Journal*. Scott was talking the language of serious money, and it was difficult to concentrate. His mouth moved without any other facial muscle stirring, and his bald head seemed too big for his body. We sat at the obligatory arrangement of sofas and armchairs at one side of his office, his seniority to Ham evident from the size and quality of the furniture. There were no adornments or personal effects in this office, and the hangings on the walls were strictly corporate art. The chair I sat in was low, as was Scott's sofa, presumably so that his little legs could comfortably reach the ground. If Scott remembered that we had met before, he did not admit it.

'Ham tells me you're a deal-maker, and that's what we need. Clients expect us to conceptualise innovative off-balance-sheet financing transactions. We need somebody who can synergise the core strengths that we have here, someone who'll go the whole nine yards for us. Is that you?'

It took a little time to snap back into the conversation, as I had not been a part of it for about ten minutes. As interviews went, this one was easy: I'd hardly done more than shake hands, order my coffee and cross and re-cross my legs.

'Well, Scott, I have a strong background in derivative and synthetic trading,' I lied, 'and I really want to get back out on the road, seeing clients and doing deals. So I think we have a good potential match.'

I had wisely decided to wear my only button-down white cotton shirt, with a dark blue suit, burgundy tie, and black loafers. Scott would not have appreciated Jermyn Street stripes. He looked at me through his rimless glasses, evaluating my vacuous comments or, more likely, wondering about his next meeting.

'Great. Let's see if we can do a deal. What's your next stop?'

'Mary Jo Garber.'

'My secretary will show you the way. Best of luck; good meeting you.' We shook hands, and he walked back to his desk. I wanted to stay and see if his feet touched the ground when he sat in his desk chair, but he stood at a computer terminal and typed something into it, almost as if he knew what I was thinking.

I left his office and stood by his secretary, a plump middle-aged white lady, another token of Scott's seniority. She looked up, smiled, and took a memo from beside her terminal.

'You all set with Mr Hines?' She got up, looking at the memo, and walked round her desk to me. 'So, it's Mary Jo next. Will you follow me, please?'

We walked in file down the long corridor, no natural light reaching us as all offices on this executive floor commanded the windows, each with a secretary sitting outside at walnut-veneered workstations, the computers silent in deference to the near-godliness of the managers who had made it to this level. I half-expected to see signs saying SERIOUS MONEY AT WORK – DO NOT DISTURB. Even the bells of the elevators were muted. She turned to me as we boarded.

'So, how do you like our weather?'

'Better than London, I can assure you. I like New York weather; it's so black and white.'

'Un-hnn,' she grunted nasally, in an expression completely devoid of understanding.

We watched the numbers light at the top of the elevator as it moved upwards, arriving at the seventeenth floor. She got out first, used her security pass to open the glass doors to one side of the reception area, and held a door open for me. This floor was all open-plan, and we meandered through a series of grey cubicles until we arrived at one with Mary Jo's name on the side. There was no one at the desk.

'Why don't you take a seat here, and I'll find out what's happened to Mary Jo?'

I did as ordered, and she left me. Phones rang, and people chatted quietly, discussing pension schemes and auto loans and health care benefits. I thought again of Sarah and I smiled involuntarily. Knowing she was only a few blocks away, and waiting for me, was the sweetest pleasure I could imagine. New York can be the loneliest place in the world, especially at the weekend, and she had come and washed away that loneliness. I thought I might be in love with her.

'Hi. I'm Mary Jo Garber.' She was short, white, and very fat. Her hair was cut like a schoolboy's, with the parting on the left side, and her face was greasy and spotty. She held out a pudgy hand that limply rested in mine very briefly. 'So,' lingering on this word, 'you must be shattered. You've seen everyone?'

'Yes, you're the last, but by no means the least,' I said brightly.

'OK.' The 'K' was pitched an octave higher than the 'O'. She was relentlessly lively, perhaps to help offset her physical appearance. 'Everything I'm going to say to you now is contingent on two things,' she continued. 'First, that you won't remember a word I say. But don't worry: nobody does. Second, should we decide to extend an offer to you, it will be contingent upon a satisfactory medical examination.'

'Fine. Understood.'

She shuffled some papers and brochures, and put them in a clear plastic folder. She was sitting opposite me, her back to her desk. 'We offer a range of benefits,' she began, and my concentration drifted off, just as she knew it would. Sarah had arrived on Friday afternoon, untouched by the flight, ready for action and food and companionship and sex, although we didn't take them in that order. She had brought one case of clothes, and didn't bother to unpack them in my room. Any caution that I had felt fell away as quickly as her clothes, and we had shared the kind of passion that I had thought was lost to me for ever. I was reliving this when I heard Mary Jo ask me a question.

'Er, no, my wife died,' I said after some hesitation.

'Oh, I'm sorry,' she said. She started off again, talking about insurance beneficiaries and multiples of salary, and I tried to stay interested. The sore on my face itched a little bit; when Sarah had seen it, she stroked my cheek and insisted that I go and see a doctor immediately. It was only a little lie, but I told her the cream was from the doctor. She was satisfied.

'Well, I guess that about covers it,' Mary Jo said. She beamed at me, and I beamed back. 'I've put together this folder of information, which should tell you everything you didn't pick up just now. And I've put my card in there, so if you have any questions . . .'

'There is one. What about the medical?'

211

'Ah yes. We have a medical facility in this building. You could go there now, but it's better to make an appointment. I can set it up for you, if you wish.'

'No, that won't be necessary,' I said very casually. 'I think I should probably wait to hear from Ham first.'

'OK, no problem. Just call me when you're ready, and we'll fix it up. You're all set; do you have any other questions?'

'No, that's perfect. You've been very helpful. I do hope we'll talk again.' We both got up, which made us stand very close to each other, and I put the folder in my briefcase. Mary Jo walked out of the cubicle first, and I followed her to the glass doors. As we waited for the elevator, we talked the unique language of lobbies.

'Where are you staying?'

'A small hotel on Lex. It's very convenient; my daughter lives on Murray Hill.'

'Wonderful,' she said. 'Where does she work?'

'It's a small publishing house uptown.'

The elevator arrived, and I turned to shake her hand. 'Many thanks, Mary Jo.'

'No problem. Enjoy your stay.'

The huge reception area at street level was full of people, some waiting for appointments, others standing talking. I walked briskly to the revolving doors, feeling as well as I had since I'd arrived. I stood on the sidewalk in the cloudless daylight and, for the first time since Anna's death, I was looking forward to the rest of my life.

Sarah sat at a booth by the window, a large mug of

coffee in front of her. The coffee-shop was nearly empty, and Louise was busy wiping tables and chewing gum. I waved at her as I walked across to Sarah. Sarah stood, put her arms around me with a big grin on her face, and kissed me. Louise approached.

'Good morning, Louise. Can I have some coffee, please?'

'You got it.'

Sarah and I sat opposite each other, holding hands over the table.

'Well?' she asked, eyebrows raised.

'Well? Yes, I think it went pretty well. They'll be in touch.'

'Is that it?'

'Yes. One interview is very much like another. They talk a lot, you listen and remember not to scratch your backside, and that's about it. Ham has obviously put in a very good word for me.'

'Did they talk money?'

'That comes next. This morning we conceptualised.' We both laughed at this, two happy lovers wanting everything to be laughable. 'What have you been up to?'

'I've read the *Journal* and the *Times*, and I bought a book about the Cape. And I've drunk a gallon of coffee.'

'You see, you're going native already,' I said, and we smiled at each other. 'Are you hungry?' I asked.

'What for?' The change of tone was immediate, four eyes suddenly burning more brightly.

'All of a sudden, I feel very tired. I think I need to lie down.'

'Good idea,' she said. 'I'll help you undress.'

Our weekend had been perfect. We had slept well, my fever had gone, and we had revelled in the anonymous hinterland of love in a foreign climate. We ate Chinese, bought huge kebabs from street corner stalls, walked in Central Park and watched Frisbees slicing through the clear air and softball games with men and boys and beautiful girls, and we held hands all the time, our separate lonely lives joining at our palms. Our unexpected, unannounced passion caught me unawares, reviving nerves and little pockets of flesh that had lain dormant for so long. London, Anna, that life, was filed away, tied with a pink ribbon and stuffed at the back of an unopened drawer of my mind.

Sarah wanted time, and I wanted Sarah. She wanted affection, and some love, but she didn't have the need to resolve issues of ownership, or make and hear statements of intent. I wanted to tell her everything, to clear away the debris of the past, in the hope that this shared knowledge would bind us together, but she didn't ask, and I wouldn't tell until or unless she did. This suspension of a contract nagged at me, because our lives together were still separate, and I wanted to make us one, in some holistic amalgam of minds and bodies that would take us on a new path, sweeping over the tracks we had made before. Uninterested and unruffled, Sarah just accepted the status quo, giving but not really taking. It hurt.

We had missed lunch, in the English sense; in New York, mealtimes meant a gentle stepping-up of the continuous grazing process that moved through Danish and bagels and doughnuts and coffee, hot dogs and heros and pizzas and doners, cookies and candy and yoghurts and ice cream. Sarah showered as I dressed. She had ordered me to go back down to the coffee-shop and wait for her.

Louise was still there, and I sat at the counter.

'Hey, howyadoin'?'

'Just fine,' I replied.

'Your daughter is so cute. You're a very lucky man.'

It took a nanosecond to pick it up, the soporific glow of sex still deadening my mind. Louise poured coffee, and I fumbled for an answer.

'Oh, oh, no, that's not my daughter,' I managed ineloquently. 'She's my . . . a colleague from London. She's just in town for a few days, and we've been catching up. No, she's not my daughter.' Methinks he doth protest too much.

'Ah, I gotcha,' said Louise, and I think she had. I picked up my mug to hide my shame, and burnt my lips on the liquid.

'Here's your colleague now,' Louise said, and she gave me the smallest look of complicity. Sarah's hair was still wet, and she looked a dream. She came over to me.

'Ham just called. I took the call because I thought it was you. Sorry.'

'Don't worry. What did he say?'

'Call him back. He sounded pretty keen to speak

to you.' Louise stood behind the counter, listening to this exchange, and I felt I was losing a friend.

'I'd better go and do it. Will you excuse me for a moment?' I rushed out in confusion, leaving Sarah and Louise to pick up the pieces. My room, our room, was quiet and cool. I called Ham, and he was there.

'Hey, old buddy, what's up?'

'I'm just returning your call.'

'Oh ya. How did you think it went this morning?'

'I was pleased. I liked the team; everyone seemed very focused on what needs to be done.'

'Terrific. Hey, they liked you too, so it seems like we might have a deal here. I've got to run the numbers past Scott, but we want to make you an offer. Are you up for it?'

'Yes, yes, definitely.'

'Good man. What are your movements in the next few days?'

'I was planning to go up to the Cape on Wednesday, spend a couple of weeks there. But I can delay that, if it's important.'

'No, you go on up there and enjoy yourself. Just give me a contact number, and we'll be in touch. Hey, I'm really looking forward to having you on the team. We'll knock 'em dead.'

'Me too, Ham. I really appreciate everything you've done for me.'

I gave him my number in the Cape, we said our goodbyes, and I sat on the edge of the bed feeling high, elated, ready for action. I didn't even think about the medical.

TWENTY

The cedar-shingled houses of Bayberry Ridge all share a common attribute: wealth. The condominium beach resort stands at the top of a sand cliff, and extends backwards towards the town of Mashpee, sprawling across the scrubby terrain with tennis courts, a golf course, swimming pools and restaurants. The high art of relaxation does not come cheap at Bayberry Ridge. A poll of residents and property owners would find the highest concentration of chief executives, politicians, senior vice-presidents and assorted money-makers anywhere in the civilised world. And the Ridge is civilised: no rose blossom withers on the stem; no screaming Kyles and Kevins and Kirstens disturb the tranquil air; no blade of grass dares to grow higher than the regulations allow. Electric golf carts glide from house to house, transporting people and luggage and laundry and victuals. These are surely the Elysian fields. The private beach of Bayberry Ridge, reached most directly by a frightening vertical staircase down the cliff, confirms this. It reaches for eternity, the swathe of pale sand unbroken by ugliness or signs of human interaction. The sea is cold and clear, the Atlantic the only miscreant accepted in this enclave of comfort.

And to here we came, two refugees from Hell, sweeping past the clubhouse and into the car park, the soft rain more like mist. The long drive from New York was dull, the endless wooded hills of Rhode Island uninspiring, and we were keen to get inside, stretch out, cuddle and kiss, and breathe in the luxurious ozone of this cape. Keys delivered, service mobilised, we drove on to the house, single-storey and set back fifty yards from the edge of the cliff. The front garden was well-tended, the shingles all in place, and the rooms freshly cleaned as part of the service, for which I paid a handsome fee. Sarah and I walked around the rooms, she seeing it for the first time, whilst I reviewed the furniture, and noted the few ornaments that Anna had brought to this place. Sarah saw them too, the pictures of a life from long ago, smiling secure, confidently facing the camera and the future.

'So this is what you did with all your bonuses,' she said.

'And then some. I haven't exactly got value for money – yet.'

We went out on to the wooden deck that linked the house to the rear world, and looked at the Adirondack chairs, painted white, and the other houses that squatted in the mist further back.

'It's beautiful now,' she said. 'God knows what it's

like when the sun's shining.' We hugged each other, and I had never been so happy in this place. She liked it, and her enthusiasm had the same effect on me as a child's does, when they force you to look again at some well-known object with less jaded eyes, through their mind and their eyes.

We unloaded the car, filled the fridge with our shopping, and unpacked our cases. These mundane tasks took on a new significance, the first time Sarah and I had shopped and packed and unpacked, looked at each other's soap and toothbrushes, behaved like two married people, married to each other. I don't think she thought about it, but I did.

You should get up early in the Cape. The mornings are superb, the clear clean air a literal inspiration, the promise of a perfect day lingering in the slowness of dawn's arrival. Sarah slept whilst I stood on the deck, a big mug of coffee in my hand, watching as others broke out into the world, invigorated by the sun and salty tang in the ocean wind. I was wearing a polo shirt and shorts with deck shoes, and I could feel the nip of the early wind. Anna had liked these mornings, sitting on the deck and drinking orange juice, planning our day together.

We'd gone to bed early, still too excited to behave like a couple, except in our coupling, and not yet ready to sit still and quiet in each other's company. The feeling was uncomfortable, but not unpleasant. We had plenty of time to weld our lives together, although I was far more anxious to do this than

Sarah. She was relaxed, and loving, and unquestioning.

As I thought of her, she appeared, her robe loosely tied around her waist and her hair unbrushed. She slid up to me, still barefoot, and hugged me, breathing in deeply.

'This is all I need,' she said.

'Breakfast?' I knew I felt a little stiff in her arms, but I didn't know why. 'We have croissants, coffee and orange juice.'

'Sounds perfect. Should I help?'

'No. Just sit here and don't get too cold.' I could hear myself sounding like a father.

In the kitchen, a small area off the main room, I promised not to push her, not to want too much too soon. I was very frightened that the wrong words now could ruin everything we had, if we had anything. I carried a big tray out to the deck, and we ate.

'If you'd like, we can take a walk on the beach after breakfast. It's private, and it won't be crowded.'

She nodded enthusiastically. 'I'm in your hands.'

She sat back in her chair and lit a cigarette, watching me. 'Something tells me that we're about to have a serious discussion,' she said, never moving her gaze from me.

'No,' I replied, a little too readily.

'What is it? Something's wrong.'

'It's just . . . I just don't want to lose this feeling. You've become very important to me, and I don't want to ruin that.'

'How can you ruin it?'

'By expecting too much. I'm well past the age for this kind of thing.'

'What kind of thing? We're two people who enjoy each other, whatever age we might be. Just accept it as that.' She said this dispassionately, an unemotional observation which she had long ago accepted.

'You're right. I'm being stupid.'

'So what's new?' she asked, smiling and raising her cigarette to her lips. 'Lie back and enjoy it.'

Such good advice to give, so difficult to take.

The beach was empty, stretching away to a tiny white point on the horizon that we would never reach, and we held hands as we walked. The sun was warm enough to overcome the chill of the ocean breeze, and Sarah wore a brightly-coloured sun dress, her tousled hair waving seductively. We were getting better at managing the silences, the awesome splendour of the land and seascape filling the gaps perfectly.

'You know Marty has a place here?' she asked.

'It doesn't surprise me. He seems to be everywhere I am.'

'There was quite a lot of talk about the circumstances of his departure,' Sarah continued. 'There are always rumours, but these were pretty hot.'

'What?' She obviously wanted me to be interested, and I was.

'Dealing on his own account through the bank's

221

books, mainly. I don't know if anything was proved, but I heard that his expenses were a really good example of creative accounting.'

'Aren't they all?'

'Everyone adds the odd taxi fare and restaurant bill, but he was apparently charging everything.'

'Then he got what he deserved, the little bastard.' Sarah's revelations hardly surprised me.

'He'll resurface, smelling of roses. Those guys always do.'

'As long as he's nowhere near me – or you,' I said, and we walked on in silence, relishing his misfortune.

We had not talked of our own situations, still separate, and Sarah seemed to have put these behind her as well, as if everything that went before meant nothing to her. She'd said nothing of her plans, and I couldn't ask, in case they didn't include me. We sat together on the sand, looking out to sea, no points to orient us. She turned to me.

'I'd like to do it – here,' she said.

'But . . . you are incredible. This is a highly respectable place. You can't just . . .'

She was taking off her dress. 'It's so exciting,' she said, just like a little girl. My mind and my body were having an argument, and I could feel which one was going to win. 'Come on, hurry up, before the neighbours see!'

My body won, and I was very glad it did.

When we had finished, and were re-clothed, we lay side by side, looking up at the sky. Now she spoke in the low voice of languor.

'You have to take things one at a time. Don't be in a hurry to get your life sorted out. What will be, will be. Anything more is just a bonus.'

'Do you really believe that?' I rested my head on my hand, looking at her.

'I don't really believe anything, but that'll do.'

'Perhaps it's different for you. But I've spent my whole life getting things in order, following some pattern, and now it's all gone. It's hard to adjust to that.'

'Then wait. You have a new job, and you have this place. That's enough, at least for now. The rest will fall into place, if you let it.'

'And what about you?'

'That's different. Do as I say, not as I do.' She laughed, and pulled my face down to hers.

'Shall we get some lunch?' Our talk was too painful. Maybe she was telling me that we had no future, and maybe she wasn't, but I didn't want to find out yet. We got up, brushing the sand off us, and headed back to the house, quiet and lazy, still holding hands.

'Kick the sand off your feet and get your ass down here. I promise you it'll be worth it.' Ham's call had come as we were finishing lunch, and he was insistent.

'We'll pick up the tab for your flight. We've booked a room at the Waldorf. We can sort out all the details in the morning, and you can be back in your beloved Cape by early evening. There are some people you have to meet; the team's looking really good.'

I looked across at Sarah, who was smoking and watching me. She angled her head and raised her eyebrows, giving her casual consent to my trip.

'I'll call you when I get in.' I tried to sound energetic and thrusting. But it was a poor impression.

'See ya then.' Ham put the phone down.

'Don't worry about me,' Sarah said. 'I'm a big girl, and I speak the language. I'll have plenty of fun. I need a break from you anyway – you're wearing me out.' I still felt uneasy when she referred to our lovemaking, and I wondered if she could see me blush.

She came into the bedroom as I packed. 'Don't worry. I'll be here when you get back.' She stroked my spine as I leant over my case. 'I might be drunk, but I'll be here.' I was realising how much I needed her, and I didn't want to look up as I folded and re-folded a shirt.

'I hate leaving you on your own. And I hate leaving you.'

'It's only one night, and I'll be fine. I think the natives are friendly.' I stood up and turned to her quickly, hugging her tight, pulling her in towards me as close as I could.

'I'd better call the airline,' I said, and walked away to the phone, not letting her look into my face.

When I returned to the bedroom, she had finished my packing and had closed the case. 'Just remember,' she said with a smile, 'always wear a condom!' The thought froze me, and I changed the subject.

'I'll call you when I get to the hotel, just to see you're OK.'

'Fine. I'll be here.'

I was focused, and I was fresh. I'd slept well, the hangover of the sea air still in me, and I was ready to talk and listen.

Ham was similarly animated. 'Here's the deal. You come in as senior vice-president, reporting to Scott, with a strong dotted line to Walt and me. Between you and me, Walt will be gone by year-end. We're lining you up to take his place. You get a base of one-seven-five, plus profit-sharing, which is very good. All the other crap will be handled by Mary Jo.'

One hundred and seventy-five thousand dollars sounded very good, but I showed no emotion.

'You'll be on the road a lot, talking to clients, putting deals together. We'll ring-fence you from the paperwork; you just have to bring in the business. Sound good?'

'It sounds ideal, Ham, but I was hoping for a little more on the base.'

'What did you have in mind?'

'Closer to two hundred.' This was the critical moment, the time when I demonstrated my belief in my own value. There was a long pause. I drank a little coffee, and looked at Ham as he wrote the figure down on his yellow pad. For the first time since Anna's death, I was asserting my own worth.

He looked at me, shaking his head. 'Jeez,' he

exhaled. 'I'd have to run that past Scott. Is it a deal-breaker?'

'It's important to get things right at the start.'

'I'll see if I can swing it,' he said, and I knew, as well as he did, that I had won.

'I want you to meet some other people, some of the guys you'll be working with.'

'Excellent. Now?'

'Yup.' He got up, and went to the door of his office. 'Let's go.'

We walked down the hall to the elevators. When we reached them, Ham put his arm round my shoulder. 'Great to have you on the team. You're gonna love it.' We travelled to the seventh floor, talking about the weather on the Cape. When we got out, I could see that this was the trading floor, encased in thick glass walls, the madness and shouting completely cut out from the lobby. Ham keyed in a number on the security lock, and we walked into the zoo.

'Guess this makes you feel right at home,' he said as we walked across the floor, avoiding traders as they pushed their chairs away from their desks, ready to jump up and shout orders or simply to slump back in anguish at deals lost. 'You'll have your office on this floor, but we'll put some protection between you and these animals.'

When we reached the other side of the room, we stopped to look at the action. Ham clearly enjoyed being here, apart from it but able to watch, secure in the knowledge that he could return to the serenity of his floor.

'I have to admit to being less than honest with you,' Ham said, grinning. 'I haven't told you the best bit yet.'

'Oh,' I said warily. 'What's that?'

'We just hired the best deal-maker in the business. You'll be working very closely with him. Once you have the clients, he'll make sure we can execute properly in the markets. We're really excited about having him on board.'

'Great. Who's that?'

'An old buddy of yours. There he is now – over there.'

In the hugeness of the room, it had been impossible to focus on any particular face amongst the screens and screaming, but now I stared hard towards the area where Ham's finger pointed. The air-conditioning had obviously worked efficiently to dissipate the blizzard that he normally created, but there was no mistake. Slouched at a desk, phone crooked into his shoulder, abuse dribbling from his mouth, sat Marty. Even at this distance, it was clear he was giving somebody a very sore ear.

Ham was watching me closely. 'You never thought you'd be working with him again so soon, I bet.'

This was no time to let personalities stand in the way of two hundred thousand dollars, plus bonuses. 'No, but I agree with you. He's a brilliant trader.'

'Let's see if we can catch him for five minutes,' Ham said, as we walked towards him. As we got nearer, my stomach starting lurching, and my hands, ears and face grew very warm. We stood behind him as he finished his conversation.

'Get this straight, cocksucker, there's no more business from this desk for you. Your line has just been terminated.' He tossed the receiver on to the desk with a flick of the wrist.

'Same old Marty,' Ham said.

Marty looked over his shoulder and, if he was shocked to see me, he didn't betray it. He turned his head back slowly to the screens in front of him, then picked up the phone and started on another call.

'Marty, if you have a couple of moments,' Ham said, and Marty's shoulders sunk as he breathed out in frustration.

He swivelled round in his chair to face us. 'Yeah?' He looked at both of us with the same air of boredom.

'I wanted you to meet your new colleague,' Ham grinned. 'You two go way back, from what I hear.'

Marty squeezed his mouth so that the jowls creased, and he faintly raised his eyebrows. 'Yeah, well, what's history is over. This is the real world, and I've gotta get back to it.' He waved his arm at the room around us, but sat still.

'I'm looking forward to re-joining it,' I said.

Marty's body seemed to convulse from its very centre, and he sat up. He blew a short noisy breath from his nostrils. 'It could be harder than you think,' he said after a pause, and turned his chair back to the desk. Ham and I walked off together.

'I'll say one thing for Marty, he's consistent,' I said when we were out of earshot.

'Don't worry about it. You won't have any trouble

228

from him. He's a pussy cat if you know how to handle him.'

The problem was, I didn't.

TWENTY-ONE

It started on the flight.

When I'd reached the shuttle terminal at La Guardia, I had felt tired, still reeling from the shock of seeing Marty at such close quarters. Ham had got approval for my salary, and I should have been celebrating, but I was empty, and I sipped on a cup of stale complimentary coffee. Between the buzz of Manhattan and the quiet of the Cape, I was suspended and uneasy. I called Sarah, and told her the good news, which she received with genuine enthusiasm and congratulations. She promised to have 'a bottle of something good' on ice for my return. But my lassitude turned to something worse once I was on the plane. I drank two glasses of apple juice, leaving the beer nuts untouched, and I began to shiver. I felt I was coming down with flu, and willed myself to recover. My hands felt dry and cold, and my scalp contracted uncomfortably. I pulled my jacket tight round me, and asked the stewardess for some tablets. Illness was uncommon to me, and I couldn't remember feeling worse.

In this sick state, my mind started a journey of its own, revisiting Anna and her things, dragging back the past in a messy recollection of the life I'd left behind. I thought of Barham and Challis, and wondered whether they'd made any progress on the case. It worried me that they hadn't been in touch. I wanted things resolved, as long as that meant that I was untouched by them, and able to move ahead with Sarah to another life. Sarah was there, somewhere in my rambling thoughts, but blurred and indistinct, whereas Anna kept on returning to remind me of what I had done, and lost.

By the time we touched down I felt awful, hardly capable of carrying my small case, and shaking violently. Now my whole skin was too small for my frame, and all my clothes were too loose, even the socks slipping in my shoes. I decided to hire a limo and driver, and arranged it with a cheerful woman in the arrivals lounge. The building was cold, but no one else seemed to notice. I needed to sleep, under thick blankets and soft sheets, just like my mother had provided so many years ago. I'm a good patient when I'm ill – I just pass out and ask for nothing, sweating out the fever, and I was sure I could do it again. I briefly considered whether this sickness was simply a reaction to everything, the mind sending a clear message to the body, but it was too real, too much an actual physical condition, to believe this.

I needed the heater on in the car, in spite of the evening warmth, and I curled into myself and crouched into the corner, the driver sensing that I didn't want to talk. Sarah, Sarah, Sarah – she would be waiting for me, ready to receive me unquestioningly, to put me to bed and give me hot lemon, to soothe away these aching thoughts and shivers. I must have blacked out in the car, into a delirium of jumbled images and echoing voices, and was woken by the driver as we approached the Mashpee rotary, the roundabout that marked the centre of life for this little community. I croaked some directions at him, and we drove on towards Bayberry Ridge. The wealthy were still at play, out on the courts and the fairways, and the sight of their expensive pursuits in progress was gladdening.

The car eased to a halt at the picket fence of my house, and I tipped the driver as he carried my bag to the front door. I pushed it open, threw the case down, and looked for Sarah, just as I had once looked for Anna when returning from a business trip to New York. The house was cool and subdued, and I walked to the kitchen area to pour myself some water.

As I drank it, a voice behind me said: 'If you're tired after that flight, you should really come straight to bed.'

I looked round to see Sarah standing at the bedroom door. She was wearing a black silk and lace teddy, with three pearl buttons down the front. She looked too good to touch, too perfect for masculine hands to rub against her, and I stood speechless and senseless before this beauty. She slinked her way over to me, and undid my tie.

'You look awful,' she whispered. 'Come and lie down and I'll make it all better.'

Mentally, and physically, I was unprepared for this welcome, and I remained where I was, not able to express whatever I was feeling, which was confusing.

'God, are you all right? You really do look terrible.' She still had her arms round my waist, and was leaning away from me to look into my face.

'I don't know what it is. I feel pretty dreadful.'

Sarah immediately snapped into action, and pulled me by the hand into the bedroom.

'Get undressed and into bed,' she ordered. 'I'll get you some pills.' She left the room and I did as she said, the movements all painful and very laboured. She returned with a glass and two tablets, and put them on the bedside table.

'Are you cold? Do you need blankets?' I was lying under a single sheet, and I nodded towards the wardrobe.

'Please. There should be some in there.' She pulled two dusty blankets out, and unfolded them on top of me.

I smiled weakly. 'It's so strange, being nursed by a woman dressed like that,' I said. 'My mother would definitely not have approved.'

'Well, anything to help the patient's speedy recovery,' she replied, and sat on the side of the bed. She felt my brow, and her warm soft hand ran back into my hair. If I was going to be ill, I could think of no better comfort.

'I don't think you have a temperature,' she said.

'You'd better try and sleep it off. Do you need anything else?'

'Just you,' I said with my eyes closed, and she stroked my head until I drifted away.

When I woke, the fever had taken hold. I was frying, and the sweat was chilling the sheets. The curtains were drawn, and one bedside light was on. I felt photophobic, the dim light drilling through my irises and into my brain. Sarah walked in, a wet flannel in her hand.

'You're really burning up,' she said, as she dabbed the flannel over my face.

'What time is it?'

'Late. I think we should change the bedding. Can you bear to move?' She held my dressing-gown, and I rolled out of the bed as she put it on me. I was bent at the waist, trying to make myself small in an effort to keep the fever away.

'There you are. Get back in quickly.' I climbed back in, and the fresh sheets felt wonderful as I shook and shivered, a new nausea adding to the symptoms.

'Just sleep.' She placed her mouth lightly on my cheek, a loving demonstration of care.

'What will you do?'

'I have a good book, and plenty of booze. I think I can manage.'

'Sarah – you're fantastic.'

'I know. It's all going on the bill. Now rest. I'll be back later.'

The bed heated quickly, and the heat worked to move me back to the twilight of rest. The Dali-esque visions that danced in my mind were broken periodically as I turned over and briefly woke, but I stayed sub-conscious for most of the night, the bed all mine, but the pain shared and lessened.

I was weak, but alive, and dry. The sun filtered through the flimsy, unlined curtains, and I could hear the familiar noises of the Cape world outside. I levered myself out of the bed, and put on my dressing-gown. With my hand against the wall, I walked unsteadily towards the main room. Sarah was in the kitchen, preparing something.

'Hi,' I said, and my voice sounded unrecognisable. She turned swiftly, and looked at me sternly.

'Get straight back into bed. What the hell do you think you're doing?'

'I feel much better,' I remonstrated.

'You have just spent twelve hours fighting a fever. You are not leaving your bed today.'

'I think some fresh air might do me some good.'

'Then I'll open the window in your bedroom. Now go.'

I nodded in sullen agreement, and returned to my bed.

She followed me. 'I don't know what you did in New York, but I hope it was worth it. I told you to use a condom. You were pretty bad last night. And shouting – I should think everyone round here could have heard you.'

'Oh God,' I groaned. 'Did I say anything terrible?'

'No, you were fairly incoherent. I was hoping I

might have picked up something juicy, but there was nothing. You did shout "Don't do that" several times, but that was about it. Your secrets are safe.'

'Actually, I'm quite hungry. Is it lunchtime?'

'I'll bring you something. Do you like soup?'

The question stung me. Here was the woman I wanted to be with, who shared my bed, nursing me through some mysterious fever, and she didn't even know if I liked soup.

'No, I hate it.'

'Good, because we haven't got any. I'll make you a sandwich – and coffee?'

'Sounds great.'

Some time later she returned with a big tray, with plates of sandwiches, coffee for me, wine for her. As I ate, she talked.

'I walked a lot yesterday, around the development and along the beach. I could really get accustomed to this. I'd even take up golf, if I thought it'd help my chances of staying here. Did you know they had a huge health club here? I worked out there – pretty half-heartedly, but it made me feel better about the booze and ciggies.' This last remark was followed by a large gulp of wine. 'If you're up to it tomorrow, we could go to Martha's Vineyard.'

'I'd like that. I'm sure I'll be fine tomorrow.'

'So how did it go yesterday? You haven't told me anything.'

'Well, I have a job there, and we agreed the package. But there is a down-side.'

'There always is,' she said. 'What is it?'

'Marty. He's started work there, and I'll have to work with him, pretty closely.'

She considered this. 'Can you deal with him?'

'I think so. I won't be working for him, and Ham will protect me, as long as I deliver the business.'

'Are you going to tell me about the package?'

'It's good. I've got a base of two hundred, plus bonuses. I think I can live on that.'

'Yes, it sounds as if you'll survive. They must really want you.'

'It seems so. Of course, it's all subject to a medical,' and I laughed as I said it.

'Of course, over here they're paranoid about AIDS and drug abuse. When is it?'

'I have to fix a date. I'll wait until I've recovered, then go back to get it done.'

I was tired again, and she recognised the signs, clearing away the lunch things and rearranging the bedclothes.

'Get some rest, and get fit. We've missed out on a lot of serious screwing, and we need to catch up.'

This was hardly classic bedside manner, but it inspired me. I curled up, and slept soundly and dreamlessly.

By the next morning, I was fine. Sarah wouldn't let me eat breakfast on the deck but I got dressed and sat with the fat Sunday papers in front of me. I didn't really want to go to Martha's Vineyard – there would be too many tourists, and I was happy in this private world. Sarah sat down next to me on the sofa.

'Are you up to a little conversation?' she asked. 'There's something we need to discuss.'

'I'm all yours,' I said, tossing another section of the paper on the floor.

'I don't know how to tell you this, and I don't know if I should,' she began.

'If it's about your shady past, forget it. I already know; it's common knowledge.' I smiled, but she didn't.

'You remember the day you got fired?'

'I'm unlikely to forget it,' I said.

'And you remember that the police interviewed me then?'

'Yes,' I said, a little more concerned now.

'Well, when you went away, and I was still in London, I got a call – from the same policeman.'

'Yes?'

'Yes. He was called Barham, and he was very friendly. He said he needed to tie up some loose ends about Anna's case, and could we talk? It seemed reasonable, so I agreed.'

'And?'

'He came round to the flat one evening, on his own. He was very polite, and he had a glass of Scotch. He asked me about you.'

'I knew Barham had found out. Marty told him.'

'Do you know why Marty told him?'

'Spite, I suppose.'

'Yes, but not against you. Against me.'

'Why? What has he got against you?'

'Before we got together, Marty had tried it on with me. He was very clumsy, and arrogant, and I turned him down. He didn't like that.'

I shook my head in disbelief and anger.

'Marty's dangerous and vengeful,' she continued. 'You'll have to watch your back twenty-four hours a day. But that's not why I'm telling you this.'

'Go on.'

'Barham wanted to know about us, how long we'd been seeing each other, and he was very determined to find out the exact date we first . . . got together, as he put it. A lot of what he asked was going over the same ground as before, when he saw me in the office.'

'He has to do this. It's part of his job.'

'I know. But he asked me more: how well I knew you, your thoughts, your emotions, your state of mind. He asked how you'd reacted to Anna's disappearance.'

'And what did you say?'

'Nothing very much. I told him we were involved, but not that close. You seemed to be coping well. That was all I knew.'

'Did he ask anything else?'

'Yes.' Sarah moved on the sofa and rubbed her hair back from her face. She took a cigarette and lit it. 'He asked me to . . . to watch you, to keep an eye out for any signs of strange or irrational behaviour, and to let him know if I saw anything.'

'Did you agree?' This was said in a calm, slow tone, no hint of terror in my voice.

Sarah's response was immediate. 'Christ, of course

not. I told him if he wanted a spy, he'd picked the wrong person.'

'What did he say to that?'

'He was sorry if he'd offended me; he hadn't meant it in that way at all. He understood my reaction entirely. He was very apologetic. He said he was merely trying to protect me, and I told him I could look after myself.'

'Was that it?'

'Pretty much. No – there was one other thing, that he said when he was leaving. He asked if you'd ever mentioned prostitutes, what you thought of them. I told him we'd never talked about that, and he was satisfied.'

'I wouldn't worry about this at all. It was kind of you to tell me, but it sounds pretty routine stuff to me. I'd just forget all about it.' I put my hand on hers, and stroked it.

'I have now. That's all in the past, your life and Anna's, and it's none of my business. I don't want to know about it. I take you for what you are to me, not what you might have been to someone else.'

In those words, as they fell from her beautiful lips, was the thing I had dreaded, and longed for, the most, and the sickening, abhorrent feeling that bolted through me was joy, a detestable delight that we were now locked together by a common bond, a strand that was woven around us in a tightening knot. I held her in my arms, the rope of shared expectation binding us close, and her warmth and strength spread gently into me. Now she could be, would be, mine forever.

TWENTY-TWO

'And you're sure you'll be OK?'

We sat by the window, coffee and brandy in front of us, with cigarette and cigar smoke fogging the view between us, relaxed and relaxing. We had eaten clam chowder and saltines, soft-shelled crab, and key lime pie, and our noses both shone with the redness of two people unused to the sea air and sunshine.

'I've gone native. I wouldn't know what to do in London. The neighbours are looking after the flat, and I don't want to look for a job. This is where I want to be. You go – I'm staying here.'

All week I had tried to convince Sarah to come back to London with me. I didn't want to visit the house on my own, going back to a strange and unfriendly world that I was getting ready to box up and store away. She was determined to stay put. The long days of sun and love had cleansed me of the virus, and I was sure that I was fit to make the final break. But Sarah was my insurance, my guardian against the lurking gloom and uninvited memories that Redesdale Street harboured. In this week, my confidence had grown in our partnership, the tendrils twining around us, but I still dreaded leaving her.

'I'm going to get some tennis lessons – the pro looks gorgeous – and I shall buy some trashy books and work on my tan. I'm enjoying being a bimbo.' She was so sure of everything, and her absolute certainty was unsettling. She rarely debated anything: Sarah knew what she wanted to eat, when she wanted to make love, what she should wear, and what I should do, and it all appeared effortless, and right. This was what I was searching for, but it still worried me, as it left no room for negotiation and compromise.

'It should only take a couple of days, a week at the most. I've got to sort out my affairs with Douglas, and I'll check in with Barham.' I'd told her this before, and recited it again more for myself. I'd also told Ham of my plans: the bank was going to arrange an apartment for me in Manhattan, and we had agreed a start date. The loose ends of life after Anna's death were being plaited together for me, and I was trying to weave Sarah into that skein. It wasn't easy. We had carefully avoided any discussion of her plans, although I wasn't even sure that she had any. Her independence imbued everything she did and said; I didn't know whether she was locking me out of a secret compartment of her life, or whether I was locked into one. At the end of this time with her I still knew very little about her, and perhaps that was one of her attractions. She didn't have a mysterious past, she just didn't seem to have a past at all. The only thing I felt I knew was that I couldn't, and wouldn't, let her go. I would fight – would she?

The Californian chardonnay and the brandy made me bold. I was going to ask her a question I hoped she might answer. I was about to speak when she read my mind.

'Did Ham tell you where this apartment is?' she asked.

'It's on Fifth, somewhere in the fifties. They use it for visiting executives and dignitaries. I'll stay there until I get settled.'

'Where will you look for a place?'

'I can't really decide. I'd like to go uptown, into the eighties, but I don't know how much I'm going to have to pay. The service charge on these places is often more than the mortgage.' We weren't getting very far.

'Don't you know someone who can help you decide? It seems crazy to buy a place before you know the market.' At last she presented an opportunity, and I took it.

'I was thinking,' I said. 'If you had some free time . . .' It was a weak way to start, but I let the thought fight its way through the tobacco smoke.

Sarah smiled. 'I wondered how long it would take you. I always knew you had an ulterior motive.'

'Well, I just thought, if you wanted to . . . I mean, it's entirely up to you,' I stuttered.

'Buy me another brandy and stop waffling,' she said. I caught the waiter's eye; he had introduced himself, but I couldn't remember his name. Sarah was enjoying my discomfort. The brandies arrived, and I leant over towards her, taking her hand in mine.

'I'm not going to ask you to do anything. I know you have your own life, and your own priorities, and I'm happy with this, just as it is. You're very special, and I don't want to ruin what we have, if we have anything. Only you can know that.' It wasn't eloquent, and it wasn't what I wanted to say, but it was the most I could let her know.

'That's sweet,' she said.

I waited for more. Nothing came. I took some brandy. 'But I don't know what you want to do. I always seem to be asking you to wait for me.'

'I've got plenty of time,' she said. 'You're getting yourself sorted out. I'm happy to watch, and I'll help you if I can. We both know this isn't the real world, but that doesn't make it any less exciting. I don't want to go back to the real world just yet.'

The real world – of Marty, and mortgages, and money – lay beyond the sea that we overlooked, and it was too far, and too cold, to swim, especially alone. I'd done the deals with everyone but her. We didn't even have a draft contract to negotiate with. I tried again.

'You're right, of course you're right. We've both been through a lot recently. I should be very happy with what I've got.'

246

'But you're not, are you? You think you've lost everything, and you want to replace all of it, new for old, just like claiming on insurance. But you'll probably find that things work out better if you don't try and do that. I bet when you get back to London you'll end up throwing away most of your furniture, and your knicks and knacks. That'll be good – you shouldn't keep relics of the past, you should trust your mind to hold on to memories.'

How could she be so knowing, and so wise? Was I really so transparent? I felt as if she was right inside me, catching my thoughts before I knew about them, forestalling the need for consideration.

'If I were you,' she continued, 'I'd rent something. I'd rent the furniture too. Go and live somewhere anonymous, for as long as it takes to build up a new life for yourself. That sounds easy, I know, but you can't simply buy a ready-made environment. You're not giving yourself a chance if you try to. If you want to make a fresh start over here, you've got to dump everything. Otherwise you'll always be in limbo between the past and the present – and the future, if that's possible.'

I listened to this with a growing sense of nausea. Lightly, effortlessly, she was unstitching the threads, even as we held hands and talked about matters of life and death. I sighed in anguish, as if the effort of pushing against this wall had taken everything out of me.

'But don't let me tell you what to do,' she said. 'You have to follow your own instincts.' And she

247

laughed, and drank, and the immediate pain was over, to be followed by the lingering ache that sensible, rational advice always delivers.

I sat in the huge foyer, with marble cladding and a large directory of departments and services hung on the wall behind the security guards' desk. At ten-thirty in the morning, traffic was light, with few interesting people walking past me. A small man with spectacles and a bulging tan briefcase half his size sat at right angles to me, and he studied a mass of papers and documents that were clearly to be the subject of his meeting with the bank. My overnight case lay on the floor beside me, and I fidgeted as I thought about the cold stethoscope and the sharp needle that I was shortly to face.

I had decided to take the medical before going back to London. If there was anything wrong with me, I wanted to know before I started work. The fears that had been so overpowering after Barham's news had dulled considerably, and I was confident that I would receive a clean bill. I told myself one more time that sex with Anna had always been natural and, more importantly, infrequent. I had nothing to worry about, but it didn't stop my armpits tingling hotly.

A woman walked towards us. She looked at me and the little man.

'Mr Sardanis?' she asked, her eyes flitting between us. Mr Sardanis got up and introduced himself, his papers flying to the floor. They both scooped them up, and left me alone. My sweat glands were now putting in overtime, and I shifted my weight and straightened my trouser legs. I looked around casually, and caught sight of him as he came out of one of the banks of elevators. I had no newspaper to hide behind, nothing to act as force-field, and he headed straight for me. I decided to stand up and face him head on.

'Hi Marty,' I said loudly and confidently. I didn't extend my hand.

'So, you're really gonna do it. I say one thing for you, you've got balls.'

'How's business?' I was determined to be friendly.

'Shit, but I'm working on it. Hey, you still screwing Sarah? She's some hot number, eh? A real ball-breaker. Have you got her up the rump yet? She loves it in the dirt-box.'

'Thanks, Marty, I'll let her know you asked after her.'

'I bet you don't. But just remember – I was there before you. Think about that next time you give her a good shafting.'

'Good seeing you, Marty. I'm really looking forward to working with you.'

'Yeah, right.' He sloped away, a lizardly retreat with feet dragging along the floor, and the sinews that held me together loosened and forced me to crumple back into my seat.

Giving blood was a positive pleasure after seeing Marty. I even watched as the syringe filled with the almost black liquid, which looked healthy and plentiful. I had to take my shirt off, and do some exercises on a step, and I gave a sample of urine. The medical rooms were brightly-lit and busy. A woman in a nurse's uniform handled all the fluids, while a man in a white coat listened and tapped and prodded at various parts of me. It seemed no more vigorous, or rigorous, than the dozens of medicals I'd had in England, and it was over quickly. I was told I was all set, and they'd only be in touch if they needed to do anything else.

I had some time to kill before going to the airport, and I ended up in the coffee-shop at the Lexington House. Louise was there, and her welcome was warm.

'Hey, stranger, howyadoin'?'

'Pretty good. You'd better watch out, though; I may be coming to live here.'

'No kidding. That'd be neat. You got a job here, or what?'

We talked, punctuated by the occasional interruption of lunchers seeking the special – chicken à la King – and Louise really wanted to know everything, all about the Cape, and where I would live and, I suspected, how my love life was shaping up. I thought Louise would make a good Samaritan: everything she said was finished with a question mark, drawing more information out, and making me feel that everything would be just fine. As promised, the special was quite special, and I followed it with cherry pie.

'Yes, I'm off to London to pack everything up.'

'I guess you'll be real sad to leave all that stuff behind?'

'I don't know. I'm very excited about moving over here, and things are pretty quiet in London. I don't think I'll have time to feel sad.'

'Well, if you ever get lonesome, you know where to come.'

'You have yourself a deal,' I said, and I left her a very large tip. I walked out on to Lex feeling masterful, in control, and nearly as excited as I'd told Louise I was. This city would suit me. I could handle Marty, and the thousands of Marty-clones that festered in every building. The ambiguities of London life were far worse than anything he could throw at me. I belonged in this place, where everything was cut and dried, dealing and trading was part of life, where everyone knelt on the banks of the river of money and scooped out what they could.

I picked the one cab driver in New York with an Anglo-Saxon name – Jimmy Green – and a passing understanding of English, and we raced to JFK as he told me of the time his wife had been to England to see a relative. He didn't want a conversation, so my role was easy – I merely clung on tight and listened, grinning and grunting in equal measure to prove I was still alive and attentive.

As I wasn't paying for the flight, I was going first class, and I sat in the private lounge with other heavy-hitters from the wealthy world and skimmed through a few business magazines. I felt as if I were going abroad – 'The past is a foreign country; they do things differently there' – and this no man's land was strangely enervating. I called Sarah, to rebuild links with my home base.

'The flight's on time, I have a large Scotch in front of me, and I'm ready for action,' I said.

'Good for you. Do what you must, and then get out of there. If you linger, you'll be lost.'

'Don't worry. I have no intention of staying a minute longer than is absolutely necessary.' I meant it; already I missed her. 'I just wish you were with me.'

'You're a big boy. You'll manage. So will I.' She sounded dreamy, as if she might be lying down.

'Everything OK there?'

'Perfect. I have my tennis lessons booked, and I've been shopping.'

I now remembered phone conversations I'd had as a teenager, when there was nothing more to say, but neither wanted to call off. This was different; Sarah was obviously ready to say goodbye.

'Take care. Do what you think is right. You only get one chance.' I couldn't be sure, but it sounded like a warning.

'I will, I promise. Trust me.'

She laughed. 'That's the last thing I'll do. Be good. Bye.'

And the line went dead. I stood for the longest time with the receiver in my hand, which was warm and wet, and I had the uncomfortable feeling that something had just been passed to me which was hard to interpret, and would need to be analysed slowly and carefully. I put the phone back in its cradle, and wiped my hands on my trousers. I needed some more alcohol; the old fears were making a comeback.

TWENTY-THREE

Something in her eyes told me; or rather, something that was no longer in her eyes. The light that had glistened so brightly in the early days was gone, replaced by a flat and dull film of impenetrability. This could have been the shift from love to like, from passion to respect, but I knew it was something more. The vigour and verve had evaporated, replaced by mute acceptance of boredom and a lassitude that was hard to handle. The same words were still exchanged, the rituals still observed, but there was no commitment to them; we could have been communicating in sign language, for all the sentiment that passed between us.

At first the changes were slight: there were fewer kisses, and more silences, less to discuss and more to repress, and the urge to burnish our love diminished. Imperceptibly, a fissure grew to a chasm, and we stood on either side, unable to make eye contact across the yawning divide. There was no hostility, no bruising, no blood, just apathy. The feeble tide of life washed us along, no motivation to swim against it or hold on tight to each other. It was never discussed, and never acknowledged.

The rooms of the house grew larger, as if to accommodate the new distance between us. The kitchen table was vast, and our simple meals could not disguise the flat expanse of pine and sorrow that stretched before us. The sitting room was avoided. We moved from hall to kitchen to bedroom, the only room where we still shared a common space, without looking at the gaps in between. Home had become a memorial, but the war it commemorated was beyond our memory.

The battlefields of office life were easier to handle, and I only felt happy in the officer uniform I wore from Monday to Friday. I stopped calling home from work – I had nothing to say. The dollar was strong, the franc was weak, and everything else was grey. It never occurred to me that I should change course, that I could intervene and shout 'Stop!' and think again about our lives, my life, her life, and how to line them up. And no one else would tell me, for no one else could care, especially if I didn't. But I did care, in a quiet and abstract way, and there was no one to tell.

So when I arrived back at Redesdale Street, and the house was just as I had left it, there was no new sensation of emptiness. I dropped my bags in the hall and walked down to the kitchen, and it could have been any time. Only the scent was different – an absence of life that left a distinctive tang in the air. I poured a glass of Scotch, and waited. I waited for noise, for a hint that I was still alive inside this tomb. The lethargy that this silence pulled over me was numbing, and I waited for it to pass. That was now my luxury; I could wait for the demons to disappear.

Mary Jo Garber had given me the name of a company that specialised in transatlantic removals, and I had called them to arrange packing and storage. A sharp-suited representative announced himself at nine o'clock in the morning, and he and I moved briskly round the house, assessing the job in hand. This was the opportunity to close the chapter, ditch the past, and move on to my new life, and the previous night I had gone round the house and marked all the furniture that would not be moving to New York with me.

'You're not taking very much with you, are you?' the rep said.

'No. New life, new start. It isn't worth keeping.'

'Do you want us to dispose of it?'

'Could you arrange that? It would certainly help.' I had no desire to try to sell it.

'Leave it to us. We'll remove everything, and store what you decide to keep.'

Suddenly I regretted coming back. If I'd spoken to this man on the phone, from the Cape, I would have told him to get rid of everything; now that seemed impossible. Perhaps I should have let Sarah handle it. The rep and I moved on, and he scribbled notes on his clipboard.

'It'll take us two days to clear the house,' he said, as we sat in the kitchen and drank coffee. 'At the end of the first day we'll have moved all the non-essentials, and closed up all the rooms you're not using. Everything will go to our warehouse, and will be stored until you give us instructions.' This man had repeated these words a thousand times, and had stood sentry as lives were packed away and hidden in air-conditioned obscurity.

'When can you start?'

'We have a team that could be here tomorrow, if that's not too early for you,' he said. That was fine with me, and I told him to get to work.

After he left, I went out and bought some storage boxes, determined to follow Sarah's advice and clear out the relics of the past. I started work in our bedroom, and after thirty minutes I had packed away all Anna's clothes, which were to go to the local charity shop. I couldn't decide what to do with mine, so I left them in the wardrobes. On the bed, I placed all the ornaments and framed photographs, mostly of the children, until the room was clear. I put all Anna's toiletries in a black bag, and carried this downstairs and left it in the hall. I worked through each room, storing few items, filling black bags with rubbish that had been so valuable, and so unnoticed, up until the day Anna disappeared. I worked silently, and carefully, and threw away everything that I couldn't decide what to do with.

By mid-afternoon, I had finished. The house was bare, stripped of every identifying feature; all the prints and pictures were off the walls, and the rooms looked big and soulless, but I felt exorcised, and I looked forward to the arrival of the removal men.

When Emma had left home, I took over her room and used it as my study. This was the place where Anna had no control. I had a computer in here, and my golf clubs, family photos, piles of papers, and unopened books on finance. I had never used it for anything more than storage, and the desk was full of expired guarantees for appliances, ten-year-old bank statements, paid utility bills, and drawings that the children had done for me. Now I sat at the desk, and threw the papers into a black sack. The surface of the desk was dusty and scratched, and I wiped it with my sleeve. As I was clearing more papers from it, I noticed a little calling card, and it stopped me dead.

Madame Lavender invites you to sample her fragrant pleasures at her luxurious apartments. Telephone on 668 1453 to make your special appointment.

I remembered the evening in Lucho's when Ben had given it to me. Neither of us realised its significance then, but now it was the one part of my life with Anna that wouldn't, couldn't, be thrown away with all the other paper and cardboard. This squalid invitation, secretly printed and distributed in a hundred phone boxes, stung with every word. The memory of the grubby flat in Melrose Street, the 'luxurious apartments', and the cupboard full of clothes and switches, returned to me in total recall; and in that recollection I thought of Ben, and all his friends, who had visited and stayed and practised all their depravities with my wife, never realising her identity or recognising the destruction of her life.

I also remembered Barham's face as he watched me take it in, searching for signs of recognition. I turned the card over in my hand, and put it in my pocket. The face of Anna that stared at me from the desk-top was now ambiguous: she was smiling, but only with her mouth. The eyes were dead and still, and I tried to think when it was taken. Was she already Madame Lavender, or was she merely planning her great escape? It didn't matter; I put the picture, frame and photo, in the black bag, and tied it up tightly.

'Is everything OK?'

Carole, the embodiment of everything Anna had turned out not to be, stood at the front door, her eyes almost imperceptibly looking over my shoulder into the house.

'Yes, fine, many thanks for all your help. Come in.' She stepped inside, and I led her down to the kitchen. 'I'm sorry about the mess; I've been packing up all day.'

'Oh, so you're going to move,' she said, surprised.

'Yes. I'm actually going to the States. I've been offered a job there.'

'Golly, that's wonderful. I expect you'll be sad to leave this house, though.'

I thought about a reply as I got a bottle of wine from the fridge, and then decided her statement would suffice. 'Would you like some wine, or would you prefer tea?'

'Wine would be wonderful,' she said, sitting at the table. I poured two glasses, and sat opposite her. 'So, when do you leave?'

'The packers start tomorrow; I'll supervise that, and clear up all the other matters, then I'm gone.'

The other matters, Carole obviously thought, included solving the mystery of Anna. 'Have the police discovered anything?' she asked.

'Not that I've heard. They didn't contact me when I was away.'

'No; when they came to see me, they said it would be very difficult.' Barham had been a busy boy.

'I'm sorry; I had no idea they'd call on you. I hope they didn't put you out. They can be remarkably insensitive.' I hoped she might tell me what Barham had asked her.

'Oh, don't worry, I think it was just routine. It's odd, isn't it? You live next door to someone, and it takes something like this to . . . to get to know each other.' We laughed a little, both slightly nervous, if for different reasons. 'I'm afraid I wasn't much help to them.'

'Well, anyway, I hope that's the last you'll hear from them. Cheers.' I raised my glass and we drank. When Anna drank wine, she left a strong trace of lipstick on the glass; when Sarah drank, whatever the drink, she took a large swig; but Carole, without make-up or appetite, drank as she was, impressionless.

'I can't decide whether to rent the place or try and sell it. The market's so bad.' I moved the conversation back to territory that was as familiar as the weather.

'Yes. They've just taken that one down the road off the market. No one came to look at it, and it was on for three months.' I shook my head to show her I was fascinated by this news, but I couldn't have cared less.

'Have you found a place over there?' she asked.

'Not yet. I'll probably rent at first, until I know what I want. My daughter's out there, in Manhattan, and I'm hoping she can help me.' This was another lie: I couldn't even recall telling Emma that I was moving. Sarah had usurped everything and everyone; only she needed to know about my plans.

'So you'll have some friends out there; that's good.'

'Yes, that's good,' I agreed. I didn't have any friends here, so anything was an improvement. Emma, of course, might not agree.

'Well, look, if you need any help, just let me know. Anything at all.' Carole got up from the table. 'Thanks for the wine. I have to get back. Just wanted to make sure everything was all right.'

'Thanks, Carole. I really appreciate it.' And I did; here was a woman of no importance, offering unquestioning help, and I liked her for it.

'Do drop in before you go,' she said as she walked down the front steps. 'We'd love to see you, if you're not too busy.'

It was six-thirty. Carole was going back to her children, to cook for her husband, to carry on as before. It must be interesting for them, living next door to a family that had shattered into a million splinters. They'd probably talk about it over their fettucine and salad, and wonder how it ever could have happened. They should have asked me; I was ready to tell someone.

By my reckoning, I had called Sarah five times since I'd arrived back in London, and five times there had been no reply. There was no reason for her to sit by the phone, and no reason for her to call me, but I would have liked to talk to her and find out what she was up to. I tried hard to accept this silence as a token of the strength of our relationship, and a sign that I needed to tidy up the past before I went back to her. Her message had been clear, so I worked towards the objectives she had set for me.

I had managed to speak to Barham: no, he had no further news. The man they had arrested had been released without charge, as they had insufficient evidence to make a case, but they were still working on it. Yes, he would keep me informed of developments. He didn't mention Sarah, and neither did I.

I left messages for Nick, and he eventually called back. He sounded pleased that I was going to New York; he said a clean break was exactly what I needed. He was doing fine, and he would try to come over to the States at Christmas. He didn't suggest we should meet up before then. This was a kind of security that I felt good about.

It had taken twenty-four hours to sweep away the physical detritus that Anna's death had left behind, but the cleansing was not over. I knew, just as Sarah had known, that I had to erase the memories in my head, to chase away the demons that danced in front of me as I slept. I couldn't start my life in New York until it was done. My cranium bubbled with things I could no longer keep inside it, so I had to find a ventilator, to let out the pressure as the steam hisses out of the streets of Manhattan. I think I'd known all along how to do it, and I was confident it could be done. I sat at the desk in my study, blindly thoughtless, the plan clear and clean, and I smiled as I saw the beauty of what I'd conceived. My muscles were loose and my nerves were at rest. I had never felt so calm.

TWENTY-FOUR

I am still obsessed by the news.

When the packers arrived, I asked them to leave my study until last. I put the television and radio up there, and watched and listened to all the bulletins. I felt really good; the cold sore had all but disappeared, and I had slept in the marital bed, no longer frightened by the memories.

The men worked well and quickly, closing up rooms as they emptied them, until only the study, kitchen and bedroom were left open. I wanted to call Sarah, but in my new mood of optimism I thought I could leave that until I was sure of the day I would fly back to her. No news from her meant good news. She was enjoying herself, preparing for our time together again, and I didn't want to intrude on that. We had the rest of our lives to be together and talk.

I had spoken to Douglas. I didn't want to see him, and I must have made that pretty clear on the phone. I promised him power of attorney over my affairs, and wished him well. Douglas was a boring little man with boring little problems, and I wanted no more of his world. The break with the past must be clean and decisive. I was enjoying myself.

Kate I would not speak to again. I was never sure that she liked me very much, and there seemed no need to try to be friendly. I could always send her a change of address card, a change of life card.

I walked round the house, looking in rooms that seemed huge, closing doors and locking windows, with a growing sense of elation. I was purged, and instead of a vacuum ahead, I had a new life mapped out for me. Sarah was mine, and the job was mine. Life was back on track, and the derailment of Anna's death was almost forgotten. She had broken too many rules, and she deserved her punishment. Barham probably thought that, too, and was already busy on much more pressing matters. Who could blame him? A bored housewife had played with fire, and got burnt. They might never close the file, but they weren't going to spend too much time worrying about it. And neither was I.

I rang the airline to check for seat availability over the next few days. I booked a flight for the following day. I couldn't see any reason to stay. I'd done just as Sarah had ordered. I had one last loose end to tie up: I had to go and see Emma. I called her at work, and told her what I'd been up to.

'That's great news, Dad. When will you be back?'

'Tomorrow evening. We need to talk; can I see you then?'

There was a pause as she thought. 'I'm meant to be having dinner with Henry,' she said finally.

'You can see him any time. Aren't I more important?'

'That's a very unfair question,' she snapped.

'Sorry, baby, I didn't mean it like that. I'd just like to see you, that's all.'

There was another long silence. 'OK. Let's meet for a drink. Do you know Top of the Sixes?'

'Yes. What time?'

'Seven would be fine.'

'I'll see you there. I'm looking forward to it, baby.'

'Bye, Dad.' The line clicked dead. I sat at the desk, every sound echoing through the empty house. I decided to go out to the King's Road for the last time, a stranger in my own land. I loved it.

Top of the Sixes is on Fifth and 53rd, and is reached by a special lift that whisks you past the floors of offices below it. The view is spectacular, and it is therefore very popular with out-of-towners and tourists. I didn't feel like a tourist; I was at home here.

The flight from London was on time, and the cab took me straight from JFK to the building. I was a little bit early, and I basked in the early evening light that filtered through the plate glass windows. Conversation around me was soft, and most of the drinkers were wearing smart clothes, an obvious sign that they weren't natives. My hands rested on the table beside my drink, and I saw my wedding ring again. It came off quite easily. I studied it closely, and then put it in my pocket.

Emma arrived at ten past seven, alone. If she was sorry for being late, she disguised it well.

'How was your flight?' she asked without the slightest hint that she really cared.

'Fine. I feel great.'

'You look much better. Have you lost weight? That chill must have taken it out of you.' She hugged me tight, and we sat down.

'No Henry?' I asked, relieved.

'No, I'm meeting him later. Isn't he great? He's going to be a really fantastic writer. Everyone thinks so.'

'I'm sure he is,' I said unconvincingly.

'You two got on like a house on fire. He really likes you.'

'I'm honoured.' I was treading on eggshells, but I didn't care. She was still my daughter, and his opinion of me was far less important than mine of him.

'Anyway,' she said, wisely shifting gears, 'tell me about your news.'

'It's pretty simple. A friend of mine offered me a job here; it's exactly what I want to do, so I accepted it. I start next month.'

'Where are you going to live?' she asked, with a small hint of nervous expectation.

'The bank will put me up in one of its apartments at first. I haven't even thought about where to go after that. Maybe I'll rent somewhere in Manhattan.'

'You'd be crazy to do that,' she said enthusiastically. 'Manhattan's a zoo, and it can be very lonely.

You need company, people your own age. Go up to Westchester and get a nice Colonial. You can have a garden, and plenty of space. You'd be much happier.'

I knew what she was telling me, and I said it. 'Emma, I'm not going to cramp your style. The city is very big, and I'll have my own life to lead. You needn't worry.'

'Dad, that's the furthest thing from my mind. When I moved here, I was incredibly lonely. I knew one person, and she lived miles away. I had to work really hard to build a life for myself here. I just don't think you should have to go through the same grief I did.' She sounded sincere.

'So you think Westchester would be suitable for an old man?'

'It's not that at all. You'll simply have more room to breathe, and you'll get more for your money. I bet all your office buddies live out of town.'

'I'll think about it. There's no rush.'

We ordered drinks, and she sat back and pushed her hair away from her face. 'Tell me about Mummy. What really happened? You haven't told us everything.'

'I spoke to the police the other day. There are no new developments, as they say. It's a mystery, to me and them. I'm telling you everything, I promise.'

'You and Mummy weren't very happy, were you? Nick and I both know that.'

'Then you're both wrong. Every marriage has its ups and downs. You'll discover that when the right man comes along. But we had a good relationship, and we were happy. Did Mum say something different?'

'Not as such, but she sounded depressed whenever I called her. She thought you were working too hard.'

'So what's new? That's a simple fact of life. Mummy knew that. It was part of the deal.'

Emma pursed her lips, and shook her head slightly. 'I wish I could talk to her now,' she said, and she was on the verge of tears. 'I miss her a lot . . . I really miss her.'

I took her hands in mine across the table, and squeezed them. 'We all miss her, baby. And wherever she is, I know she misses us. We just have to carry on as best we can without her.'

'Sometimes, when I'm very depressed, I get angry that I don't believe in God. At least then I'd have something to hang on to.' This was the first time I could remember Emma raising religion as an issue. Was she blaming me for failing to provide spiritual guidance?

'You still have your family, baby. We're still here. We're all hanging on.' It was the best I could do.

'Would you have preferred another boy? Were you disappointed when I arrived?' This was serious talk, obviously saved up for some time.

'I was delighted when you arrived. Doesn't every father want a daughter? You were everything – are everything – I'd hoped for. Surely you know that?'

'I suppose I do. You just have an odd way of showing it. But it'll have to do.'

'Fathers worry about their daughters. It's only natural. I'll always worry about you; you can't change that. But I promise to do a better job in future. You have my undivided attention.'

'What about Nick? Did you see him in London?'

'No, but we spoke on the phone. He's happy, enjoying life. He might come over at Christmas. Maybe we can all get together.'

'I'd like that. Nick and Henry would get on terribly, though.'

'Let's cross that bridge when we come to it,' I said with the wisdom of a father.

'So what's your plan now? Are you going up to the Cape tonight?'

I shook my head. 'No. I'm staying here tonight, and I'll fly up tomorrow.'

'Do you have any plans for tonight? Henry would love to see you again.'

I was sure he would, especially if I paid. 'Baby, I'd be very bad company. I'm planning to have one more drink, and then I'm going to crash out. That's very kind of you, but I'll pass for tonight. Send Henry my best wishes.'

'Well, if you change your mind, give me a call. We're not going out till ten.'

'I'll be long gone by then. Let's have another drink.' I was amazed by her agreement to this. Emma was relaxing in my company, and didn't feel the need to run away any more. Things were going right in my new life. I decided to push my luck. 'Look, why don't you come up and stay one weekend soon? I'd love to have some more time with you – catch up on everything and start again.'

It was a delicate moment, and Emma sensed it.

Having accused me of walking away from her, she could hardly refuse the offer, but she wasn't sure how to accept it. She leant forward to pick up a book of matches and lit one, watching the flame flare and then diminish. 'On my own?' she asked, still holding the match.

'I'd like that,' I replied.

Another pause. 'That'd be super,' she said at last. 'I'd love to do it.' Her affirmation caused us both to sigh silently, and we sat and looked at each other for a while as the ramifications of the deal sunk in. 'Will you keep the house on the Cape?' she asked when we had our drinks.

'I plan to. If I can sell the house in Chelsea, I'll pay off the mortgage on it. I could go up there most weekends. That's why I don't think I need much space here. I'm going to be working my tail off in the new job, so I only need a place to eat and sleep in during the week. But one of my new resolutions is: nothing's cast in stone. I haven't made any decisions yet.'

'Good for you. You were getting too set in your ways. This'll be really good for you.' And she meant it.

I wasn't frightened of the city at night. I knew my way around; I swaggered with the confidence of one who'd lived here all his life, and nothing could touch me. I walked with my bag down Fifth, not alone, but part of the scenery, someone the tourists came to see, someone they made films about. I was at the centre of the centre of the world, no past to care about or be defensive of; this was how Pinocchio felt when the strings fell off him. I even sang his song, as I walked past the Rockefeller Center and St Patrick's Church. As I walked and sang, I realised that the bag I was carrying was full of old clothes, useful to the old self, but now redundant. The baggage of the past needed to be ditched, and it was hanging from my hand. I considered dropping it as I walked, but thought again. I didn't want my underwear to cause a bomb alert in mid-town. I held on loosely, determined to jettison the load at the hotel.

I arrived at the Lexington House at eight-forty-five, greeted by the night staff with the same effusion as always – 'Hi. Howyadoin'?' – and the same piece of chewing gum rolling and clicking in the receptionist's mouth. I checked in, got to my room, threw the useless bag in a corner and slumped on to the bed, deliciously lumpy and solid. I weighed my options: a few drinks in the Pink Poodle, watching the transvestites and time-worn hookers while drinking expensive watered whisky; dining at the Four Seasons surrounded by celebrities and pushers; walking downtown to the Village; or sleeping, preparing, saving myself. As these attractions presented themselves, my body decided for me, and I passed out.

When I woke up, I wanted to be well. I wanted it to be the morning, the dawn of this new life. Neither condition was obtained. I was very hot, clothes sodden, muscles heavy, and the night was as black as it gets in the city, fought off with a million mega-watts of human light. I pulled myself up, and ran through the aches and pains I was feeling. A shower was called for, so I took one. I stood shivering in the bathroom, and dried myself with the towel that trebled as a flannel and bathmat. I dragged my feet across the floor, and scrambled back under the covers, the familiar shaking and shivering starting again. Perhaps I was allergic to sleep in Manhattan. I switched on the bedside lamp, and shuddered myself into a wandering delirium, where Anna and Nick and Emma roamed freely, and Sarah stood just beyond the horizon. From time to time an enormous convulsion from the core of my soul jackknifed me from one side of the bed to the other. This was the psyche at work, filing late at night, ordering the swirling mass of fears and doubts into darkened niches, tidied away and for my eyes only. Behind the tremors and the rigours, I was pleased to watch my mind getting ready, the physical pains a small price to pay for the absolution I would gain. In the morning I would be clean, finally at the end of the new beginning.

TWENTY-FIVE

'Wild night, huh?'

Louise looked knowingly at me, my neck barely able to restrain my head from tumbling on to the counter. The thick mug of thick coffee stood steaming before me, and I asked Louise for orange juice. She smiled, the smile of one who has seen too many hangovers to be impressed by any other alibi, and I hadn't given her one. What should I say? I didn't sleep well because I was rearranging my life? That kind of talk would definitely consign me to the funny farm in Wheeze's eyes.

In fact, I looked worse than I felt. At six in the morning, I had given up the struggle and got up. I needed the fresh air of the Cape, and Sarah's embrace, to fortify me. The coffee and juice would keep me alive until then. I had slipped Lenny a ten dollar bill to get rid of my luggage; he was surprised, pleased, and obedient. All I had were the clothes I stood up in, my wallet, passport and keys to the house. Travelling light, I was on my way home.

After the first mug of coffee I was ready for solids,

and I ordered a minor league breakfast of eggs and home fries, refusing all the suggested garnishes and additions. I ate slowly, reading the paper and avoiding any thought of last night, last week, last year. This was the real deal: here and now, today is the first day of the rest of your life. I just wanted to get on with it, for it to start.

And it would start, naturally enough, with Sarah. That confidence, the firm belief that she was waiting too, stayed unshaken in me. When she had talked me through her advice, and it sounded like a warning, I was scared. No woman since my mother had ever read the rules to me, and I found it hard to take, harder to understand. But now I understood completely; the terms of our agreement were disclosed. I had fulfilled my obligations, and her silence was the final test. Go about your Herculean tasks, she said, and come back to me unencumbered and free to treat. I'd done it all, and all for her.

I couldn't help thinking how well things had turned out. I had made things happen, and turned them to my advantage. Fate was not so kind, but I was smarter; where life had threatened, I had fought, outmanoeuvring destiny and making better deals elsewhere. That was me: the ultimate trader. I could buy and sell anything – money, property, life itself – on the margin, and come out with a profit. Sarah, the job, Emma – these were the gains of a smart investor, the king of arbitrage. The dealing would go on, accumulating wealth and health and wisdom, the counter-parties to each trade the sorry losers, soon forgotten and never mourned.

This realisation of worth, of self-esteem and value, had grown within me during the days with Sarah. She understood the trader's mind, unlike Anna, who wanted ... Well, who knows what she wanted? It didn't sound like she did, so how could I? But Sarah ... she had all the answers, and was right on the track with me. We would trade together, not with each other, but against the odds, the fates, the world. And that's a pretty tough combination; but when you're a trader, a really stellar trader, you can get away with murder.

The cooling, rarefied breezes of Bayberry Ridge served to clean my head of any lingering thoughts and doubts about those fast-fading days, that other world of which I had once been a citizen. Anna seemed no more than a brilliant super-nova in the constellation of my existence, fascinating to watch but even the image, as much as the reality, soon dispersing on the retina. I dropped in to the clubhouse and picked up some mail, then walked up past the tennis courts, where earnest men frantically chased the hope of one searing backhand, one terrific ace, that they could bore their wives with all evening. Late afternoon barbecues were already sizzling, fresh expensive meat being cremated by men who knew no better; women sat silently, sipping wine coolers and smoking menthol cigarettes.

I savoured the atmosphere, the tang of wealth and relaxation, as I reached the front door of my house.

It was open, and I walked in to find a maid at work, plumping up the cushions as her final task.

'Good evening, sir,' she said in Hispanic tones.

'Hi,' I said, half-ignoring her, looking around for Sarah. The house looked antiseptic, sterile, empty; there was no delicious smell of Sarah and her aura, no vital signs to indicate inhabitation. The maid retrieved her trolley, nodded and smiled, and left, closing the door behind her. Normally, I love a clean house; my mother used to clean before and after our daily visited, and I grew up with the fragrances of polish and disinfectant as much as stews and pies. But this freshness was oppressive, as if it hid the evidence of a crime.

Every room was perfect, as if it had never been lived in. No pots and pans lay drying on the draining-board, no damp towels hurled casually on the bathroom floor. There were not even indentations on the furniture, the cushions filled and full, no trace of someone's recent presence on the seats, no body-prints or fingerprints to hint of Sarah's touch. And, in the tiny seconds that it took to check all round, I knew. Of course I knew; how could it be otherwise? What had she said? 'If you want to make a fresh start over here, you've got to dump everything.' And that, I now knew, included her.

I went out on to the deck, close to nature and reflected money, and watched the burning sun. I wanted some tears, some palpable demonstration of my loss, but they refused to come; perhaps the ducts had given up for lack of practice, perhaps the mind

278

had moved ahead, anticipating pain and silently disseminating some metabolic analgesia.

I was slumped against the rail when I heard her voice.

'Well, well, the wanderer returns,' she said brightly. I turned to look at her, and she seemed to shine with all the qualities I had ever looked for in a woman. I stumbled towards her, hugging her violently and clenching my fists behind her back.

'Where the hell were you?' I mumbled into her hair.

'Where do you think?' she replied. 'At the health club. I wanted to be in peak physical shape for your return.'

'And are you?'

'Why don't you come to bed and find out?'

'You scared me,' I said as I took a drag from her cigarette. 'I thought you were helping me to follow your advice, and baling out so that I could start afresh.'

Sarah leant up on one elbow and studied me as I lay there. Her eyes seemed almost completely black, with only the vaguest trace of whites at the very edges.

'You think I'd give up on you, after everything we've been through? I may be dumb, but I'm not stupid,' she said, and she laid her head on my chest. I took it as a signal to begin, to unlock the bolted vault of my secrets and let her see inside more clearly than ever before.

'You've no need,' I started. 'There's no obligation to stay with me.'

'I know that. I want to be with you – don't you understand that? It's my choice.'

'You don't ... well, you don't feel any sense of unease? After all, Anna wasn't even buried when we began our affair.' I needed to dance around the issue, testing the strength of her feelings before going on.

'Things don't always work out as neatly as we'd like,' Sarah said blandly. 'What matters is we're both enjoying ourselves, so let's not worry about the chronology too much.'

'But I want to get all that straight,' I said. 'It was you who pointed out that I was trying to get my old life in order before setting out on a new one, and I'm nearly through. But there are some things that need to be said once, and then consigned to history.'

'Oh God,' Sarah said in mock horror, 'I feel a truth session coming on. Spare me from that, I beg you.' I laughed a little with her, but it was unconvincing. She moved her hand down on to my crotch and squeezed gently. 'Why this obsession with the past? Why not just take what we've got, and be content with that?' She began rubbing me slowly, making it difficult to stick with my plan.

'Because I have to be sure.'

'Sure of what?' she asked, still stroking.

'Sure that what is past is really past, that it can't come back and destroy us. There are so many reasons why you should leave me, and I want to deal with them all now. That's the only way I'm going to be able to face the future with any confidence.'

Sarah pulled herself up and straddled me, her hands gripping the flesh on my chest. She moved her hips back and forth, never once taking her eyes off me, in the first flush of a sexual trance. This was not how I had wanted it to be; she seemed too manic, too frantically interested in fucking to care about anything else, to see that I needed much more than a physical solution. But there was no denying her power and her will, and I succumbed as I always had.

TWENTY-SIX

'No. This is your party, and it has nothing to do with me.' Sarah was on the move, and her voice had an edge to it that transmitted much more than her words.

'I don't want you to disappear without trace. I want her to know about us. You've become a very important part of my life, and I'm not ashamed of it – or you.' I was standing in the middle of the kitchen, calling after her as she skipped from room to room.

'That's very sweet, but I'm not thinking of you,' she replied as she swept past me. 'I don't want to be involved in all of this. It's personal to you, and I don't fancy the idea of playing gooseberry while you and Emma get yourselves sorted out. It's a no-win situation for me, and I don't like those very much.'

Sarah had finally come to a halt opposite me, her arms folded and her face set sternly. I put my arms out but she didn't move, and I realised that this was a battle I was going to have to lose. I loved her for her independence, and I couldn't now ask her to compromise it for me. At the very back of my mind was a small relief that she was so decisive, that she seemed to have enough common sense for both of us, and I gave in gracefully.

'Where will you go?' I asked, already debating the finer points of the peace treaty.

'I have some friends on Long Island. I haven't completely cut myself off from the real world yet.' Sarah knew how to deliver a message, and I received it clearly.

'And you'll come straight back?'

'Here we go again,' she said. 'You still haven't learnt about this relationship. We're grown-ups now. We do what we want – both of us – and that's the deal. When have I ever asked you to do anything for me? It doesn't work like that. We're both here because we want to be here of our own free will, with the emphasis on free. I don't want you on a chain, and I don't want to be on one either. Just let it roll for as long as it can. That way neither of us can get badly hurt.'

She was so much stronger than me, and acceptance of that fact was uncomfortable. Just when I thought I had her she would wriggle away, teasing me with an endless game of hide and seek, light and shade, yes and no. I had thought, on that first night back with her, that we had gone beyond this phase and were now a partnership, ready to take on the world together, but still she fought against me when it suited her, instinctively recoiling from that alliance. We weren't equals in the struggle, and she knew that I knew.

'I know,' I said. 'But you can't blame me for trying.'

'Actually you're quite wrong. I can blame you – a lot – but I don't. You haven't yet realised that it isn't the rules that have changed, it's the game. You're not what you used to be. You're someone different now, someone playing on a field where you have no experience. You've never been here before, so it's only natural that you want to try and bend the rules to make them more understandable. I'm trying to teach you, but you've got to pay attention.'

'OK,' I said, desperately wanting to defuse the situation. 'I hear you. I'm sorry I said what I did. I'll try not to let it happen again.'

Then she came forward and put her arms around my waist, pushing herself against me. 'Good boy,' she murmured in my ear. 'You'll soon get the hang of it.'

The rain had not let up since Sarah had gone. I sat nervously on the sofa and tried to read the papers, but my thoughts wandered uncontrollably as plans and problems presented themselves to me in a long stream of bullets, each one punching a hole in my confidence. The imminent arrival of Emma, so soon after Sarah had left, was steadily undermining all my assumed composure, and the weather seemed to reflect my sense of unease, with growling black clouds unleashing torrents of stinging cold water on to a place that had previously been so bright and clear.

Even though I couldn't see it as such at the time,

this moment, as I sat alone with only anxiety for company, was the turning point, when I was forced to leap forward or jump back, into a new life or back to the old. I was facing up to a past that now had no relevance, and was seeking to consign it to history for the very last time. In having Emma here, as two adults trying to be friends, there were aims on my silent agenda that she'd never need to know. Emma had been my daughter, my child, an asset I'd shared with Anna, but I no longer wanted her to be like that. I wanted to see her as separate – from me and from my former life – so that she too could make that step ahead into the new order of my world as it was soon to become.

I knew she'd be tired, and I knew that we had two full days to redress the sins of the past, but when Emma arrived we were awkward and clumsy in each other's company. I opened a bottle of wine and we sat facing each other, nervously worrying about those silences that two real friends would accept as part of the deal. We talked about the rain and the forecast, and what we might do the next day, but the talk was incredibly small and I felt that I'd lost her before we'd even begun.

Then, at dinner, she surprised me. She had the blush of alcohol on her cheeks, and her eyes were too bright. 'Do you remember that holiday we had here?' she asked.

'I certainly do. I've always thought it was the best holiday we ever had.'

'Isn't it strange how things like that happen? That

holiday is one of the best memories I have. It's as if some almighty power had pre-ordained that we should have a good time, and was even prepared to alter our memory to make sure it stayed that way forever.'

'Why do you say that?'

'We did have a good time, but there was a feel of ending about it all, quite a lot of sadness in fact. I suppose we all knew that it was the last time we'd all be together, and that made it bitter sweet. And then of course there was Mummy.'

Emma saying that brought it all back to me: I remembered the accusations Anna had made, and the way in which she had criticised me for being consistent. Even now the faded sharpness still hurt.

'What do you mean?'

'Good old Dad. You were always two paces behind the rest of us. That holiday was agony for her, but you probably never even noticed. Men don't on the whole. For you it was all a big adventure, just an opportunity to have some fun and show us how much you loved us. For two weeks every year you thought you could make up for all the time you hadn't spent with us, and that we'd be satisfied with that. But that was the last time, wasn't it? Since then Nick and I haven't figured much on your radar screen, have we? And I think Mummy saw that coming, and it really hurt her.'

'Hold on,' I said, still struggling to take in what she had just told me. 'There are compromises that we all make, and decisions we all take, which we think at the time are for the best. But it's not awfully fair of you to start revising history now, with the benefit of twenty-twenty hindsight, and tell me that I was a bad father. I can't accept that.'

'I'm not saying you were a bad father. I don't think you're any different from any number of fathers I've seen in action with friends of mine – quite the opposite in fact. It's merely that Nick and I wanted a bit more, and Mummy too. We'd have gladly traded a lot of what was on offer materially to spend more time with you, and get to know you better.' The effect of this was slightly corrosive, eating into me and forcing me to fight back even when I didn't want to.

'Can I let you in on a little secret?' I asked her. 'My father never hugged me as a boy – not once, to my recollection. He hated physical contact. He literally shied away from it, still does. He couldn't ever find a way to show what he felt about me and my brother, but I've never doubted his love for a moment. I've learnt from that, and I've tried to be more demonstrative than he was with me. Excuse the cliché, but you're a product of your upbringing, however much you try and fight against it. I've tried my hardest to give you something that I didn't get, because I think it's very important to improve all the time. I don't have any regrets about how you and Nick have turned out, and I think I deserve some of the credit for that.'

Emma waited, perhaps regretting what she'd said. I wanted to get this knocked on the head once and for all, and I was no longer prepared to be berated over what I had or had not achieved.

'You are a complete enigma, do you know that?' she said at last, smiling a little. 'Do you know how long I've waited to hear you defend yourself, to stand up for something and take a position? Mummy once told me that the only time you'd ever overruled her was when you were adamant that I should go to boarding school. In everything else you deferred to her wishes – parenthood by proxy. Do you know what that did to her – and us? It made us feel as if you didn't really care, as if having us was simply another acquisition that you needed to make but couldn't find the time to maintain. I know that's a harsh judgement, and I don't believe it's true, but that's the perception you left with us.'

'How could you seriously think that I didn't care for you? That's so fantastic it's beyond the realms of imagination.' I was quite annoyed by now; Emma, not yet a fully formed woman, was listing my inadequacies with all the poise and conviction that only youth can muster.

'Because that's precisely the impression you gave. You were locked inside a glass cage – or maybe we were. In any event, the result was the same.' She stood up then, and tossed her napkin on the table. 'Shall we have some more wine?'

'Yes, of course,' I said distractedly, and went to the fridge for another bottle. She followed me and we stood together in the kitchen area.

'This is all water under the bridge,' she said as I

opened the bottle. 'What's done is done. But I know why you've got me up here this weekend, and it isn't guilt that's motivating you. You're not looking for my forgiveness, because you don't think you've done anything wrong. What you want is affirmation of your new life – my seal of approval on whatever it is you're planning to do next. And that's fine, and perfectly understandable. But I reckon you owe it to me to try and understand what went before, and how I feel about it. I'm always going to be your daughter first, a friend second.'

How could she know these things? How could she have seen so quickly what was going on in my mind? She was too young to have this insight, but perhaps what she had said was right. I'd spent so little time getting to know her that I shouldn't have been surprised by her intelligence.

'You're wrong,' I said. 'I wanted to see you because I love you, and because I need you. Yes, I'm hoping that I can carry you along with me into whatever future I have, and I don't want to lose you. But I don't need your imprimatur, just as you've never sought mine.'

'And there's the difference. I'd have loved to talk to you about my plans and dreams and hopes and fears, and to hear you tell me what you thought of them, but you were never available for that. We never moved on to that higher plane.'

We walked back and sat down at the table again. I filled our glasses and lit a cigar.

'Are you sad?' Emma asked, much quieter.

'Sad? About Mummy?'

'No, not about her. Just generally.'

'Why should I be sad?'

'I don't know. It just seems that there's always been this superficial gloss to you, as if nothing ever really gets to you, puts you up or down. Nick and I once discussed it, how you seem so determinedly calm about everything. That's very unhealthy.'

'I'm just built like that. I'm not a moody person.' I couldn't follow this line of questioning at all.

'So how would you describe yourself? You see, I don't know. If I were asked to act as a character witness for you at the Pearly Gates, I wouldn't know what to say.'

'I wouldn't waste too much sleep worrying about that. I'm just Dad, and that's all there is to it.'

'How will you ever get closer if you won't let me in?' she said.

'There's nothing else there, Emma. This is me – what you see is what you get. There are no hidden depths. Why do you want to make some up?'

'Because I need them,' she said very quietly. 'Because I need to understand what makes you tick. I'm part of you, don't forget, and yet I've never really felt like that.' She drank some wine and thought hard before speaking again. 'Sometimes, when I'm on my own, I talk to you. I ask you about things, and seek your advice. I've always done it. It's a silly little fantasy, but I keep on doing it anyway.'

What's that song – 'Killing me Softly'? Emma was certainly doing that. 'And what do I say?'

'You're kind, and wise, and you make everything all right.'

'But you're talking as if I were dead,' I said before I thought. She had no answer for that – or, if she did, she kept it from me.

TWENTY-SEVEN

'My parents were very good to me. My father travelled a lot, but I don't remember missing out on
fatherly love and attention. My mother looked after
my brother and me very well. She claims that my
brother was horrid to me as a child, but I don't
remember that either. It's funny how your mind
erases the bad things, like the weather. The past is
always sunny. I don't think it ever rained in my
childhood. I loved boarding school, although my
mother thinks I had a terrible time. Sometimes I
think she must sit at home and dream up new ways
to worry about her children, now they're grown up
and have lives of their own. But it's pretty fanciful,
the stuff she worries about, and her memory is completely selective. Dad, of course, has no second
thoughts; he's always been completely sure that
everything they did was right. Fathers are like
that.

'I still don't think about leaving home. We always
used to joke about the fact that I didn't take my
silver napkin ring, which was a Christening present,

293

and that I wouldn't really have left until I took that with me. No offence, but when I was ill and you were with me, I couldn't help feeling that what I really wanted was to be looked after by my mother, in her bed, just as I had been when I had measles or mumps. I expect I'll always think like that. That's why Anna was so good for me; she knew how to behave like a mother, even from the earliest days. They say men marry their mothers, don't they? I wonder if that's true.'

We were sitting on the deck, the remains of dinner and a fresh bottle of wine in front of us. The tip of my cigar and her cigarette were glowing ever more brightly in the fading evening. Sarah had not asked about my weekend with Emma, and now her serenity had returned. She sat with her legs pulled up under her, listening as if this were the most fascinating story she had ever heard.

'I never really spent much time on my own. I met Anna when I was quite young, and I'd had a pretty miserable time before that. I lived in a flat in Fulham, and I was terrible at looking after myself. I lived on toasted cheese sandwiches and omelettes, and I went back to my parents quite often. But that's not why I married Anna. I really loved her. She had everything I wanted, and respected, and I knew straight away that she was the right girl for me. God knows what she saw in me. Safety, I suppose. She wanted security, and she wanted to give up work and have babies. Doesn't that sound old-fashioned? We were the last of the nuclear families.

'I never questioned the values that I'd inherited from my parents. Even at Oxford, when I should have been irresponsible, and worrying about the big issues, I behaved in a middle-class way. I grew my hair – everybody did – and I had motorbikes, but I clung on to the beliefs that Dad had passed to me in the genes. I didn't want to change the world; I didn't see that it needed changing so much, anyway. And I worked pretty hard, which was a rarity in those days. Everybody thought they could get a job simply by being there, but I wanted to do well. I don't know if it made any difference. I don't really care, either. I'm a great fatalist: what will be, will be.

'Anna was clever. She could have been successful in her job, but I don't think she had the drive. Her parents had conditioned her, just as mine had, and she didn't see the need to push herself intellectually. So we were pretty well matched. But the children were a shock, and I don't think we ever recovered fully from them. By the time they left home, we had nothing more to give to each other, but I didn't notice because I was still climbing the corporate ladder. Anna was left at home, living on the scraps of my success. It sounds so easy now, telling you all this, but at the time it just didn't occur to me that she might be looking for something else.'

Sarah leant her head to one side in response to my last remark, suggesting that this was new and interesting to her. I carried on.

'I know you have to work at a marriage all the

time, and my contribution was to bring home enough money to let us live our lives well. I was so busy doing that, I didn't have time for anything else. And Anna never once complained. She never suggested that things needed to change, or that she had problems with the marriage. I always asked her to come with me if I was going on a business trip, but she wouldn't. She would have loved Budapest, and I felt guilty going on my own. But I swear she didn't want to come.

'Now, when I look at our friends, her friends, I realise how often this sort of thing happens. You drift apart, and it's so slow and painless that you don't notice it, until you have nothing left to say to each other. But I don't see what else you can do. We'd agreed on our life together, and that agreement had an implicit cost, which had to be met. That's what I was doing: meeting the cost.'

'I don't understand the problem,' Sarah said. 'Didn't Anna agree to this?'

'Of course. We didn't sit down and say, "This will cost so much, and that will cost so much," but we both knew. She knew what she was getting, and she knew the price we had to pay. It's all a compromise.'

'Did you ever talk to her about it?'

'Why should I? It wasn't a problem for me, and I thought she would have said if it had been for her. How was I to know? Most people would be very envious. We had everything; she wanted for nothing.

'And she knew I loved her. I was never unfaithful, even though I had plenty of chances. I bowed to her instincts on raising the children, except for school, and I let her do whatever she wanted. Maybe that was a mistake; maybe she couldn't handle the freedom I gave her. But I wasn't violent, I didn't get drunk, and I always accepted her decisions. I'm like that: if you present a good case to me, I'll accept it.

'We were good lovers,' I went on. The admission surprised me. I had never talked to anyone about our love. 'Obviously, the passion goes eventually, but we were good lovers.' I drained my glass, and refilled it. I blinked at Sarah. 'Why she felt . . . why she had to do what she did – well, I'll never understand that.

'When I found out about Anna, and her other life, I just went numb. I know it sounds ridiculous, but I couldn't grasp what had happened. It was so extraordinary, and it didn't fit into any pattern that I recognised. I spent a long time thinking about it, trying to adapt the knowledge to something I could relate to. But I didn't know how to deal with it, and there was no one to ask. The more I thought about it, the less sense it seemed to make. Even now, I still can't adjust to the facts.

'I kept on asking myself "Why?". I went back to the flat in Melrose Street several times, just walking up and down to see if I could find some clue, but it didn't do any good. Every time I tried to work it out, the shock of it would cloud my reasoning. No anger even – just stunning shock. What was she up to?

'I had loved Anna – you may doubt that I loved her enough, or in the right way – but I loved her in my own way, and the news blew all that away. I did all my grieving then; that's when the sense of loss and bereavement hit me. I don't miss her now. Isn't that terrible? Twenty years of my life have been chopped away, truncated if you like, and I don't miss it, or her, at all.'

'I think you're still in shock,' Sarah said. 'So much has happened to you that you just haven't had time to take it all in. It doesn't sound so terrible to me that you can't yet get a proper perspective on everything.' As always, she was being reasonable and logical; she inspired me to go on.

'Even now, I don't think the rest of the family knows what happened. They know Anna was in a strange place, and they know she was murdered, but they think the police are still trying to work it out. How could they suspect dear, sweet, reasonable Anna of such things, such things that they know nothing of? I won't put them straight – it would be pointless, on top of all the misery her death has already brought.'

Now my hands sweated, my glands pumped, and the life forces rushed round inside me in an endless swirl of blood and nerve and adrenalin. We were nearing the orgasmic moment, when all the senses would concentrate on a single, twitching pulse, ready to ejaculate in purest ecstasy. This was the passion that I needed to share with Sarah, the climactic instant when we would be truly bound together by a common fate.

'A cynic would blame it all on Ben,' I said. 'You remember Ben, the guy who worked for me?'

'He's pretty unforgettable,' Sarah replied. 'But what's he done wrong?'

'He led me to her, in a funny kind of way. We were in Lucho's one evening, and he handed me a card – you know, one of those cards you find in every phone booth in London, advertising personal services.'

'Oh that,' Sarah said knowingly. 'You know, he was quite a collector of those. He reckoned he had about three hundred of them in his bottom drawer.'

'I never knew that. It hardly matters now. Anyway, I kept the card in my wallet for ages. I forgot all about it until one lunchtime. I'd dropped a ton of money that morning, and I'd been out with a broker for a very liquid lunch. As we were finishing the brandies, he made some offhand remark about spending the afternoon with a friendly tart, and we both laughed about it. But after I'd left him I pulled the card out and had another look at it. I was pretty tanked up, and more out of curiosity than anything else, I decided to call. I got through, and I was so excited about what I was doing that I never recognised the voice. I wasn't really listening anyway, but I managed to get the address and I went round there in a taxi.'

'So you've used a whore? Am I meant to be shocked?' Sarah seemed almost bored by what I was saying, and her manner annoyed me.

'I think you're unshockable. That's what I love about you.'

'Go on with your story,' she said as she poured more wine for us.

'I made the taxi pull up down the street. I didn't want to get out right in front of the building. But then I got cold feet, and wondered what the hell I was doing there. The alcohol was beginning to wear off, and I wasn't feeling so uninhibited any more. Then I saw a guy coming out of the flat, and a couple of minutes later he was followed out by a woman. She was wearing dark glasses and a lot of make-up, and she had a long coat pulled tight around her. It was the coat I recognised. I'd bought it for her.'

'This was Anna?' Sarah gasped, sitting up in her chair.

'This was Anna. Not my version of Anna, the one I had loved so much, but still unmistakably her.'

'Christ, what did you do?'

'I stood very still, and watched her walk down the road to the corner shop. I waited for her to come back, and watched her go into the flat again. I took up a position about three or four doors down from the flat, on the other side of the road, and waited. Another man went down to the front door, looking all around, and held his head down as he rang the bell. Then he disappeared inside. Twenty minutes later he came out. I don't know how long I stayed there for, but I must have watched four or five men come and go.'

I drank some of my wine and peered at Sarah's face, illuminated only by candle-light and hard to discern. She said nothing.

'I got a taxi to Lucho's. As usual, the bar was full of people from work, and I acted as if nothing had happened. Ben was there, and pretty soon everything was back to normal. I called Anna, and we talked briefly; I listened for some trace, some little sign of guilt, but I didn't hear anything different. I wonder if she did.

'That night I didn't sleep well; sometimes I slept in the spare room, if I was late and didn't want to disturb her, and I sat up all night and got myself completely confused. My head ached like hell, and stupidly I took some pain-killers that simply fogged my mind even more. By the morning I was very groggy. Avoiding Anna wasn't difficult; I left before she woke, but I didn't give her a kiss goodbye.

'I went to work, but I couldn't see the screens properly, and at lunchtime I gave up and went out for a walk. Every woman I saw on the street seemed to look at me oddly, as if they knew what Anna was doing. I jumped into a taxi, and went back to Melrose Street. I stood where I had been the night before, and waited until Anna arrived. Before I had a chance to move, a man went in. Stupidly, I never even looked at him, he just looked like a thousand other men in grubby coats with grubby minds. When he had left, and I was satisfied that she was inside alone, I crossed over and stood at the top of the stairs. I really didn't know what I was going to do. My heart was in my throat, and I felt so sick I was worried that I might pass out. But I went down the stairs, and rang the bell. I waited forever, trapped in this little cement patio between the real world and Anna's other life. Then the door opened, and we stood facing each other.

'She didn't move. She didn't try and slam the door,

or run away. She simply stood where she was, almost defiant, and looked at me. I put my hand up to the door and she opened it a little more so that I could come in. I brushed past her and went through to the main living area.

'The flat was disgusting; the carpet was dirty, and there were cartons of half-eaten food and cans of soft drink everywhere. The smell of sin, of rotting and decadence, was overpowering. Stale sex smells like that, I suppose. I stood in total anguish, hardly able to move. The only noise in the place was the fridge, occasionally coughing into life. I looked in the kitchen, then across to the bedroom.

'She was just standing there behind me, her arms folded as she watched me. There was nothing to say. The circumstances were so bizarre that words would have seemed completely redundant. I turned round and faced her, and I knew I was in danger of throwing up. But she was much calmer, she started to walk towards me, still looking petulant, as if I had interrupted something private and she was very cross about it.

'If she'd stayed still, and hadn't tried to speak, I think things might have been different. But she kept on coming towards me, and I could see she wanted to say something. Inside me, a thermostat blew and I just exploded. I lunged at her, without really knowing what I was planning to do. I saw the whole thing in slow motion, as if I were standing to one side of the room as someone else attacked her. She didn't actually put up much of a struggle, once I'd knocked her over with the weight of my body. I pinned her down with my knees and throttled her.'

Sarah was completely still and quiet, and I savoured this moment of disclosure.

'The funny thing is, once it was over, I felt much better. My head was clear, and I felt as if I'd solved a very difficult crossword puzzle. It was almost as if I'd hit the bottom, and now was going upwards, higher and higher, as if her death was some kind of drug that put me into a steep climb. My muscles began to sing. I wanted to be walking, running – but not away from anything, just to enjoy the freedom of movement, to feel the breeze as I sprinted along.

'I looked at her for quite a while, then I walked away. It was so peaceful, so quiet, and it just seemed that the constant roaring in my ears had finally stopped for good. It was over.'

Sarah's small voice finally broke the spell. 'I thought you said that she was beaten around the head after she was strangled?'

I had to laugh at this. It was so typical of her to want to know every last detail so that she could get things straight in her mind. 'She was. Before I left I hit her with a glass ashtray. I wanted to be sure she was dead.'

We fell into silence again, and I revelled in the sweet glow of confession, especially to Sarah, who represented all my future hopes and dreams.

'God, I am so sorry,' she said after an eternity.

'For what? For whom? Justice has been done – not that justice that wears wigs, and judges you on legalistic grounds, but natural justice, the moral code that's much more substantial. She wronged me, and was made to suffer for it. The human law has triumphed – a triumph of the will, if you like. It doesn't need the interference of officials and regulators, scratching around for clues and evidence and all those shoddy, sordid details. This is pure.'

'I understand all that,' Sarah said, and she seemed to be wiping tears from her cheeks. 'You've no need to justify your actions to me. But she put you through so much, she must have made you suffer so horrendously to drive you to do this. Now I just want to make it all right for you and blow away all the pain and misery. Will you let me do that?'

This was the cherished moment, when Sarah nailed her colours to my mast and we became a single entity, unable to exist without each other, connected by force and need and desire and history. I could feel the pulsing excitement within me, a vicarious thrill derived from her submission, and I smiled in the dark as my whole body throbbed.

She got up and moved to me, climbing on to my lap and wrapping her arms round my neck. She ran her fingers through my hair and showered small, light kisses on my eyes and nose in a display of love that transcended the mere physical. She held on to me as if her life depended on it, as if she might be safer were she actually inside me. The feeling was enormously powerful.

Before sleep that night I went to the bathroom, and vomited heavily until only bile was left in my stomach. The emetic worked; as I rinsed my face in the basin, I caught sight of myself in the mirror, and my whole face had changed. It was younger, fitter, happier than I remembered, and I grinned at the sight of it. Nothing could stop me now.

TWENTY-EIGHT

My first day at work, and already Ham and I were working on a deal. Only five days had passed since I'd told Sarah everything, and yet that seemed like eternity. We had turned a corner and were heading in a different direction, the past consigned to the trash with the disdain it deserved. Exorcising all the old memories had proved to be a masterly stroke. Sarah was relaxed and happy, staying in the Cape until I had something permanent fixed in Manhattan. Things could not have worked out better, and my confidence returned in huge waves.

There was still the nagging doubt about the medical; I'd received a bland letter telling me that further tests would be required at some stage, but I didn't dare ask for more details in fear of setting off alarm bells. The cold sores and fevers had long since disappeared, however, so I decided that Anna's final legacy had gone to the incinerator with her.

Looking back, I might have made some mistakes, some misjudgements of character, but I had always managed to overcome these and retake control of my destiny. Nothing should have been different about this time; I had never been so much in control, so completely in charge of events – and yet I failed to notice the moment when kismet took over.

I was standing in the trading room when that moment came, when the dream was over and crunching reality slammed through the door. Ham and I were working on this deal, and Marty's advice was needed. The three of us stood debating the issues, surrounded by the screaming, bawling madness of traders and squawk-boxes. The intercom on Marty's desk buzzed into life; a nasal voice whined the message.

'Marty, I have a call on fifty-three, can you take it?'

He wheeled round, picked up the receiver and punched a button on the dealer-board. He listened, then held the phone out to me.

'Someone for you.'

I took the receiver. 'Hello?' I raised my eyebrows at Ham, to indicate apology and frustration.

'Hi, it's me.' Sarah's voice was still as sexy as the first time I heard it. 'Sorry to interrupt on your first day, but I had to call.'

'Look, is there any chance I can call you right back? I'm just a little tied up right now.'

'This can't wait. Just give me two minutes to explain.'

I looked despairingly at Ham and Marty, holding up a finger to indicate that I wouldn't be more than one minute. I sat down at the desk and leant towards the screens so that my conversation couldn't be overheard. Marty and Ham continued to talk at my back.

'What is it, Sarah? Are you OK?'

'Yes, I'm fine. Well, actually that's not true. I'm feeling like shit, if you must know. But that's not why I rang. I wasn't going to call you – in fact they told me not to – but I really couldn't go on until I'd got things sorted out with you. Must be catching, mustn't it, this need to get everything resolved?'

'You're not making any sense, Sarah. What exactly are you talking about?' As I asked her this I was aware of a commotion behind me, and some voices being raised, but this was usual in the trading room and I tried to ignore it.

'Oh God, let's get right to it, then,' she said in a long sigh. 'You remember I told you that the detective – Barham – came to see me?'

'Yes.' Now the room around me had gone silent, save for the low growl of one voice over a loudspeaker announcing price changes. I looked around, but at first I couldn't see through the bodies between me and the door. Then they parted. There were two uniformed bank security guards, with two other men, and one guard was pointing at me. Sarah was talking again, and it was hard to concentrate.

'And you remember that I told you that Barham asked me to keep an eye on you, and I told you that I'd refused?'

'Sarah, what has this got to do with anything?'

The two guards, flanked by the other two men, were walking towards me. My throat closed, and the

309

room began to rotate. The receiver slipped in my hand, the sweat running freely. It was only when one of the plain-clothed men reached me that I recognised him: Barham.

'I just wanted to tell you,' Sarah said in the sweetest tone I'd ever heard from her, 'I lied.'

I dropped the phone, and Marty caught it. He spoke into it.

'Way to go, Sarah. I always knew you had it in you. All the time the bastard's shafting you, you're shafting him right back. I love you Brits, I really do.'

Whatever was said in reply I didn't hear. I could hear Marty laughing, and that laugh never left me. It still echoes like tinnitus, ringing and jarring inside my skull. It will never leave me, his laugh. It was the last free thing I heard.